Bronwyn Rivers grew u
She moved to the UK to
Oxford on nineteenth-ce
academic researcher and bc
She now lives in Sydney
The Reunion is her first novel.

Bronwyn Rivers grew up in Newcastle, New South Wales. She moved to ... 1998 to take a doctorate at the University of ... on nineteenth-century women's novels, and was an academic researcher and book reviewer in England and Australia. She now lives in Sydney with her husband and two children.

La Zona is her first novel.

The Reunion

Bronwyn Rivers

CONSTABLE

CONSTABLE

First published in Great Britain in 2025 by Constable
This paperback edition published in 2025 by Constable

1 3 5 7 9 10 8 6 4 2

A CIP catalogue record for this book
is available from the British Library.

ISBN: 978-1-40872-079-0

Typeset in Adobe Garamond Pro by SX Composing DTP, Rayleigh, Essex
Printed and bound in Great Britain by Clays Ltd, Elcograf S.p.A.

Papers used by Constable are from well-managed forests
and other responsible sources.

MIX
Paper | Supporting
responsible forestry
FSC® C104740

Constable
An imprint of
Little, Brown Book Group
Carmelite House
50 Victoria Embankment
London EC4Y 0DZ

The authorised representative
in the EEA is
Hachette Ireland
8 Castlecourt Centre, Dublin 15,
D15 XTP3, Ireland
(email: info@hbgi.ie)

An Hachette UK Company
www.hachette.co.uk

www.littlebrown.co.uk

For Matthew, Sam and Thomas

Author's Note

The Australian bush can be treacherous and has claimed the lives of hikers. It is important to note, therefore, that all characters in this work are completely imaginary and no resemblance is intended to the behaviour or motivation of any real person, past or present.

Prologue

It had been all around them the whole time, throughout their ordeal. Running through veins and through leaves. Through heads and hearts, through branches and tree trunks. It ran through the young limbs of Ed Fletcher, while he lived, just as surely as it ran through the bodies of the friends who had accompanied him into the forest.

Heedless of their distress, it had gone on, performing its tireless work in every living thing and deep within the ground, just as it does now. Gathering into rivulets, then streams, and into the creek that starts way up in the impenetrable bush. Into the narrow river, through folds of grasslands, down through the valley in which the Fletcher homestead still stands, though the white iron lace that rings its grand balconies is now peeling and cracked.

Now the morning sun reaches across the crinkled velvet expanses of the treetops, tips over the cliffs ringing the valley, lights up the cockatoos screeching through the abyss, then touches the homestead. The paddocks lie still in the sun, the animals and birds wander and fly.

Then everything freezes. A gunshot explodes the air. Four people see their friend collapse.

Just for an instant afterwards there is an answering silence. And in that silence the minds of the five friends spin outside of time, out across the valley and into the bush, up through the winding gullies and secret places, past the creeks, the birds with their careless song and the creatures scurrying and still, to an empty clearing, heavy with memory, which looks like any other.

Chapter 1

They were just having a weekend away to catch up with some old friends – at least that's what they had each told colleagues and families. None of the five former schoolmates had admitted their reluctance as they discussed the trip. But they all eagerly agreed to meet at the old cafe before making the last leg of the journey down into the valley, and it wasn't for the view, spectacular though that was. No one put it into words, but they wanted to check each other out, take their last chance to prepare, before arriving at the Fletcher house.

Their everyday tension had clung to them as they stuffed last-minute items into bags and checked with neighbours about cats and keys. Then they reached the motorway, their cars sped up and they leaned back a little in their seats. The wide road curved out into the countryside, freeing itself from the tendrils of the city, and their moods lifted a little with a sense of escape, despite themselves. Perhaps the weekend would be okay. Perhaps they were worrying about nothing.

Each car in turn left the main road, then took another turn-off and another. They passed through towns, then villages, then hamlets. The cars grew dustier, and the potholes became deeper. Clusters of gum trees in paddocks started to reach over the narrow road and became a forest that grew thicker and thicker and pressed in against the bitumen in hypnotic patterns of green, until the fields disappeared and all they could see was a tunnel of leaves.

And the whiff of escape evaporated, as images of the weekend ahead formed and reformed in their minds.

'I remember now,' said Hugh, who was travelling with his wife, Charlotte. 'This forest goes on for ever. The road always felt like it was never going to end.'

Charlotte glanced at the clock. 'And then, all of a sudden, it would appear.'

They rounded a corner and indeed, there it was. A small weatherboard cafe with faded green paint, set back a little from the road, surrounded by an orchard.

The car crunched to a halt on the gravel forecourt. Hugh got out immediately and stretched his cramped muscles, then rested his fists on his hips. The place seemed deserted, but between the lace curtains a sign in one of the windows was turned to 'open'. Someone should be able to get them a coffee at least.

He watched as Charlotte lifted herself carefully from the car. She flicked her hair over her shoulder, smoothed her shirt over a curving hip and glanced around.

'I wonder when the others will arrive,' she said.

'You think I'm clairvoyant?' The words just slipped out of his mouth.

Charlotte pressed her lips together and looked away.

That familiar stab of guilt. He sighed. Enough. He charged inside the cafe to grab a menu, clattering the plastic strips of the fly screen.

It was annoying that he even had to be here. Charlotte had eventually convinced him that they did have to accept the invitation but, really, they could all have met up in the city. It would have been more convenient for most of them – and he could have made it to the footy on Sunday morning and then to the pub with his mates.

And there would have been less danger of the past escaping from where it had been safely stowed.

When he re-emerged from the cafe, Charlotte had chosen a table in the orchard at the side and another car was pulling up. The driver got out and waved, and Hugh immediately recognised Alex, with his pale skin and floppy hair. From the passenger side of the car, a larger man with dark hair clambered out more slowly.

'Oh my god,' said Charlotte under her breath. 'Is that . . . Jack?'

Hugh whistled quietly. 'He's really stacked on the kilos.'

As the two men approached, Hugh stood to greet them. Charlotte smiled and smoothed her hair.

Alex looked at Charlotte's rounded stomach. 'How is it going? You feeling well?'

Hugh heard Charlotte murmur her usual response. The idea of having a kid was great, and of course Hugh was proud. It was maybe a bit scary too, but he was sure there would be nothing he couldn't handle. He'd be fine. They'd be fine.

They took their seats under trees that glowed in the late-afternoon sun. It was a hot day and they were glad of the shade.

Alex looked around the orchard. 'This is a nice place.'

The others nodded. The silence was filled with the hum of insects.

5

At the sound of another car arriving, Hugh looked towards the car park. A lean woman with fair hair emerged from the hatchback. She held one arm a little stiffly. She raised a hand when she saw them and picked her way across the grass.

'Laura.' Hugh stood to kiss her.

She hadn't changed too much. Perhaps she was a bit thinner than she used to be.

Alex murmured his hello. Hugh noticed that Jack knocked against the table slightly as he also rose to greet her.

After Laura had ordered inside the cafe, she took her seat and looked around at the group. 'God, when was the last time we all saw each other? Feels like for ever.'

'You all came to the wedding.' Charlotte was speaking carefully. 'Surely you haven't forgotten already?'

'Of course not,' said Alex quickly. 'It was beautiful.'

Hugh suppressed an urge to roll his eyes. Did Alex never get sick of saying the right thing all the time?

But Charlotte looked pleased by Alex's comment. 'I wanted it to be special. We wanted it to be special.' She turned to Hugh.

'Yep.' Hugh gave a quick nod, then looked away. That damn wedding. It had been so much trouble.

'Hel-lo-ha!' cried a grey-haired man, who approached with a tray and clanked it down on their table. He handed out their drinks then stood back and put his hands behind his back, stretching a little.

'So, you folks going on to Nanganook then?'

After a moment Alex said, 'Lost Valley.'

'Oh.' The man paused. 'The Fletcher place, eh? Sad business, with Robert.'

'You know the Fletchers?' asked Alex.

'Everyone around here knows everyone else. But the Fletchers always kept to themselves – even before Robert passed away.' The man stepped a little closer. 'Word is, things are going downhill a bit, on the farm, with Martha Fletcher there by herself.'

Hugh looked at the waiter. 'Thanks. I think that's all.'

'Righty-oh.' The man gave a nod. 'Well, sing out if you need anything.'

They all watched him walk back to the cafe.

When he had disappeared, Jack cleared his throat. 'That doesn't sound great.' He pushed his glasses up his nose and looked around at everyone. His voice was slow; slower than Hugh remembered. As though talking was an effort. 'Honestly, I was wondering if we would all show up for this trip.'

Hugh couldn't help stiffening. He stole a glance at the others.

'I mean, was anyone else a little surprised to be invited out here, to the house, for the weekend?' Jack went on. 'No one would ever say we're Martha's favourite people.' Jack looked from face to face.

Hugh followed Jack's gaze. He saw Laura examining the surrounding bush.

'Martha was the one who suggested the five-year memorial,' said Charlotte.

'Yeah, but that was just a few hours. In the city. Neutral ground,' said Jack. 'And I thought she seemed pretty tense then.'

Hugh thought back to the previous meeting, five years ago. Jack was right; it had hardly been a relaxing afternoon. They had gathered at a cafe near Sydney harbour. The conversation had been hard work. At the end, Martha had stood and made some speech about how much Ed had appreciated all of them as friends. What she said was nice enough but the whole occasion had felt pretty stressful.

Charlotte said, 'It's hard to say no to Martha. After . . . what happened, with Ed. And now there's Robert's death.'

Hugh remembered Ed's father Robert from their school days, but he'd been a bit of a distant figure. Charlotte was right. It was hard not to do what the grieving wife and mother asked.

Alex chewed his lip. 'Perhaps she's using the anniversary to smooth things over? I mean, it's been ten years.'

'What do you all think is going to happen?' Hugh forced a grin. It was annoying that they had to come, but they were here now, and there was no need to stress about it. 'It'll be fine. We'll get through this commemoration thing for Ed that she has planned for Sunday. Then we can all go back to our lives.'

Hugh looked around the table, took in the nods from the others then leaned back in his chair.

The insects continued to whirr.

Charlotte put on a bright smile. Hugh recognised that smile. She thought she could make everything okay by sheer force of will. 'Perhaps we can even enjoy having a weekend away together,' she said. 'I'm looking forward to catching up with you guys.'

Alex nodded. 'You're right. Maybe a picnic. Or a drive to one of the lookouts. Hey, there used to be a great view, just through there, right?' Alex waved at the bushes. 'How about we take a look?'

That was exactly the sort of thing Alex would suggest. But they might as well. Clearly no one was in a big hurry to get to the house. Hugh peeled himself from the seat and straggled through the low scrub with the others.

After a short walk they mounted a set of steps. Then the sky opened up around them.

On three sides an ocean of forest stretched out to the far horizon, ridge after ridge of eucalyptus interleaved with sudden gullies. Bird calls pierced the sunny afternoon, and the treetops rustled with gentle shifts of warm air.

The only break in the vista was the valley that opened up on the fourth side. It was surrounded by high cliffs, great gashes of orange stone, and at its base far below lay acres of rolling grassland. On the far side, a two-storey homestead, ringed with verandas, perched like a doll's house. The Fletcher homestead. The only sign of human habitation in the whole vast landscape.

They all fell silent.

Hugh saw Charlotte turn her head and he followed her glance. Laura was standing a few steps from the others. As they watched, she shivered.

Charlotte said, 'Laura, what is it?'

Laura turned to them. 'It's always the same, no matter where I am. I can't bear the sight of the bush any more. Every time I can't help but think, if only we hadn't gone on our walk.'

Chapter 2

Ten years previously

'It's going to be a hot one.' Alex stood on the front veranda of the Fletcher homestead and surveyed the valley. It would be a very warm start for their walk.

'It's going to be a great one.' Alex saw Ed Fletcher shoot past and dash down the stairs, his arms full of nylon and the straps from a backpack trailing behind him. Ed was always zipping about. He plonked the load on the lawn.

Another pile of equipment walked past after Ed. Alex saw Hugh's red hair poking around it as he made his way down the stairs, then placed his pile next to the others.

It was good that they were planning carefully. Of course, they'd been on hiking trips as a group before at school, with teachers, but Alex had never been walking just with other friends and no adults. He reminded himself, again, that Ed and Hugh were very experienced hikers. It would all be okay.

Alex looked past the veranda of the house and the gleaming paint of the ironwork and took in the valley. Brown grasses stretched out beneath the early-morning sun, cliffs looming over them on all sides. The big tractor trundled across a paddock below the house with two farm hands riding on the back. A couple of blokes were carrying building supplies around to the extension work at the back of the house. In the distance three men wrestled with fencing wire.

Martha Fletcher emerged from the house and stood next to Alex. She looked towards the workers. 'They've been out for hours already. They'll be wanting morning tea soon.'

Alex tried to think of a response. He nodded towards the far side of the garden. 'The roses are looking nice, Mrs Fletcher.'

He saw Mrs Fletcher smile briefly and he was pleased with himself for coming up with the compliment straight away.

'Thank you, Alex. It's been hard keeping them going lately, what with the drought and all this heat. I reuse the washing water.' She brushed her hands against the apron that spanned her comfortable figure then pushed a strand of dark hair behind her ears. 'But I can't stand around here all day; I better get the muffins out.'

She disappeared back into the house, and Alex wandered towards the others. They were sorting their equipment. Alex had already made sure he had everything required for the trip together; his stuff was all neatly gathered in a pile.

The sun caught Laura's long fair hair as she sat on the grass nearby. She closed her eyes, pressed her fingertips together and took a deep breath. 'What a gorgeous day.'

It was good the way Laura tried to appreciate the world around her. He should stop and really notice things like she did.

'You're not taking that, are you?' Hugh stood nearby, his fists resting on his hips. He nodded at the small painting set next to Laura's backpack. 'Hardly essential equipment.'

'It's the most essential thing. There'll be so many beautiful views. It's basically why I'm coming.'

Alex was not surprised when Hugh rolled his eyes.

'So why are you coming then, Hugh?' asked Laura. 'Not to get out into nature?'

'I like getting away with my mates,' said Hugh. 'And the countryside around here can be challenging walking. It's good to test yourself.'

'Test yourself! It's the end of school – we made it through a whole six years; we're free. Some of us want to have fun and enjoy ourselves,' said Laura.

'Don't worry – I'm bringing some "fun".' Hugh patted his own backpack. 'Of the liquid variety.'

Ed passed Hugh and Laura carrying a box. 'Catch!' He threw a couple of chocolate bars at them and grinned. Jack was standing to the side, marking a small piece of paper with a pencil. Ed threw a bar at Jack's head then looked over Jack's shoulder. 'Are you seriously checking your possessions off a list?' Ed laughed. 'I suppose that's the sort of care and effort that made Jack Zhang dux of St Stephen's College.'

Jack pushed his glasses up his nose and eyed the box of chocolates. 'And that's the sort of crowd-pleasing shit that made Edward Fletcher the school captain.'

Alex turned away. They seemed so easy with each other. He had never really had that kind of banter with anyone.

He turned to Charlotte and Laura. Laura reached over to her bag and pulled out a floppy hat with a big cloth flower.

Charlotte's face softened. 'That's such a Laura hat.' Charlotte pressed her own cap against her head, then flicked her golden hair over her shoulders. She glanced around to see who was watching.

'What do you think, Ed? Like my new top?' She smoothed it against the curve of her waist.

'Our gorgeous Charl – as always.' He gave her a noisy smooch on the cheek.

'Oh stop!' She pushed him away, but she was smiling.

Alex noticed Ed wink at Laura. Then Laura rolled her eyes slightly.

Martha emerged from the house with a tray of muffins. 'You might as well take some of these. They won't keep, and they'll do for your morning tea. And don't forget those.' She picked up a cardboard box and began to distribute packets of trail mix between the piles of equipment. 'Oh bother, there aren't enough.' She frowned. 'That's Rachelle's fault. I *told* that girl to order more of them.'

Ed walked past and slung his arm around her shoulders, his dark curls rubbing against her hair. 'It's fine, Mum – we'll cope.'

Ed took a map from his backpack and unfolded it with a flourish. Alex leaned closer. Hopefully the route wouldn't be too onerous.

'We'll walk in along this trail, follow that ridge.' Ed's finger traced a line. 'Then we can either head this way, and camp at Stockman's Rest tonight. We can refill our water there. Or we could go to Blackett's Flat; there's water there too. Then onto the Nanganook valley the next day.

'I reckon Stockman's Rest.' Ed's voice was decisive.

'Wanting to take it easy, are you mate?' Hugh grinned. 'I reckon we could make it a bit further.'

'Well obviously. If it was just you and me, I'd have us running the whole route in one day. Half a day. Make it really interesting. But we've got to plan for the group.'

'I think you're getting soft.'

'It's called being responsible.'

Alex knew Hugh was just trying to wind Ed up, but it was a relief that Ed was holding his ground.

Ed looked up at the sound of a raised voice. 'Oh crap.'

Martha stood in front of the house, berating a young woman wearing an apron.

Ed sighed. 'Mum always needs someone to blame. She'll be having a go at Rachelle about the damn trail mix. I'd better go settle them down.' He hurried over towards Martha.

Hugh turned to Jack who was still checking his itemised list. 'Tent – tick. Jacket – tick. Girlfriend – *tick!*' Hugh nodded at Laura, who was standing a little way off, chatting to Charlotte.

Jack grinned. 'Frustrated you don't have a girlfriend to take?'

'No, mate – being single is a gift. For I am young and free.'

'Whatever you say.'

Alex thought Hugh probably was jealous. Alex was slightly jealous himself – not of Laura; he wasn't interested in her. But the fact that Jack was so settled into a relationship. Alex had never had a girlfriend. It wasn't that there was someone in particular he was longing for, but the idea of having someone who was interested in you and your life; who was in your corner with you against the world – who wanted to help you. That was very attractive.

Then Ed clapped. 'Okay, guys, time to get everything into those packs. We need to get going soon. Make sure you have everything – especially sleeping bag, waterproof jacket, water bottles.' He jogged lightly on his feet, as though poised for flight.

'Yes, Mum!' called Hugh sarcastically.

A dull roar in the driveway signalled another truck arriving. A man in his late forties leapt down. Ed's dad.

Robert Fletcher walked to Martha and stood near her, watching the activity.

Alex leaned over his bulging backpack then hoisted it onto his back with a wide swing. He turned towards the others.

He saw Jack wander over to Laura and take her hand. Laura gave him a quick smile, then let his hand go and set off towards the others. Alex frowned. It was an odd little moment.

Quite apart from thinking about their safety, Alex was also wondering how they would all get along together, out in the bush with no one else around. They'd known each other for six years, since they had been thrown together as a house group in their first year at high school. Boarding school made for intense relationships quickly formed, and they had gathered, almost for survival, under their unofficial leader Ed.

But as they'd grown older the differences had emerged. Ed and Jack were close friends of course; Ed and Hugh bonded by being competitive about sport and physical prowess; and now Laura and Jack were in a relationship. But objectively they were a bit of an unlikely group. Charlotte had her own gang of similarly pretty, popular girls to whom Alex would never dare speak. Laura was super nice, of course, but Alex privately thought of her as a bit of a hippy and he bet Hugh did too. And Alex couldn't quite quash the thought that if he hadn't been put in that house group at the start, the others would never have been friends with him at all. He just wasn't as confident and sociable as they were.

Still, they had gone on regular hiking trips with their house master over the years, so when the idea of a trip by themselves to mark the end of their school years was raised, it was naturally assumed they would all go as a group. Alex wondered whether this would be their last hurrah, whether they'd stay in touch once they were all off at university.

Alex saw Ed give Martha a hug and then she patted him on the back. 'Love you, darling.'

'Love you too, Mum.'

Robert Fletcher had moved to the edge of the garden and was staring out over the paddocks, his back stiff and straight. Alex saw Ed run up to him. Ed went to hug his father, but Robert just nodded stiffly and Ed stopped abruptly.

Then Ed shrugged and dashed back to the others. 'C'mon – let's get this show on the road.'

'Look after yourselves,' Martha called.

'Mrs Fletcher, if you could have one of your pies ready when we get back?' Hugh grinned over his shoulder, and Martha smiled.

They crossed the garden, made their way through a gate, then set off across a paddock that sloped upwards towards the cliffs. Ed was at the front and the group soon stretched out into a line behind him. Alex was happy to bring up the rear. He could adjust his pace to how fast the others walked.

He took a breath and forced himself to relax and take in the valley landscape. It was a lovely day, and they were going to have a great trip.

Back at the farm, Martha and Robert stood together watching.

'Hope those kids'll be sensible.' Robert's face was stern. 'Hot few days ahead.'

'They'll be right. We've spent enough time with Ed, hiking around here. And he's a good leader.'

The mother and father squinted in the sunlight as the group bobbed against the paddock, shrinking until they were just dots high up near where the bush began. The cliffs around the valley stared down impassively.

Then the dark line of forest swallowed up the six tiny figures.

Chapter 3

'Whoa!' Jack gripped the armrest in the passenger seat of Alex's car. 'Better slow down.'

A moment ago, the road had been a sinuous strip of bitumen overhung with leaves. Now the trees disappeared. One side of the road rose in a high cliff and on the other a vertiginous drop opened up to the valley below.

The road twisted in repeated hairpin bends, the car swaying this way and that and, with it, Jack's stomach. On they drove, each slope winding around into another, again and again, ever downwards.

This road. Appearing in his dreams all too often, and even popping into his mind unexpectedly during the day sometimes. Over and over, this journey. Going back down the bends, through the forest, back to the Fletcher house. Burrowing down through the thick walls of green.

As the bends finally straightened out and they entered another forest, Jack rubbed his face. He remembered the moment that the email from Martha had arrived, inviting them to come and stay for the weekend. Badly laid out, with random capitals and punctuation, it showed she was clearly not at home with computers.

It had been all too much to deal with; he just put it aside. These days it was hard to face up to any kind of decision. Navigating through a day was like wading through mud. Curled up on the couch at home, ignoring the work he should be doing; that was his favourite pose.

But then the phone calls started. Was he going? After a while Alex said that the others would all be there and he had arranged to give Jack a lift; and it was easier just to give in to that momentum.

Seeing everyone again at the cafe just now after all those years could have been weird. They had mostly gone their separate ways with their lives. But that first chat had been okay. It seemed like the others had come on this weekend out of the same sense of duty that had tugged at him. And the bond between them seemed to still be there, faint but discernible, despite all their differences; the long arm of the past reaching out to grab them, whether they wanted it to or not. They had been through so much together, both before and after the walk into the bush with Ed. They were the only ones who really understood each other.

Now, amid the gloom of the forest, there was a flash up ahead. In a moment, the leaves melted away and they were suddenly surrounded by rolling brown grassland. Unconsciously, Jack let out a sigh as the car freed itself from the last of the trees.

The road through the valley farmlands came to a dead end at a wooden gate. The house wasn't visible from the road, but 'Fletcher' was marked out in faded letters on the crossbar. Jack eyed the peeling paintwork. Then Alex turned the steering wheel, and the car began to pitch and roll up the rough track.

They crested a rise and suddenly the house stood before them. Jack pushed his glasses up his nose. He would have to get out. He would have to do this.

He clambered out of the car. The engine ticked as it cooled in the silence. Warm air pressed around them

A large two-storey house of dark brickwork with a steeply pitched roof loomed over them. Both storeys were ringed with verandas protected by white iron lace.

Jack's gaze softened. He could see the past selves of his friends as they lounged on the verandas and chased each other across the lawns. They were ten years younger, their faces carefree, grinning as though all the world lay before them, theirs just for the taking. These, at least, were friendly ghosts. He glanced across at Alex. 'This feels so familiar.'

'But it's also different; look.' Alex nodded at the house and Jack followed his gaze. Alex was right. The paint on the iron lace was peeling and a couple of woodwork panels on the gables were hanging loose. Several planks were missing on the wooden veranda, and the corrugated iron roof was stained with rust. It was a striking change from when they used to visit as school kids; back then everything had been kept in such good condition.

Jack turned to look back the way they had driven. The valley lazed in the afternoon sun. Cliffs reached up above it on all sides. Jack looked along the thin line of road back between the grassy paddocks, but he couldn't see where it met the pass back up to the cliff top. Their exit was invisible among the trees.

As if their escape route had disappeared.

'Boys! You're here at last.'

Jack turned to the woman who had suddenly appeared behind them, then had to suppress a cry of surprise. Martha Fletcher's skin hung from her lean frame almost as loosely as her worn set of clothes. Her arms were folded in front of her, the fingers working at the cloth near her elbows. Martha would have been in her late fifties, but looked at least ten years older.

'So good of you to come.' Martha was smiling but it didn't reach her eyes. Her face was framed by grey hair going white. 'Dear Jack.' She reached out and took his hand in both of hers. Jack forced himself to smile through his shock. 'You were such good friends with my boy.'

He nodded. It was true. Jack and Ed had been very good friends. Since the start of high school. Best mates. Jack still wasn't quite sure what had made Ed pick him out among the crowd of twelve-year-olds bobbing uncertainly around their new school, with their blazers too big and their shoes still shiny. Ed's face had suddenly appeared at his elbow on the way to a geography class, his blue eyes bright in a face alive with humour.

'Come with me.'

Jack stared back at him. Who was this boy? Had they met? 'Uh – why?'

''Cause I've got a fun idea.'

Soon enough they had been ensconced behind the sports grand-stand, chewing their way through Ed's stash of sour lollies, sipping on cans of fizzy drink that he'd magicked up from somewhere.

'So, top three test batsmen of all time?' Ed looked at him, eyes narrowed.

'Oh. Uh, Bradman, Tendulkar, Sobers . . .'

'No, no, no – I said top test *batsmen*, not all-rounders.'

Ed had been typically energetic in this discussion, as in all that had followed over the years. Whatever activity was at hand, he would throw himself into it. It was part of his appeal.

Eventually Jack had been the one to suggest that perhaps they needed to get back to class. The sugar high had given him jitters which had combined with nervousness about facing up to those strange new teachers.

But Ed had led the way, confidently sauntering back to the main buildings.

'You two! Where do you think you're going?'

Ed's expression was wide and clear. 'Sir! We thought we saw a boy heading off by himself towards the lower fields. Thought we'd better check he was okay, sir.'

Somehow the teacher had bought it.

As they'd re-joined their class, Ed's sidelong grin had a triumphant air.

Now Jack stood awkwardly in front of the house, Ed's mother gripping his hand for too long. 'Mrs Fletcher,' he mumbled.

'Martha, please. After all we've been through. And you're both grown men now. Not like . . .' Her eyes darted about, not settling on his. Her voice trailed away, and she finally let his hand go.

Jack cleared his throat. 'Martha I was – we all were – so sorry to hear about, ah, Robert.'

She turned at looked at him suddenly, but then glanced away. 'Yes. Thank you.'

'Alex.' She took the other man's hand. And at the sound of another car on the track, Jack turned with relief.

Martha peered at it. 'Is that Charlotte and Hugh?' Jack noticed Martha take a breath and pull her shoulders back. As the car stopped and the doors opened, she adjusted her expression.

'Charlotte.' Martha reached out her hands. 'Are you keeping well?' She gave the younger woman a tight smile.

'All good, thanks.' Charlotte patted her stomach and flashed a wide smile. 'It's so lovely to see you.' She reached up and smoothed her hair.

Jack remembered that if Charlotte felt awkward in a social situation she would overcompensate, and she looked a little awkward now, unsurprisingly. Martha's smile was more like a grimace.

'And Hugh. Did you have a good trip?'

'Yeah, great, thanks. Hope you're well, Mrs Fletcher.' Hugh nodded at Martha then turned as a small hatchback appeared in the driveway. 'Here's Laura.'

The car pulled up in front of the house and the door opened.

Martha walked to the car. 'Dear Laura. So good to have you here.' She reached forward and pulled Laura into a hug. Laura looked across at her four friends, catching Jack's eye.

Jack held his breath.

That old, stabbing thrill. It was almost comforting. He wondered whether enough years had now passed to enable the gap between them to be bridged – then he impatiently dismissed the thought. It was impossible, of course.

He studied Laura's face. Time was, he could read all of her expressions. But not any more. Was she tolerating Martha's embrace? Or comforted by it?

Martha turned back towards the house. 'Now, how about you bring your bags and I'll help you settle in.'

They gathered their luggage and trailed behind Martha along a brickwork path clotted with weeds. Jack noticed the overgrown shrubs and long grass that clearly hadn't felt a mower in a long time. Back in the old days Robert kept the homestead lawns as smooth as a bowling green. Jack saw a wide dip in the lawn filled with straggly bushes. He was sure there used to be a rose garden there.

Martha stopped suddenly and turned towards them. 'You're all very quiet.' She gave a sudden barking laugh, and Jack started. 'Don't look so gloomy. You're all young and healthy.' Then her face softened, just as suddenly. 'You always used to enjoy visiting. It's still a lovely place. You need a rest from city life.

'And then, on Sunday, we'll come together to remember Ed. I've got something really special planned.'

Chapter 4

The group stood in the dim entrance hall surrounded by suitcases. Light filtering through the stained-glass door showed black and white floor tiles and picked out dust motes drifting across the high space. Charlotte could see a staircase curving up into the darkness above them.

'Perhaps I should give you a tour? It's been a while since you were here.' Martha started up the stairs. 'I'll show you to your rooms first.'

At the top of the stairs, Charlotte stood for a moment, puffing. Being short of breath at the slightest exertion was another fun side effect of pregnancy. She tried to breathe more quietly; she must look so unfit and awkward. She flicked her hair over her shoulders and smoothed it down.

It was going to be just like any other weekend away. It was going to be fine. Sure, it would be a bit sad, and Martha could be difficult, in her grief. And Ed's death had been awful, obviously. But ten years had passed now, and even if was duty rather than their own choice for a getaway that had brought them here, there was no reason why old friends shouldn't all have a nice time catching up.

She could see the hallway stretching in both directions. There was a musty smell coming from the frayed carpet. An old wooden dresser stood at the halfway point, covered in piles of linen. She took a breath. It was warm inside the house and warmer still upstairs.

'This way.' Martha set off and they all trailed after her.

'Charlotte and Hugh, I thought you could be in here.' Martha pushed a door open and stepped through then looked around the room, smiling expectantly.

It was a spacious room with French doors leading onto the veranda. But most of the carpet was grey, rather than the cream that was still visible at the edges, and the diamond-pattern wallpaper was coming loose in the corners.

It was also dusty and untidy. The bed was rumpled. The crystal dressing table set, with its perfume bottle, brush and comb, was shoved to one side to accommodate a stack of dog-eared magazines. A pile of blankets appeared to have been abandoned on the top of a tallboy. It was a far cry from the spick and span house that Charlotte remembered from their visits when they were at school.

Charlotte looked around then realised that her shock was probably registering on her face. She summoned up a smile. Be a good guest, she told herself.

'It's great, Martha. I remember, Laura and I were actually in this room back . . . back then. I remember that wallpaper.' She stifled a sneeze. 'Leave your bags for the moment.' Martha turned to the door. 'You might as well all come while I show you around.'

The next room was for Jack. It was also very untidy and clearly hadn't been dusted for some time. Martha looked at the bed. 'Oh dear, it's not made up.' She frowned.

That frown. Charlotte remembered the frown from their schooldays. It had appeared whenever Martha was not happy with something, and it was soon followed by identification of a guilty party.

'It's the cattle agent's fault.' Martha's tone was sharp. 'He called me when I was about to do this room; he distracted me.'

'It's fine Mrs – Martha,' said Jack. 'It'll be easy for me to make up the bed.'

Martha led them along the hall. Charlotte noticed little curls of peeling paint on the walls and ceiling.

'Here's a bathroom you can all use.' Martha waved through a door at a narrow room with pink tiles, a spotty curtain and a chain hanging from a cistern.

'And the spare linen is here, if you need anything.' Martha opened a door near the bathroom. A moth fluttered out.

'Hey, that's quite an impressive collection.' Hugh nodded at the cupboard. One half was filled with folded fabric. The other had rows of tiny boxes and bottles spilling over the shelves and sticking out of half-closed drawers.

Charlotte watched Hugh. Hopefully he wasn't going to make some sarcastic joke. He seemed to be unaware of how some of his remarks affected people.

He seemed particularly unaware of how some of his remarks affected her. He was just so short with her, lately. She had hoped that the pregnancy might repair some of the bumps in their relationship, but they seemed to be growing along with her stomach. Perhaps this weekend, with its change of scene, might help them. Get them away from the regular routine.

She took a breath and made herself smile. In any case, the baby, when it arrived, would certainly bring them together. She rubbed her bump again. Yes, this one would surely arrive safely.

Martha nodded at Hugh. 'Yes, my medicine cabinet.'

'Oh right – you used to be a nurse, didn't you?' Alex looked politely interested.

'That was a while ago now, before Robert and I were married. I always found the training useful, though. More than once I've given doses from here, or bound someone up while talking to the ambulance service. Nurse or not, out in the country you need to keep supplies.'

She shut the door firmly and moved down the hall. 'That's my bedroom.' She waved through an open doorway. 'And, Alex, you're in my sewing room. There's a divan you can sleep on.' She stepped back to show him.

'Oh . . . wow.'

Martha followed their gaze then smiled. 'Oh yes. My little collection.'

Tiny crocheted figurines, miniature animals and people, covered every surface. They gazed at the new guests, their expressions blank.

'I have to keep myself busy in the evenings somehow. I thought I'd keep them all together in here.'

They were even lined up on the floor.

Charlotte only just managed to stifle a kind of horrified laughter. Quite apart from their creepy gazes, the sheer number of the figurines, all the hours and hours of work they represented, was deeply unnerving. Frantic, somehow. She mustn't make eye contact with the others; that would definitely set her off.

She heard Alex clear his throat. 'It's all good, ah, Martha. No problem. Plenty of room for me.'

'I knew you wouldn't mind. You were always so accommodating, Alex.'

'What's in there?' Hugh nodded at a closed door.

'That's my study. That's private.'

Martha turned and headed down the corridor. She turned a corner then stopped. 'Laura, you're in Ed's old room. I thought you'd appreciate that.' She reached for Laura's hand and gave it a squeeze.

Charlotte noticed Jack looking away, down the hall. Jack had always maintained that he was over Laura. But it wasn't too hard to imagine that he was lying to himself. Charlotte had seen the way he had been looking at Laura at the cafe.

Everyone else peered into the room. There was a perfectly made bed. A stack of school textbooks lined up at the back of the desk. A shelf with a set of cricket trophies, gold figurines frozen, mid-bowl. All neatly dusted.

Charlotte couldn't find anything to say. How was Laura going to feel, staying in this shrine to Ed?

Martha turned suddenly, and Hugh and Alex had to jump out of the way as she charged between them, her lips pressed together and her eyes a little watery.

'We can go down now.' She disappeared around the corner, towards the stairs.

Charlotte turned to the others. She could see her own dismay written on their faces.

Little tendrils of worry began to creep around Charlotte's

stomach. And that wasn't good for her. She rubbed her rounded belly. Her doctor was always trying to reassure her. But she couldn't help it; she lived with a constant, low-level awareness that something might go wrong at any moment.

Laura ran her finger along the hallway dado rail then held out the thick dust so the others could see.

Alex nodded. 'I mean, I'm no perfect housekeeper. But compared to what Martha used to be like . . .'

'Time was she would have died rather than show guests through a house in this state.' Laura shook her head. 'It's just such a shock.' She looked along the hall. 'We'd better go down.'

They caught up with Martha at the foot of the stairs. The older woman's smile was back in place, but her hands were working at the cloth around her elbows again.

'You remember, that's the sitting room.' Through the open door, Charlotte could see faded brocade drapes and rows of leather books. Two large Chesterfield couches stood in the middle of the room, stuffing inching its way out of both of them.

'I think we'll eat in the dining room tonight.' Martha waved through another open doorway. A long table was already laid with cutlery and tall glasses. 'Give us a sense of occasion for our first meal together in years, yes?' Martha eyed each of them in turn. 'I'm looking forward to having a really good talk.'

Chapter 5

Laura followed right behind Martha as she led the way down a passage under the stairs. They emerged into a large kitchen. A table occupied the centre of the room, while a couch and dressers piled with plates sat along the walls.

Laura noticed that the lino was grubby as well as patched and peeling, and, from across the room, she could see streaks of unwiped food on the benches. Laura's concern inched up a notch. Poor Martha's grief seemed to be overwhelming her.

'The cellar is down there.' Martha indicated a small doorway with stairs disappearing downwards.

Politely, Laura took a few paces down the stairs and peered into the dim space. She turned and found Jack hard on her heels. Their eyes met before she looked away. Bloody hell. Would he ever let go of the past? He didn't look happy. The weight gain wasn't a good sign, and he seemed slower, more lethargic than she remembered. Probably depressed. But – that was not her problem. She pushed past him, back up the stairs to the kitchen.

Before the trip, she had warned herself that it wouldn't be easy seeing everyone again, and she sure had been right. The chat at the cafe had gone okay, but she had felt the tension throughout her body, the urge to hold herself a little separately from the others. She took a breath. There were so many emotions there, lying coiled around their dreadful experience. It was to be expected that some strong feelings would come up.

The thing was, this weekend could actually be a time of healing. Surely enough time had passed for that to be possible, for them to move forward into a place of sharing and understanding?

Now Martha said, 'You would have seen, the cellar's pretty empty. I think most of the wine is gone, but we do keep some cans and supplies. The pantry is through here.'

They followed Martha into a large storeroom.

'This had to be big, because back in the day they didn't get supplies delivered very often, so they were always in bulk.' Martha nodded at a cupboard. 'More supplies in there; more water.' She waved at a set of hooks on the wall. 'There are all the keys to the sheds and outbuildings; not that we usually keep them locked. And the keys to the utes.'

'And what's that?' Hugh inclined his head at a tall cupboard.

'That's the gun cabinet.'

Ugh. Laura couldn't help but grimace.

'Don't look so horrified,' said Martha. 'You need them, out here in the country. It's always kept locked.'

Hugh opened the door. 'Not at the moment.'

Three long dark rifles were lined up in their racks. They really were horrible things. A shelf above held small cardboard boxes.

'Oh, dear.' Martha looked concerned. 'That's not good. I really must get onto that. Straight away. It's hard, since Robert . . . I find it more difficult to attend to all these jobs. Let's look outside.'

Poor Martha. Perhaps Laura should offer to help her with something. Not now though; let Martha finish her tour.

They crowded out onto an open area of wooden decking under a corrugated iron roof. Laura had to pick her steps carefully, between boards that were coming loose from their nails.

'Whoa, what happened there?' Hugh nodded towards a low weatherboard structure built out from the back of the house that seemed to be on the point of falling down.

Typical Hugh, launching forth without any tact. Laura reminded herself to quell her irritation, to be generous to her friends. To show kindness. But it didn't help when the others came out with their old annoying habits, right on cue.

'Oh yes, the laundry wing,' said Martha. 'It was repaired a number of years ago, but obviously not very well.'

Laura remembered there had been building work going on around that part of the house at the time of their bushwalk with Ed. But she wasn't going to mention that. Let Martha bring up Ed when she was ready.

'We had some wear and tear,' Martha went on. 'I need to get onto fixing that too. Unfortunately, the paint was delivered before the building materials.' Martha nodded at a couple of cans that were stacked near the back door.

The Martha they used to know would never have left things lying around out of place like that. But Laura kept her mouth closed. Instead, she gazed out across the valley. Mile after mile of grassy paddocks, not a house in sight.

Laura remembered that this was the only farm in the valley. Back in the day, Robert used to tell them repeatedly, with a note of pride, that it was 'one of the most isolated farms on the east coast'. Ed would mouth the phrase along behind him and they would have to try not to laugh.

Ed. He just kept popping up, whatever she was doing or thinking. And that was going to keep happening, this whole weekend.

Laura took a slow breath. She should just be in the moment. The evening light was beginning to turn pink. It was still very warm after the hot day. The valley was huge, and it was all so very quiet.

'Must get a bit lonely sometimes,' said Charlotte to Martha, with a smile.

Laura bet that smile was an effort for Charlotte. Charlotte would be horrified by the isolation, away from any opportunity for social interaction.

'Oh I'm quite used to it, after all these years,' Martha replied. 'Still no mobile coverage – but at least there's the satellite internet now, and they made sure that thing could project a little way around the house. She nodded back through the kitchen door towards the dresser where they could just see a white modem shoved behind some plates. 'That's one thing that's changed since you were here.'

Alex smiled. 'Connected to the twenty-first century, like it or not.'

Laura suppressed a frown. Did Alex have to be so jolly? Surely, he didn't really feel like that? Of course, everyone didn't have to be constantly gloomy, just because it was the anniversary of Ed's death. But the cheeriness, at least from Hugh, Alex and Charlotte was grating, considering this was meant to be a memorial weekend.

'Now. You young people should have some fun.' Martha waved at a large wooden box. 'Here, I got out the old set. You all used to love using that.'

Laura met her friends' eyes.

Jack shook his head. 'I don't know, Martha. I'm not sure we . . .'

'Go on!' Martha smiled.

'It's been so long,' said Hugh. 'I don't think we're really still into it.'

'I insist!'

Laura could see Martha's smile becoming more fixed, her jaw lifting.

They mustn't let Martha get stressed. Laura opened her mouth to persuade the others, but Alex got there before her. 'Come on, guys; it will be fun.'

'That's the spirit, Alex.' Martha nodded. She turned towards the kitchen. 'Now, where are my manners? I'll get you some drinks. I bet you boys would like a beer or two. You go ahead and get set up.'

Martha's voice trailed off as she wandered back into the house. Laura glanced from face to face. No one said a word as they gathered the box of mallets and hoops and headed down to the lawn.

Chapter 6

Martha stood in the middle of the kitchen, wondering why she was there. She was sure she had walked in here for a good reason.

The sound of talking drifted in through the window. She turned and frowned. Then she heard the clack of a croquet mallet against a ball.

She wasn't imagining these noises, remembering them from so long ago, as she often did. Ed's friends were really here, visiting. They were here because she had invited them in memory of Ed's death. And soon it would be dinnertime and she had come in here to the kitchen to cook dinner.

She turned to the fridge, opened the door and stared. Surely, she would have ordered something specific to cook for them on their first evening. Ah yes, she was going to do some lamb cutlets. But where were they? It was hard to find anything among the mix of bottles, packets and leftovers that were crammed in the fridge. Eventually, she found the cutlets wrapped up in butcher's paper and took them to a bench to begin preparing.

After much rooting around in a drawer, she found the chopping knife and vegetables and set to work. But then after a moment her hand slipped. A bright drop of blood appeared, and she pressed against it with her fingers. Her hands were shaking slightly.

She made herself take a breath. She had known it was going to be difficult, having them here, at the time of the anniversary. Of course, it was a shock to see them again. They were so present in her mind that the reality had been a bit of a jolt. But it was okay. It was. And it really was a big help that Laura was among them. Dear Laura. That girl had been such a comfort to her, over the years. Such a warm and caring young woman.

She was reminded of past times when they had visited. When Ed had still been here. She kept seeing the friends' faces of ten years ago superimposed over their current ones. They hadn't changed as much as she herself had, she knew that, but the changes were still there, in slightly thinner faces, wiser looks. The problem was, when she saw those younger faces, she kept looking for that other precious face that she would never see again.

People were concerned about her being out here, those few friends who had stayed in touch in the face of her misery. Especially now with Robert gone. Patricia, in particular, had often tried to convince her. It was time to move to the city, take a smaller place, let someone else run the farm.

Dear Patricia, she meant well. But that wouldn't be possible. This place was so connected to Ed. She couldn't leave. It would be like leaving him behind. When the grief was particularly painful, she could sooth herself by imagining the sound of his feet, as he ran down the stairs too fast despite her constant admonishments to slow down. She could hear his tread in the hall. If she closed her eyes, she could imagine the door opening and him appearing before her. Sometimes she could even feel the arm that he would sling around her shoulders as he looked down at her and reminded her of how much taller than her he was. And it helped, it really did. If she moved to some poky apartment in the city, free of memories, Ed would not be able to come with her.

Martha scrabbled in a drawer and eventually found a Band-Aid and pressed it against the tiny cut.

There was no need to be nervous. As she had told herself, she would see how the evening panned out, take it as it comes. But if it didn't go well, then at least she had a plan, and she had prepared well. Everything was ready to go, if it was needed.

Chapter 7

Alex swung his mallet between his knees. It hit the ball with a satisfying clunk, and sent it shooting across the grass, where it knocked another ball that was waiting expectantly just in front of the hoop. He had made a great shot. Unfortunately.

Sure enough, here it came. 'Damn you!'

Alex already knew Hugh was going to be more irritated than was really justified by a setback in game of croquet. The thing was, the shot was a complete accident – in fact, he had been trying not to hit Hugh's ball. He didn't want to annoy anyone further.

This trip had always been a bad idea. No good could come of it. Raking up the past like this held all sorts of dangers. But as soon as he saw the emailed invitation from Martha, he'd known it would be hard to decline. Then Charlotte had called, and Laura, and it had become clear that the others would all be going. So there was no way he could refuse to attend. Then Charlotte had somehow manoeuvred him into to offering Jack a lift, because Jack didn't have his own car. So here they all were.

Now he said, 'Sorry, Hugh. I can retake that. I think I might have fouled.'

Hugh was standing with his fists on his hips. 'No, you didn't foul, Alex.' Hugh sighed irritably. 'It's okay to try to win in croquet, you know. It's just a game.'

Alex chewed his lip. He shouldn't be nervous being around these people he'd known for so long. He thought, not for the first time, that he would rather have spent the weekend working. At least he never felt like his clients were judging him. They were just grateful for help to get back on their feet after their time in prison. He didn't have to worry about whether he fitted in with them, because there would never be any expectation of a social connection; no need to spend Friday nights getting pissed with his colleagues, like the kids from school seemed to do who were now lawyers and bankers.

Alex went to his ball. There was no choice but to put it straight through the hoop, and then onto the central post. Laura, Charlotte and Jack clapped from the edge of the lawn. Alex saw Charlotte saunter across the grass and pick up a mallet. She flicked her hair over her shoulder and looked around, checking to see who was watching. She gave the ball a decisive whack and watched it shoot confidently across the grass, and right past the hoop. She laughed, handed the mallet to Jack, then went to stand with Laura.

He let out a breath slowly. Just relax and enjoy being here.

As the game went on, the thwack of mallets against balls echoed back against the high walls of the house and were interspersed with occasional screeches as cockatoos wheeled overhead.

Hugh threw his mallet down. 'Well, I'm ready for a break now.'

They settled on dusty wicker chairs that were scattered at the edge of the yard. Hugh reached into the esky that Martha had provided and pulled out a beer. Alex could see Charlotte watching Hugh's arm, but she didn't say anything.

'Anyone else want one?' Hugh glanced around.

'I think I might need one.' Jack sighed. 'Dining with Martha tonight. It's not going to be the most relaxing meal, is it? She's wound up like a bloody top.'

'She's not the Mrs Fletcher from back in the day,' said Charlotte. 'The calm, competent hostess.'

Jack said, 'But she wasn't like this five years ago, was she? When we met, for the last memorial?'

Alex scrunched his face. 'It's been ten years since the walk. I'd have thought she would have gotten better, not worse.'

'Perhaps it was losing Robert that has kind of pushed her over the edge?' wondered Charlotte.

'One thing seemed a bit strange to me . . .' Jack leaned forward slowly. 'Did you notice that there aren't any photos of Ed in the house? Like, not a single one?'

'I guess she doesn't want to be reminded all the time.' Hugh shrugged.

'She wouldn't be reminded.' Laura's voice was soft. 'She would be thinking of him all the time, photos or no photos.'

'She does have that bedroom,' Charlotte noted. 'His old room. All his stuff, just . . . sitting there.'

They fell silent.

Alex saw Jack pull some papers and a small bag of leaves from his pocket.

Hugh looked over and gave a whistle. 'Hey, Jack. Now you're talking.'

Charlotte glared at Hugh.

'We'll go sit over here,' said Hugh. 'Away from you. Now, Jackie, my mate.'

The scent of the pot was sharp against Alex's nose. Hugh and Jack had hardly moved away at all. Hopefully Charlotte wouldn't stress about the smoke.

A dark shadow had crept across the valley and now covered most of the farmland, although the air was still warm. The cliffs opposite glowed orange in the last rays of the sun. Lights from the house began to gleam.

'So how's it going with you then, Jack?' asked Hugh. 'Still writing that PhD? What was it – the molecular structure of the rare Amazonian troutfish or something?'

Oh dear. Hugh was often funny, but sometimes when he'd been drinking, what he thought was funny wasn't so amusing to other people.

Jack turned his head slightly. 'Rainbow fish. It's Australian, not Amazonian.'

'Been a while now, hasn't it?'

'Six years. Yes. Thanks for reminding me.'

'Wanna tell me what it's about again?'

'Not really.'

Hugh looked at Jack and shook his head. 'You could have been anything. I mean, you were top of the year, top of the school. Goldman's, McKinsey would have snapped you up. Could have been earning a fortune by now.'

Bloody hell. Hugh must be able see that it wasn't exactly tactful to remind Jack about the ambitions he'd had. Did he not care? Was Hugh going to 'remember' that Jack had dropped out of a medical degree?

Jack simply shook his head.

Hugh's eyes wandered towards Jack's expansive girth. 'And I'm not sure this degree is doing you any—'

Out of Jack's sightline, Charlotte kicked Hugh and he fell silent. But not for long.

'Weren't you seeing someone?' Hugh asked. 'What was her name? Jenny?'

Jack looked down, rolling another joint. 'Julie. Just a bit of a difficult patch at the moment.' He paused to draw on the rolled paper. 'She's actually moved out. For a bit.'

Alex saw Jack glance at Laura. Laura immediately looked away.

'Okaaaay.' Hugh paused, then turned to Laura. 'And how about you? You still working at the same place? What were you, office manager?'

'Assistant manager.' Laura smiled grimly. 'Might be manager in a few decades.' She paused and her face grew more serious. Alex saw her press her fingertips together. 'But, actually, I do have some news.'

'Oh yeah?' Hugh sat up.

'I'm afraid it's not good news. I have – well I have a diagnosis.' She went quiet for a moment. 'Breast cancer.'

Oh god. Poor Laura.

'They tell me it's very bad luck for someone my age,' she continued.

Alex saw Charlotte reach over and curve her arms around Laura, who sat, unbending. 'Oh, Laur.'

'Whoa,' said Hugh. 'I'm sorry to hear that. God.'

'No, the prognosis is okay. It's just that I had a biopsy the other day and the wound is bothering me a bit.' She rubbed under her arm. Charlotte raised her eyebrows and Laura said, 'Yeah, so I need to make a decision. Whether to have the surgery. Mastectomy.'

Alex looked down. Horrible.

He heard Laura go on. 'I'm fine, really. It's not like I feel sick. Most of the work is dealing with other people's reactions.' She gave a grim smile.

She paused. 'But you know, something like this, it does put things in perspective. Makes you reconsider your choices.' Laura's gaze moved across each of them speculatively.

Suddenly Alex didn't like the expression on Laura's face. He had known a couple of people, over the years, for whom a cancer diagnosis had triggered big changes in outlook. The fact that Laura was looking around at her friends while she said this suggested she meant something involving them. And the something involving Ed was the obvious thing she would be thinking of.

But no; they had discussed that over and over again, and they had made their decision. They would leave the past back where it belonged. Let the sleeping dogs stay fast asleep.

It was all settled.

Chapter 8

'Bloody hell, what is this? The last supper?' Hugh stood in the doorway, surveying the scene.

The dark wood of the dining room soaked up the dim lamplight. French windows between faded drapes revealed the last of the evening light outside asserting itself against the reflection of the room. A table was laid with heavy silver cutlery and candlesticks. In the middle was a giant empty water pitcher.

'Shush, Hugh – she'll hear you!' whispered Charlotte.

'No, she won't.' Hugh plonked the bottle of wine he was carrying down on the table. Charlotte was being so bloody annoying lately. Her constant looking at him. It was like a burr he couldn't shake off. Perhaps this trip could be a good thing; getting away from the city with some other people could encourage her to be less clingy.

'Might pour this out while we're waiting,' he said, reaching for the bottle. No reason why they shouldn't try to enjoy their meal. He still thought the others were too worried about this weekend, even if Martha did seem a bit wound up. Old mates should be able to have a good time on a weekend away. If they had to drive all the way out here, then he at least intended to have fun.

Martha appeared, carrying a large plate. She laid it on the table then turned to them and put her hands together. 'Now, Charlotte, you here. Laura, next to me. Jack, you can go there, Hugh next to him. And Alex at the end.'

Each of them shuffled into place, sat, then turned to Martha.

'What? Oh no, no. I don't bother with grace these days.' Martha waved away their questioning glances. 'Hugh, how about you pass that plate around? Oh wait – the candles.' She stood and flitted between the candlesticks. Her hands shook a little as she flicked the matches.

Hugh looked at an empty chair at the end of the table, standing before a complete place setting. 'Are we waiting for someone else?'

Martha looked at the chair. 'No.'

'I can move it out of the way,' Hugh offered. 'Give us a bit more room.'

'That chair is for Ed.'

There was a sudden stillness. It seemed like the temperature in the room dropped a degree. Did she really just say that?

'It's my little way of remembering him. At a meal like this.'

God. It was like in that play, thought Hugh. Who was it? Bloody Banquo's ghost.

The shocked silence went on.

'So! How do you all find being back here?' Martha asked brightly.

After a moment, Alex cleared his throat. 'I'm, er, remembering all the great trips we used to have here. Back in the school holidays.'

Good old Alex. Always rushing in to smooth over any awkwardness. Shame he was often so awkward himself. Like, that grey blazer he was wearing now was just a bit too fancy – the bloke had gone and changed for dinner, for god's sake.

There was a murmur from the others. 'Yeah, good times.'

Hugh swirled the wine in his mouth, felt it go down. There was nothing like the surge of alcohol in your veins. He felt Charlotte's eyes on him again but ignored her. If she wasn't so bloody watchful, he wouldn't feel so irritated and want to drink more.

Another silence. Charlotte's forehead scrunched. Hugh followed her gaze and saw the dried food caught in the edge of her bowl. She laid her spoon down.

'I'd forgotten how long it takes to get here,' said Hugh. See, he could make small talk too.

'Road felt a bit scary, coming down into the valley,' said Charlotte.

Martha nodded. 'It's not great, is it? People always wondered why they went to such trouble to put it in, right through the national park, given we're the only property in the region. It was probably because the Fletcher who set up the farm originally was Minister for Roads. He was the Honourable Percival Fletcher. And that's also how the place got connected to the services, like the mains water.'

'Would have been pretty challenging engineering, especially back then,' said Alex.

'Yes, it was a long time ago.' Martha looked thoughtful. 'You know, there was another, older house, even before this house was built by Robert's grandfather. Percy Fletcher was given a land grant after the first explorers noticed the rich soil around here.

They were the ones who called this the Lost Valley. Percy set up a logging business; he was going to establish cattle as a local industry – but then the war came. By the twenties they decided that the forest should be a national park instead.'

Hugh didn't want Martha to launch into more Fletcher farm history, an extremely boring topic that he'd heard way too much of over the years, but he couldn't think of anything else to say.

'What about the original inhabitants? They'd been noticing the soil and everything else for tens of thousands of years.' But Jack's murmur was so low that only Hugh heard.

The sound of cutlery clinking against the plates filled the silence.

Martha hands were twitching, and she shifted in her chair.

Hugh tried to catch his friends' eyes, but they were all looking at their plates. They picked at the droopy leaves of salad that Martha had laid out.

'And how is the pregnancy going, Charlotte?' Martha looked like her teeth were clenched behind her smile.

'Oh, I'm fine, thank you so much for asking.' Charlotte turned to Martha with a big smile and started to talk about dietary restrictions. God, she was gushing, Hugh thought. She should dial it back a bit. Even he could tell that Martha didn't really want to hear about it.

'It will be so lovely for you and Hugh when the baby arrives. Such a sealing of the commitment you've made to each other.'

Charlotte looked up at Martha.

'You'll be looking after the baby,' Martha went on. 'And Hugh will be caring for both of you.' Martha turned to Hugh. 'Sometimes becoming a father can really bring out a man's gentle side.'

Hugh frowned. Her tone was so odd. It really sounded like she was having a dig at him. 'Yep, sure will,' he said, and turned abruptly to Alex. 'How's work going for you?'

Alex said quickly, 'Oh, yes, all good.'

'You were at a charity, weren't you?' asked Laura.

'Yes, I work with prisoners who have just been released, to help them reintegrate into the community.'

Of course he bloody does. Saint Alex.

'Gosh. That sounds like it could be challenging.' Martha looked a little concerned. 'But then, we all need to earn our money. To make an honest living.'

Hugh could see Alex looking at Martha strangely.

But Alex went on. 'It's actually really rewarding.' He laid his fork down, and as he began to describe the work his voice grew more animated. 'We can see people being given a second chance even though they might have done something wrong, and mostly they're grateful for our help.'

The others kept feeding Alex comments and questions. Hugh smiled grimly to himself. He bet they were relieved to have some conversational momentum which didn't involve probing by Martha, and they each wanted to keep the focus on someone else.

Hugh took another gulp of wine and looked about the room. All light from outside was gone now. There was nothing but their own reflection in the window – a ghostly set of shadow people having their own dinner behind the glass. The halting conversation hovered above the clink of cutlery against china. The warm room had grown even stuffier. And all the time Martha's smile was fixed and bright.

Martha turned to Jack. 'And how's your PhD going?'

After a moment Jack said, 'Fine, thanks.'

'You were always so smart. So good at school.' She tipped her head on one side and stared at him.

Jack moved his head slightly to look at her. 'Er, thank you.' His voice trailed off, and he looked away.

Where was she going with this? God, would this meal never end?

'Martha, we were all so sorry to hear about Robert.' Charlotte's voice was gentle. 'It must be hard for you. Here, by yourself.'

Martha looked down and nodded. Then, staring at the ceiling she said, 'You may not know. He took his own life.'

This silence was filled with a whole new horror.

Faark! Could this meal get any worse?

'Robert was an old-school father. Pretty strict with Ed. Aloof. In the end, I think he couldn't deal with the fact that he never got the chance to change that.'

'I'm so very sorry, Martha,' Charlotte said, barely above a whisper. Hugh bet she was even more sorry about mentioning Robert.

No one moved. Alex was frozen, staring at his plate.

Martha was gazing into the centre of the table with a lost look on her face.

Hugh saw Laura draw breath to speak, then think better of it. He wasn't surprised. He would have been very impressed if she had thought of something appropriate. *How tragic. What a loss for you. How are you coping?* It was all so bloody empty. They couldn't even say how much they missed him, because Martha knew that he hadn't been close to any of them.

Finally, Martha looked up. She glanced around the room as if she had just woken up and was a bit confused.

'It's been very warm lately, hasn't it?' she said. She looked at their plates. 'Time for dessert, I think.'

When her footsteps through to the kitchen had died away, Hugh said in a stage whisper, 'Oh my fucking god.'

Charlotte grimaced at the others. Jack started to speak, but then Martha's footsteps sounded again.

She carried a large plate with an air of triumph. 'You all love blancmange, don't you?'

Hugh couldn't remember ever eating anything like the pink gelatinous mass that wobbled on the plate, but he was pretty sure he wouldn't have loved it if he had.

Martha began to ladle out large servings. Hugh saw Charlotte peering at the opaque jelly as if trying to see through it to the other side.

'Thanks Mrs Fletcher – Martha,' said Alex. 'You've gone to so much trouble for us. With this meal. And having us to stay.'

'Oh, it's no trouble, Alex. Don't worry.'

Hugh moved the blancmange around a little on his plate.

'But, you know, there is something,' said Martha. 'That you could all perhaps do for me.'

Hugh noticed a look pass between Martha and Laura. Laura gave a tiny nod. He straightened up. What were these two up to?

Martha picked up her napkin and twisted it, as though wringing out water. She put it in her napkin ring, then began to twist the ring.

'I know you were young. You were all affected.'

Hugh felt the room go still.

'But now. The years have passed. You're older. You've had all this time to think.' Her eyes darted this way and that.

All eyes in the room were glued on hers.

The room was absolutely silent. Hugh took a breath. The air seemed thicker, harder to breathe.

'Perhaps you've remembered something. You know, you can just tell me, if you have.'

For a moment, Hugh felt himself back in a clearing in the bush, with Alex, Jack, Charlotte and Laura. Standing in a ring, near a giant turpentine tree.

The same kind of silence, back then, had slowly reached into their throats and stopped up their voices. The same creeping horror as now, curling at their skin.

Now, in the dining room, Martha's words were slow, emphatic. 'On the walk with Ed. What really happened?'

Chapter 9

Ten years previously

Martha and Robert Fletcher had taken the opportunity for a cuppa on the veranda of the homestead. They didn't often get to meet during the day, with Robert busy in the paddocks and Martha supervising staff, but Robert had been working near the house and Martha had a cake that needed sampling.

Martha enjoyed the energy that arrived with Ed's friends. The house was always so quiet when Ed was away at school, which only highlighted the contrast with the holidays. And she must do a reasonable job at hosting because the friends kept visiting. It was quiet again now the kids were off on their walk, but they'd soon be back, shouting and clattering up and down the stairs and eating everything in sight.

In the meantime, it was nice to have a moment with Robert. Martha felt the heat of the tea slide down her throat. It was still refreshing, despite the fact that the air pressing around them as they sat on the veranda was very warm. She could hear the occasional whisper of a soft breeze through the nearby trees, and saw the grass flatten and stir.

Another movement caught her eye. She dipped her head down to peer over the top of her glasses. 'That can't be the kids already? They've only had one night away. They were planning for at least three, weren't they?'

Robert looked up from his farming journal.

'Look, up there at the edge of top paddock.' Martha nodded, but didn't take her eyes off what she had seen.

Just at the point where the thick green of the bush met the yellow of the paddocks, she could see some small figures. The coloured lumps on their backs could well be backpacks. They shimmered in the heat rising off the grass.

The figures left the green of the forest and began to bob across the paddock.

'I'll get the binoculars.'

Robert returned after a moment and peered towards the bush. 'Yes it's them. They're back early.'

Martha stood up. 'But – there's only five of them.'

The couple stood silently for another minute.

Then Robert, looking again through the binoculars, said, 'It's Ed. Ed's not there.'

The warm air seemed to grow thicker. The valley was suddenly quiet.

Martha said, 'He must have been hurt.'

'We'll drive up and meet them,' said Robert. Without another word, they made their way to the ute that stood beside the house, fired the engine and turned towards the track.

The sinking feeling in Martha's stomach grew stronger as they rocked across the uneven ground and neared the group in the paddock. As the ute approached, the kids started to run, and now Martha could see the faces of Charlotte, Laura, Alex, Jack and Hugh, drawn and anxious.

'Oh, god,' Martha whispered.

Robert pulled the handbrake and they both stepped out.

The kids crowded around Martha and Robert. Their faces were streaked with dirt and sweat. Martha could smell the sourness of perspiration. She heard their laboured breathing.

They all began to talk at once.

'Calm down.' Robert's sudden, deep voice silenced them. 'What happened?'

'You need to get a rescue party, now,' said Jack. 'We'll show you on the map.'

Laura's face was twisted in distress. She burst out, in a shriek, 'Hurry! You have to hurry!'

Chapter 10

Jack's throat was dry. He looked around the dining table at his friends. They all had their gaze fixed on Martha. Jack tried to think of a response but, as was all too common these days, his brain just wasn't firing.

This silence was excruciating.

Alex was the first to speak. 'Martha, we went through everything that happened. At the inquest.' His voice rose.

Martha's voice was low and urgent. 'Listen. This is just for me. Nothing else needs to change,' she went on. 'I'm not going to make a fuss. It's just so I can know.'

Jack's mind slowly spooled back ten years, and then the intervening years seemed to flash in front of him in a jerky time-lapse.

For a moment his friends' expressions shifted, unformed. The decision seemed to hover in the very air. Would they tell her?

Alex's voice rose again. 'Martha. There's nothing more to say.'

Martha's face was crumbling, but she hadn't given up. 'I just need to know.'

Now Jack could see his friends shaking their heads, as though sorry for her hurt and murmuring comforts. His own throat was jammed up. The momentum was set. No one was going to talk.

Martha looked from face to face. She looked out of the long windows as if appealing to the twin dinner party that was reflected above the lawn. She pressed her lips together.

After a long moment, she turned back to them. 'Okay.' She nodded. 'Right!' She got up with a start. She whipped out the plates from Hugh and Jack and brought them down together, with a clank that was softened by a squish of sugary foam.

Jack saw Charlotte eye the crockery, alarm on her face.

'I'm sure you've got lots to talk about. You don't want an old woman like me here, cramping your style.'

Jack started to protest, hearing the others speak at the same time.

'No, it's fine.'

'Let us clear up, please.'

As Laura, Alex, Hugh and Jack stood and started to pick up plates, Charlotte heaved herself to her feet.

Martha paused and looked around the room vaguely. She started towards the door. Then she turned back to them. 'Well, yes. I think I might. Good night then. I hope you all . . .' She paused. She nodded. 'What? Oh, yes, I hope you all sleep really well.'

The silence after she left went on and on as they stared at the empty door frame.

Jack let his breath out slowly.

Then Laura moved. With a stiff expression she began to stack plates.

Jack reached for a plate to gather up. Movement seemed very difficult.

The others joined in, avoiding each other's eyes. The only sound was crockery and cutlery jostling together.

Later, in the kitchen, Jack stepped backwards from the sink suddenly as the water shot out of the tap, hit a spoon and sprayed up at him. He adjusted the water, squirted a little detergent and placed a handful of cutlery into the water.

The others were unloading piles of crockery onto the table, their faces looking slightly ill in the yellow light from the bulb hanging in the centre of the ceiling.

'Well, that was fun.' Hugh's speech was slurring. 'We're going to have a great weekend, I can tell.'

'Oh, shut up, Hugh.' Charlotte thumped a tray down. 'You're not helping.'

'Charlotte, you should sit down.' Laura turned to her with concern. 'You look tired.'

Charlotte stopped. 'You know, actually, I might. You've got no idea how exhausting it is, just being pregnant.' She picked up a napkin and fanned her face. 'But hey, Laura, you should sit down too, I mean . . .'

'No, it's fine.' Laura carried a set of plates to the sink. 'I'm not in treatment yet. I feel normal. I'll grab the rest of the plates.' She headed out into the kitchen passage.

Jack looked back from the sink. Hugh stood, swaying slightly, a loose grin on his face. Charlotte was glaring at him. Even Alex was silent.

Jack gathered his energy and said, 'I'll just go help Laura.' It would be a good opportunity to chat to her away from the others.

He went through the dim passage and was about to go into the dining room when he heard voices from the sitting room and drew near to the door. Inside, Laura was next to Martha, talking intently. They stopped as soon as they saw him.

'Oh sorry.' Jack took a step backwards. 'I didn't mean to interrupt.'

'I was just going up to bed,' said Martha.

'And I was about to get the rest of the plates,' said Laura.

She squeezed Martha's hand, then passed Jack and walked into the dining room. He followed her and started piling up the crockery. He studied her as she gathered the bowls. What was going on behind that face?

He made an effort to speak. 'Laura.'

'Hey, can you get the rest of these? I don't think I can carry any more.' She left the room abruptly.

Damn it, he just wanted to talk. Okay, he wanted to talk to get a better sense of what she thought of him these days. But now he had no choice but to follow her back into the kitchen.

Jack could see Hugh clowning around, waving his arms wildly and pretending to fall to the floor. His arm almost knocked a plastic thermometer off its hook near the door frame. He, Alex and Charlotte were laughing.

'Shut up!' said Laura urgently.

'What?'

Footsteps in the hall stopped, then faded away.

Laura looked back through the door to the hall. 'Fantastic,' she said crossly. 'That was Martha. Hearing us laugh like drains. Now she thinks we're all happy as Larry on the anniversary of Ed's death. Nice.'

It was so uncomfortable seeing her angry like this. 'It's okay to laugh, Laura. It has been ten years.'

But Laura just shook her head again.

After the plates had been cleared into the dishwasher and the hand washing done, Hugh said, 'Anyone up for another drink?'

Jack took a breath. 'How about we go up to the roof? Remember how we used to hang out there, back in the day?' He could feel those dried leaves tucked away in his back pocket. Okay, so his 'occasional recreational smoke' was becoming a little too frequent. But it was just so tempting. So effective as an anaesthetic. And the roof would be a good place to indulge, especially after that awful dinner.

'I don't want a drink, obviously,' said Charlotte. 'But I'd like to see the view again. And it might be a bit cooler up there.'

Laura looked out the window. 'There's a bit of a moon. Let's go take a look.'

Chapter 11

In the hallway of the first floor of the house was a pull-down ceiling flap which gave access to a little ladder into the roof cavity. From there the group had to shuffle out through a casement window onto a small flat area between the sloping roof and a low wall between two gables. Hugh went first, Laura next, and then the others.

Laura leaned back and gazed upwards. A vast black sky stretched above, the milky way clouding across the middle of an extravagant wash of stars. Then she let out a long sigh. She shivered at the beauty of it. 'That's stunning.'

'So is that.' Jack gave a slow nod towards the fields.

He was right. The valley lay dreamlike in its stillness, lit a ghostly grey by a waxing moon. Gum trees in the surrounding paddock rustled into movement. The warm breeze washed across the group as they sat on the roof, then it subsided. Theirs was the only building in the whole silver landscape.

It was all so beautiful, Laura thought. Such a contrast with all the chaotic emotions that this trip was bringing up.

Out of the corner of her eye, Laura saw Jack pull a little packet from his pocket, and then she noticed Hugh's approving grin. Jack leaned back and began fiddling with some papers, his movements deliberate. So, he was quite a keen user now. A bit of a smoke now and then was pretty common among Laura's friends, but there was a line, and heavy usage was rarely a sign that someone was calm and happy with their life.

Jack lit the joint, took a puff, then passed it over to Hugh. 'I can't help remembering sitting up here with Ed.'

'Yeah, we used to hide up here to drink beer.' Hugh grinned.

'We could hear Martha calling for us. She could hear us talking but couldn't work out where we were!'

'I was always nervous,' said Alex. 'Mr Fletcher was a bit of a dragon, I thought. I was convinced he was going to find us and go mental.'

'Ed wasn't bothered. I remember him sitting there, making faces as Martha called out, and she was getting more and more frantic.'

'He could be so funny.'

'Everyone loved him.'

'Bloody Ed, and his endless charisma.'

'Yeah, he sure had everyone at school wrapped around his little finger. All the teachers.'

'Hey, do you remember when Ed hosted the country party here?' Hugh was looking around. 'It was such a crazy evening.'

Laura nodded. 'The music just went on and on, all night. Robert eventually showed up and cut the power, remember?' It had indeed been a fun night. From a happier time.

'I remember waking up down in the bottom paddock. No idea how I got there,' said Jack.

'And we were all so stunned that studious Jack had drunk too much.'

'It was pretty wild,' said Alex.

Chapter 12

Eleven years previously

'Almost there.' Ed looked back from the driver's seat and flashed a grin at the passengers, who all whooped on cue.

Alex was sitting in the back, squashed in against a window. He joined in a millisecond after the others.

'It's going to be such a blast.'

Alex nodded and smiled along with the other boys sitting on the back seat. There was another cheer as the Fletcher house came into view, and they began to trundle up the driveway.

'Better put that out before Mum sees you.' Ed nodded at Hugh, who blew a cloud of smoke out the window then stubbed out his cigarette on the dashboard.

'Your mum should be less worried about one little cigarette than all the other stuff in the boot.'

'What she doesn't know won't hurt her.'

'Just as well – we are going to get so wasted.'

Another cheer.

Alex smiled again, although it was less at the prospect of all the drinking and mostly at the fact that he was here, sitting in the back of the car with the others, on their way to the party.

Ed's country party had been all anyone had spoken of for weeks. Now term was finally over, and this car was just the first of many that would arrive full of students from their own school and the network of friends across other schools, all journeying out to the country for the ritual of lots of booze and loud music on a family property.

As a member of Ed's house group, along with Hugh, Charlotte, Jack and Laura, Alex could probably have assumed he'd be invited. But he always had a sneaking worry that perhaps the others might decide he just wasn't cool enough. So he had been relieved as well as pleased when the invitation was casually tossed at him by Ed. Probably it was nothing to Ed. The guy wouldn't know what it was like to wonder if he would be included in some key social event because he probably had always assumed, correctly, that he'd be at the centre of things.

Alex remembered telling his parents. They had dropped into school briefly to fix some paperwork and the house master had suggested Alex might skip a period to see them.

'By the way, I won't be coming home straight away at the end of term. Ed Fletcher has invited some people back to his parents' farm. There'll be a lot of kids from other schools. So I'll spend a day or two there, get a lift back to the city on the Sunday or Monday.'

Alex had made his voice carefully offhand, but he couldn't help smiling. However, his mother had just looked vaguely at him and said, 'That's nice, dear.' She had gone back to examining the camellias in the courtyard of the office building, and his father had checked his watch, put his arm around his wife and said they'd better be going.

'So, kids, less about the drinking in front of Mum and Dad, okay?' Ed nodded at his passengers as the car drew up near the house.

Alex could see Mr and Mrs Fletcher waiting on the front veranda. Ed got out and ran to them. Mrs Fletcher gave him a hug, and Mr Fletcher nodded.

When his friends got out of the car there were handshakes for Mr Fletcher and nods from Ed's mother. She ushered the group inside. 'Come in for some afternoon tea before you unload.'

Alex took in the high space of the entrance hall, the grand stairway disappearing upwards, but jerked his head back when he realised he might be gawping. His own parents weren't short of money, but there was a different atmosphere here, like the dollars had been laid down a long time before and infused into the brickwork.

He stood at the back of the crowd that was jostling at the sandwiches and cakes laid out on the kitchen table. Martha stood back, smiling as the school kids ate their fill.

Then Ed shoved the rest of his sandwich in his mouth. 'I'm going to get the car unloaded,' he said, through the last of his mouthful.

'I'll help.' Alex stepped forward.

Soon there was a line of bags and boxes parading through the front door.

Alex was standing in the hallway with some bags when he saw Ed stop to talk to his parents. He heard Ed murmuring. Then Mrs Fletcher gasped and clasped her son in her arms. 'Oh well done, darling!'

Alex saw Ed's huge grin. Mr Fletcher's face softened, and he nodded at his son.

'Of course they chose you,' Mrs Fletcher gushed. 'The smartest, most popular boy in the year. Bet you ran rings around the others.'

So Ed had told his parents the news: he'd been elected school captain.

'Steady on, Mum.' Ed laughed. 'Plenty of smarter kids than me. Anyway, I'd better go organise everyone.' He barged out the door, and Alex went back to stacking the boxes.

He could still hear Mrs and Mrs Fletcher talking.

'You make too much of that boy.' Mr Fletcher shook his head. 'It's not good for him.' His face was stern.

'Robert, he's done so well. Anyone would be proud of that. And he's all we've got.'

Then Alex heard a commotion outside. Another car had drawn up in front of the Fletcher house and set off a round of shouting. Soon there were footsteps on the front veranda and another set of bags appeared in the doorway, with Ed shepherding them through.

Alex took a couple of backpacks from the new people, and carried them into the dimly lit sitting room. He set them against the wall. He saw Hugh come in and dump an armload of the other kids' stuff near the desk. Then Hugh took a few steps, fiddled with his own bag and took something out, then pressed it behind some papers on the desk.

There was another cry from the front of the house. Hugh made his way to the front lawn and Alex followed a moment later. While the others backslapped the new arrivals Alex looked over to the next paddock, which was beginning to fill up with utes. Someone had laid out a canvas sheet on the ground and a few people were standing around, waving tent poles at each other.

'I'm just going to sleep in the back of the ute,' said Hugh. 'I've got Dad's swag, anyway. Old man probably used it when he went partying in the bush.'

Then a cheer went up. Alex turned and saw that Ed had appeared on the veranda. Ed smiled and waved to his people.

Imagine having that kind of appeal, Alex thought. The world would be a completely different place.

A few hours later, the sun had set, the music was going and the cans of beer had started to do their work. With the enveloping darkness, Alex was feeling more relaxed. Someone had already vomited into Martha's rose garden at the front of the house. Ed certainly hadn't minded – and there was likely to be a lot more throwing up before the party had finished – but Alex kept himself in check with the booze; he hated the thought of the others seeing him like that. He just didn't feel like he knew them well enough. It occurred to him that he had never known anyone well enough to feel comfortable throwing up drunk in front of them, but he quashed that thought quickly.

He stood at the edge of a group of girls and boys who were chatting. He'd made a joke earlier, about one of the teachers at school, which had raised a laugh among the others, and he was still feeling a glow of pleasure from the moment.

He felt a hand on his shoulder.

'Alex, my man.'

Alex turned. Ed looked at him and the skin around his eyes crinkled. 'Hope you're having a good time, mate.' Ed waved at the rest of the party. 'Realise you don't know this lot as well as I do. But they'll look after you.'

Everyone talked about the famous Fletcher charisma. But Ed could be thoughtful as well as charming, and it was clear why people were drawn to him.

Alex thanked Ed then watched him make his way to the sound system.

The bonfire had been lit. It stood at the centre of the action, a pyramid of leaping flames. Shimmering orange light was cast around the house and surrounding paddocks. It lit up the outhouses and sheds, and even Mr Fletcher's tall radio aerial at the far end of the home paddock. Flickering images of dancing bodies flashed against the black night. A new song came on, a dance number with a strong beat. Ed turned up the volume and a cheer echoed across the space.

Alex saw Ed turn, survey his little kingdom and smile upon all his good work.

Even later. More chaos. Shrieking and running. Alex clutched at a fence post as a crowd of kids ran past him. That was the second group that had dashed past. They appeared to be playing some game. Was it hide and seek?

He thought about joining in but, as his stomach lurched, he realised he wasn't up for running around. And that thudding music from the speaker was not helping. He needed to get some air, away from the noise.

It was sure to be quieter around the front of the house. He averted his eyes from more than one snogging couple as he walked. Alex had heard about all the opportunities with girls that these country parties presented, but none of the girls he'd spoken to so far had seemed particularly interested in him.

But as he came round the side of the house he stopped. Blue and red lights were flickering across the grass and flashing against the trees. They were coming from the front of the house. He stumbled around the corner, and saw an ambulance, with paramedics loading a stretcher into the back.

Mr Fletcher was standing nearby, his face stern.

Alex jumped as a hand grasped his shoulder.

He looked down to see a girl with straggling black hair looking up at him blearily.

'Guy so drunk, he collapsed. Passed out. Got the ambulance.' The girl was slurring her words. 'Too much of this.' She waved a plastic cup of beer at Alex. 'Great party, huh?'

Without waiting for an answer, she turned back towards the music.

The persistent chirp of birds woke Alex. He prised his eyes open and realised that it was daylight. Very early, but there was light. He struggled up onto one elbow and peered out of the tent flap.

All around the paddock of the house were prone bodies. Some of the partygoers hadn't even been able to fight their way into their tent or up onto the tray of their ute.

He lay back down again and closed his eyes. But sleep eluded him, and after a while he struggled out of the tent and stood. The early air was crisp and the sky was clear. Wrapping a blanket around himself, he made his way across the rough grass towards the house. Perhaps he could quietly rustle up some coffee.

When he got to the back of the house he saw Hugh, Jack and Charlotte sitting on the back veranda, bleary-eyed.

'You're up early,' he said.

Jack poked Hugh with his foot. 'This one woke us up. Decided he had to go find his precious possessions right away.'

Hugh was looking very grumpy. 'Couldn't find it.'

Charlotte looked at Hugh. 'He's lost some cash. Probably just can't remember where he put it – he's still bloody drunk from last night. Don't worry, it'll turn up.'

Ed appeared at the kitchen door. 'Coffee, anyone?'

Alex joined in the gentle cheer.

Jack stood and clapped Ed on the shoulder.

'Ed, my mate. Last night was an absolute blast.'

Hugh looked up. 'Agreed. It'll go down in history. Legendary party.'

Alex saw the others laughing and joined in, his smile matching those on their young, carefree faces.

70

Chapter 13

'Wish Ed was here now,' Jack burst out.

Laura saw him staring out at the starlit landscape. She wanted to speak, but her throat had closed up. Ten years, and she was still too upset to talk about Ed easily. It was hard, hearing the others talk about him like this. It felt like they were stepping all over her sacred ground. She reminded herself that they were also bereaved. She didn't own the memory.

Laura thought about Martha, about the woman's endless sadness over the past ten years. It probably hadn't helped that Robert and Martha had stayed out here on the farm by themselves after Ed's death, so close to where it had happened. They were so isolated. It was hideous that Robert had taken his own life – but not entirely surprising. So now the woman had two terrible deaths to bear.

Laura looked out at the silver world. There won't be a better moment, she thought. She was nervous, but she took a breath and made herself speak. 'You know, I've been thinking.' She saw four faces turn toward her. 'Perhaps we should be more honest. About what happened. With Ed.'

The silence went on. Laura made herself wait.

Alex was staring at her closely. Eventually, he said, 'Are you kidding?'

Then Jack said, 'We went through this.'

'I know.' Laura made sure her voice was neutral. 'But that was then. And this is now.'

'What's changed?' asked Jack evenly.

'We've grown older. Hopefully more mature.' Laura looked back at him.

'Are you having one of those cancer moments?' Hugh's voice held an edge.

Laura's pulse leapt. Bloody Hugh. 'Excuse me?' She met his eye.

'You know what I mean. I've seen it before. People get a diagnosis, they want to go all deep and meaningful.'

'Okay, so perhaps it has made me think again. And that's no bad thing. Cancer or no cancer, we should all take the time to examine our lives with a bit of objectivity. Think about what's the right thing to do.'

Did it even need saying? That you should try to think about what's right and do it seemed so obvious. Of course, people were going to disagree about exactly what 'right' was, but all too often it seemed like they didn't even want to have the conversation, didn't even want to think about it.

Obviously, sometimes doing the right thing was hard. Laura was prepared to admit that she herself wasn't above reproach. Sometimes when you woke up and it was cold and windy, getting up and going to that protest march was really tough. She still felt bad about the time she'd pretended to her flatmate that her niggling cough was worse than it really was and instead of going out to the protest had stayed home under the doona. Sometimes she did feel really tempted to sneak that crisply curling bacon onto her egg roll. But when you'd made a moral commitment like not eating other sentient creatures, you had to stick to it.

And when you'd done the wrong thing, it was usually best to be honest about that.

'Laura.' Alex's face was tense. 'No. We *really* shouldn't go there.' His voice was very tight.

Laura's voice moved up a notch. She knew this wasn't likely to be an easy conversation. She was prepared. 'Well, I think it would do us good.'

'What do you mean, do us good?' Hugh asked.

Sometimes Hugh was just so frustrating. There was something about his snarky voice that always tested her patience. 'I know you're Mr Cool, Hugh, but don't you feel bad about what happened? Even just a little?'

'Of course, I do!' His voice was suddenly loud, so that Laura started back a little, but she didn't break his gaze. She wasn't going to be diverted that easily. She lifted her chin.

'We. Agreed.' Alex's face twisted. 'We wouldn't go into all the . . . irrelevant details.'

Laura saw Jack nodding agreement with Alex, along with Hugh and Charlotte.

'Laura, don't you remember what it was like, after they found Ed – how Martha reacted?' Alex pressed on. 'And everything else that happened?'

In the pause that followed, Laura thought back to that time. The media circus, the invasive questioning and distressing criticism.

'Do we really want to open ourselves up to all of that, all over again?' Charlotte looked around at the others.

Laura had to agree; it had been awful. They really should have had some sort of media manager. One of those PR people who help protect reputations after a crisis. But that wasn't relevant to the question at hand.

'Hang on,' Laura said. 'We're not proposing to give a newspaper interview. It's just Martha.'

'No.' Alex was more vehement. 'We should *not* upset Martha with this.'

Laura turned to him. 'She's already upset! Isn't that obvious?'

'Yes, I agree, she's clearly really wound up. And this might tip her over the edge.' Alex was insistent.

'Especially coming on top of Robert.' Hugh nodded. 'Holy crap. I just didn't know what to say at dinner when Martha told us. I mean, it was sad hearing that he'd died. But – *suicide?* That's so messed up.'

Laura stiffened. They had not talked about Robert, but Hugh of course waded in heedlessly.

Laura stood at the bench in her parents' kitchen, making biscuits, ignoring the buzzing of her phone. Baking was therapeutic. It was positive. It wasn't anything to do with death, or anger, or aggression – or the media.

She had learned that the phone was rarely going to have a message she wanted to read. Probably some person she knew, whom she had thought of as a friend, helpfully pointing out yet another hostile internet post.

She went back to the biscuits. Curling spoonfuls of mixture, one by one. Pressing knobs of buttery goo on the tray. She took deep breaths, as the counsellor had told her to.

The phone buzzed again, and then kept buzzing. She sighed and let the call go to voicemail.

A minute later, another call. Then another. She finally relented and played the voicemail, and as she heard Charlotte's words, her face dropped.

'Oh my god, Laura. It's awful.' Charlotte's voice was breaking. 'He's tried to – hurt himself. Call me, soon as you get this.'

Soon afterwards Charlotte arrived at Laura's house. They hugged for a long moment. They gripped each other's hands as they sat together in the back seat, Laura's mother glancing at them in the rear-view mirror as she drove.

Then, through her tears, Laura felt a new emotion. She realised she was actually furious – furious with him. She kept pushing the feeling away, ashamed. But it persisted; she was angry, she really was. Didn't they all have enough to deal with, without him doing this?

She stomped up the front steps of the hospital, glancing at Charlotte's tearstained face as the doors opened and the antiseptic smell washed around them. They were all grieving; they were all stressed. What was so special about him?

Their footsteps echoed through long polished corridors. When they arrived at the ward, a nurse glanced at them sympathetically and pulled aside the curtains so they could stand in the cubicle next to the bed.

Hugh and Jack were already there, shifting uncomfortably on their feet. Laura met Hugh's eyes. He grimaced at her, then looked down at the bed.

Laura's breath caught. She stared, fascinated, at the bandages around Alex's wrists. His long limbs stretched beneath a blanket.

She made herself look at Alex's face. It was the same colour as the sheets. His expression was wretched. He opened his mouth but then closed it and looked down again.

Laura's anger melted away.

The silence in the cubicle went on and on. Laura tried to speak, but a big lump was jamming up her throat.

Finally, she stepped next to the bed and took Alex's hand. 'We're so sorry. We're here for you. We'll help you.'

She nodded reassuringly at Alex as the silence returned and expanded and filled the cubicle full of miserable teenagers.

Alex caught the looks between the others. Impatience flashed over his face. 'It's okay, guys. I'm not going to crack up again.'

'Of course you're not.' Charlotte nodded soothingly. 'But I just think we need to remember how horrible that time really was. And going over all that again is not exactly going to create a happy environment, for anyone, is it?'

Laura sensed the others' resistance to her suggestion was solidifying.

She lifted her chin. She turned to Jack. 'What do you think?' It was perhaps a little bit manipulative, because Jack would want to support her. But clever Jack's opinion still held weight.

Jack pushed his glasses up his nose. 'I – look, Laura.' He paused. 'I just don't think it's a good idea. Given what we went through. How Martha reacted back then. And given what we've seen of her today. She's hardly, well, stable, is she?'

Hugh nodded. 'I agree. God knows what she might do.'

Alex said firmly, 'I definitely do not think we should go back there. No way.'

Hugh nodded at Charlotte, Jack and Alex. 'No, we'll stick to the plan. We've done the right thing, showing up for this memorial. We'll be nice to Martha, help her out however we can, get through this thing on Sunday. Then get out of here and get back to normal life.'

Chapter 14

The following morning, the valley lay still and quiet under the first rays of the sun. A cockatoo surveying the scene from a branch high in a gum tree suddenly took off, gliding across the valley and letting out a raucous screech just as it flew past the homestead.

Inside the house, Jack awoke as the screech pierced his early-morning dreams and his eyes registered the light. He dragged his eyes open and contemplated the rickety blinds.

He had slept badly. No doubt the pot and the booze yesterday evening hadn't helped. He felt an overwhelming urge to pull the bedcovers over his head, close his eyes again and let unconsciousness claim him.

But it was already too warm to be under the covers and, anyway, he knew that the relief of sleep was beyond him now.

He fumbled with the French doors and stepped out onto the balcony, his steps heavy. The boards creaked under his foot. The morning air was warm on his face and his expression softened as he saw the valley in the morning light. Even the old tractor rusting in the long grass at the far end of a paddock looked picturesque amid the gentle pastels of the scene.

He yawned and cast a glance at a group of wicker chairs. They were sprouting stray strands. He tested one chair gingerly; it seemed to bear his weight, so he sat down and leaned back.

He closed his eyes and let his muscles soften. Last night had suggested that their hopes for a simple weekend catching up were a bit optimistic. But perhaps if they stayed clear of Martha, went on a few excursions into the valley, they could still try to enjoy being out here.

'Hey.'

Jack jumped.

'Sorry!' said Alex. 'Mind if I join you?'

'Please do.' Actually, a bit of time to sit in silence and nurse his headache would have been preferable, but he made himself speak pleasantly. It was a group trip, not a solo holiday. And while Alex was not necessarily the first person Jack would choose to hang out with, he was a nice guy and usually happy to fill in any conversational gaps. Sure enough, after a few minutes Alex started on a humorous story about one of his clients, which allowed Jack to sit in silence, nodding occasionally.

Jack turned as Hugh and Charlotte appeared. So much for a quiet chill before breakfast. 'Can't believe you two are up. You were never early risers.'

Charlotte rubbed her stomach as she took a seat. Her face was creased with tiredness, her eyes bleary. 'I didn't sleep well, but that's usual, these days.'

'Yeah, and then she wakes me up.' Hugh rubbed his eyes and stretched back in his chair.

'It's good training for when the baby arrives.' Charlotte nudged Hugh.

'That's what I'm afraid of.' Hugh stared out over the valley.

Laura stepped through the French doors onto the veranda. 'What a gorgeous morning.' She stood at the railing, closed her eyes and breathed in deeply, then turned. 'Mmm, those beautiful bush smells.'

Jack let his eyes linger on her face.

'You look bright and fresh,' said Alex.

'Just did my yoga.' Laura stretched her arms.

Charlotte stared at her. 'I really wish I felt as good as you look.'

'Hey, you're growing a whole new human.' Laura smiled. 'Not surprising you're tired.'

Charlotte's face softened. 'I sometimes find it hard to believe there's a new little person in here.' She grinned at her tummy. She turned to Hugh. 'Pot of tea would be perfect about now.'

'Nope, coffee would be perfect about now.'

Charlotte stared at him for a moment, then sighed. She started to rise from her chair.

Alex said quickly, 'I'll get it; you stay here.'

'Thanks.' Charlotte glared at Hugh as she stood up, then turned to Alex. 'But I can give you a hand.'

Laura leaned on the balcony railing, surveying the scene.

Behind her, Jack rested his eyes on her back. Then he shook his head. He must let those thoughts go. He turned to Hugh, who looked as though last night's alcohol was having its revenge. 'Reckon we could make it to that lookout we used to go to?'

'Yeah, probably,' said Hugh. 'Going to be a hot one today, though. It's already warming up.'

Laura turned around. 'I don't think a bushwalk would be a good thing this particular weekend, do you?'

Jack stopped. 'Right. Of course. Well, actually we could drive there—'

But he was cut off.

It can't have taken more than a couple of seconds, although in the moment it seemed much longer. It rose up like a slow tear through fabric. It hit Jack's ears then traced a line up his arms, sending his skin tingling.

A long scream.

'Charlotte.' As he said her name Hugh was already out of his chair and taking off into the house, Laura on his heels. The adrenaline pulsing through Jack had dissipated his lethargy; he was right behind the other two.

They shot back through Jack's room, out along the hallway and clattered down the stairs.

'Hugh!' The drawn-out wail was coming from the kitchen.

They charged through the passage.

Charlotte was silhouetted against the door frame of the kitchen. She was still, staring across the room, her back to them. Alex stood frozen next to her.

Hugh, Jack and Laura came to a stop behind them.

Jack followed their gaze to the opposite wall, and his jaw loosened.

His breath caught in his throat.

He turned his eyes to the others, seeing the horror he felt reflected. Then he was drawn back, irresistibly, to that terrible wall.

Daubed in large, crude red letters was one word.

CONFESS

Chapter 15

Nine years previously

The hush in the coroner's court was so complete it was almost tangible. It stretched on, without end. Jack was sitting close enough that he could see the woman's chest rise as she finally drew breath to speak.

'These are the findings of an inquest into the death of Edward Robert Fletcher, who was seventeen years of age when he died during a bushwalking trip in the Lost Valley national park, near Nanganook, in the state of New South Wales.'

Jack still found it hard to accept they were really here, listening to these words, that this wasn't some sort of TV drama in which they had been enlisted as extras. How could this nightmare be real?

'The established facts are these: on the tenth of November 2007, a group of six teenagers aged between seventeen and eighteen set out on a bushwalk in the Lost Valley national park. The teenagers, Laura Walcott, Charlotte Davies, Jack Zhang, Hugh Chamberlain, Alexander Mead and Edward Fletcher, known as Ed, had recently completed year twelve at St Stephen's College in Sydney.

'Ed Fletcher was last seen by his fellow bushwalkers on the morning of the eleventh of November 2007, before becoming separated from the rest of the group. Ed's body was located by SES volunteers the following day, the twelfth of November 2007.'

The court was packed. Jack pushed his glasses up his nose. There was a fly buzzing at the corner of one of the high windows, from which shafts of light fell over the seated crowd. They would need fly spray. But fly spray might not reach up that high.

'This court has taken evidence from a wide range of people . . .'

Indeed, it had. Jack had thought he would never make it through that process, having to answer questions, over and over, recounting his memories. By the end he could feel them begin to blur at the edges and slip past each other.

'. . . The walk had been planned as one of the celebrations for the group finishing their schooling. Ed was an experienced bushwalker and knew the area, having grown up at his parents' property, which is located within the national park in question.

'Of the group, Hugh and Jack were also experienced bushwalkers, having undertaken a number of overnight camping trips in the preceding two to three years. Charlotte, Laura and Alex were less experienced, although they had also undertaken previous overnight camps.'

Jack glanced sideways. He could see all of them from where he sat – Hugh, Alex, Charlotte and Laura. Huddled for protection, their parents seated nearby.

'The six walkers travelled to the Fletcher property on the ninth of November and stayed overnight. They set out walking from the Fletcher's house at approximately nine a.m. on the tenth.'

Robert and Martha were near too. They both sat bolt upright, absolutely immobile, their faces turned towards the woman behind the bench as though their lives depended on what she was saying.

On the way to his seat Jack had seen the rows of men and women in business clothes clutching notepads, as well as the less-formally attired people with curious faces. Jack could now feel all their eyes on the back of his head.

At least, as he'd taken his seat, the journalists had to keep their mouths shut. Unlike those who had crowded outside the court building each day, shoving microphones towards them, trying to reach past the outer layer of family, calling to him and his friends. They had all grown used to blocking out such voices, but words would sneak their way in.

. . . anything to add . . . were you really friends . . . have you told the truth . . .

The coroner's voice again. 'The walk progressed as expected on the morning of the tenth of November. The group made various stops for meals and snacks. Records from the weather bureau indicate that the temperature in the region was twenty-five degrees at ten a.m. and reached thirty degrees at two p.m.'

The courtroom was cold. It was a freezing, windy day outside. It was impossible to imagine what the heat on their walk had actually felt like.

'The group also made good progress on the afternoon of the tenth, as they worked towards their evening destination.'

Jack fixed his gaze on the highest point of the window furthest from where he sat. This was impossible. It was like he was listening to a novel. This dull recitation of the facts could bear no relationship to their experience.

The coroner's voice went on. 'Ed's friends have explained that Ed was the group leader. He had been school captain at St Stephen's, a boy who naturally took responsibility in most situations.'

Jack remembered Ed in his school uniform, his blazer covered in embroidered awards, standing in the school hall, in the assembly yard, on the edge of the sporting fields. Everyone always with their bodies or their faces turned towards him, consciously or unconsciously. They had known that sooner or later he would make them laugh or would say something unexpected, that he would charge everyone around him with his own energy.

Jack could almost see him now, standing to the side of the courtroom, his limbs shifting inexorably, a smile twitching at his lips as he listened. This image brought Jack the familiar mix of resentment and pride. Ed Fletcher, annoyingly popular and successful – but Ed was his mate, his best mate, with his infectious grin.

That grin. Which he'd never see again. Jack pressed his lips together and stared at the ceiling of the courtroom until the water in his eyes thinned away.

The coroner's voice pressed in again. 'The evidence given indicates that Ed had carried appropriate equipment for an overnight camping trip, including approximately two litres of water, split between two bottles.'

It was hard to concentrate on the coroner's voice. What she was saying kept pulling vivid images into Jack's mind. They seemed to appear before him in that very courtroom, and he struggled to look past them at the woman calmly reading from her thick pile of pages.

'One of these bottles, a clear plastic container, was found in the bush, empty. The other was a red bottle with a distinctive platypus sticker, which Ed's friends have testified he carried with him at the start of the walk. This second bottle has never been recovered, despite a thorough search of the bushland.'

Jack felt the people behind him beginning to stir. He braced himself, certain of what was coming next in the coroner's summing up.

'A comprehensive summary of the autopsy report has been given.'

Yes, here it was.

'. . . we have heard expert evidence that it is not inconsistent with Ed having fallen against a hard surface, such as a rock, which may have happened during a period when he would have had decreased energy and poor coordination resulting from exposure.

'In the absence of evidence regarding any alternative causes, this appears to be the most likely explanation for the substantial bruising on Ed's left cheekbone.'

Chapter 16

Hugh felt the skin on his back shift, as though a tiny stream of cold water had been tipped down his spine. He could not tear his eyes away from that terrible lettering on the kitchen wall. *CONFESS*. Could he be hallucinating?

'Holy shit.' A whispered voice next to him.

If he was hallucinating, his friends seemed to be having the same vision.

The silence went on and on, as they all stared at the words, as though in time the red letters might resolve themselves into something more benign.

Hugh put his fists on his hips. He shook his head. 'Oh my god, she's really lost it.'

'Did she get on the grog, after we left her?' Jack pushed his glasses up his nose. His voice held a wondering tone. 'She must have been drunk.'

Alex said, 'I guess this *was* her? Martha?'

Hugh scoffed. 'Martha, or a random psycho who broke into the house.'

'It's awful.' Charlotte's face creased. She sat down abruptly at the table.

'She must be pretty angry.' Laura was staring at the message with an expression that Hugh couldn't read.

'I can't believe she would do this to us.' Charlotte shook her head. 'I mean – I'm pregnant. I need to stay calm. The doctor said so.'

Hugh saw Laura give Charlotte's shoulder a rub, but she still gazed at the writing as though fascinated.

'What the hell is she playing at? Where is she?' He turned to the door. 'I'm going to get her; she can come and explain herself.' He glanced back at Charlotte. 'Don't worry, babe. I'll sort this out.'

His breath came quickly as he looked through all the downstairs rooms. Then he took the stairs two steps at a time and strode towards Martha's bedroom. The door was open. The room was empty.

Hugh looked through all the other upstairs rooms, but the whole floor was still and quiet.

Everyone looked up when he returned to the kitchen. 'I can't bloody find her. I don't think she's in the house.'

'You checked her room?' asked Jack. 'The bathrooms?'

'And her bed looked like it hadn't been slept in.' Hugh shook his head. 'She doesn't want to face up to us. She must be outside.' He turned to Jack. 'Give me a hand?'

He charged outside and Jack followed more slowly.

'That crappy white ute has gone,' said Jack, pointing behind the house. 'I remember seeing it parked out the back the last night before I went to bed.'

Hugh and Jack spent ten minutes looking around the homestead yard and checking the outbuildings. But Martha was nowhere to be seen.

When they returned to the kitchen they could only shrug at the others.

'Let's try calling her,' said Hugh. 'Tell her she'd better get back here and explain what the hell she's playing at.' He patted the pocket in his pyjama pants. 'Wait, I'll grab my phone.'

He dashed out of the room and returned a moment later. 'If she's anywhere near the house she should be in range.' He jabbed at his phone. After a moment he frowned. 'It's not connecting at all.' He looked up. 'Is it just mine? Try yours.'

It only took a minute for the others to fetch their phones. But now everyone else was frowning too.

'I know there's no mobile network.' Alex looked at the others. 'But we should be able to call using the wifi.'

'Right.' Jack glanced around. 'I was on the net last night. Got the password from the back of the modem.'

'Me too.' Hugh turned towards the kitchen dresser. 'Is it turned off?'

But the little white box wasn't there.

'Has she just moved it?' Charlotte's voice was hopeful.

Hugh began shifting plates and cups aside.

Alex bent down beside the dresser. 'Well if she has, it won't be much use – the cable comes out here.' He held up a thin black cord.

'She's taken it.' Hugh's face darkened. He fiddled with his phone again. 'I noticed last night that the house wifi was the only thing the phone could connect to. And now we've got nothing. Call's not connecting. Webpages won't load.'

'Hang on. What about the landline?' Jack turned to the door.

The loud 'damn it!' from the hallway gave them their answer. He strode back in, his face grim.

'The line's dead.'

The silence went on for a long time.

'Hugh.' Charlotte's face was twisted as she looked up at him from her chair in the kitchen. 'I have a very bad feeling about this. Stress isn't good for me at the moment; you know the doctor said that.'

This was exactly the kind of needy statement from Charlotte that usually really bugged Hugh. But at this point you couldn't blame her.

'I know, babe. We'll sort it out.' He lifted his chin.

'I think we should leave.'

Four faces turned towards Alex.

Alex's lips were pressed together. Then he spoke again. 'Martha's obviously disturbed. That message is seriously weird. Now she's disappeared, which should mean we worry about her. But cutting the communications; that changes things. That's about us. That's deliberately putting *us* at risk.'

'I agree.' Charlotte nodded eagerly. 'Let's just get out of here. It's all really creepy.'

'Hang on a second.' Laura held up a hand. 'We don't know what's happened. Martha might need help.'

'And we would normally call for it,' said Alex. 'But we can't. So we should go get some help.'

Hugh stood with his fists on his hips. He felt his anger rise. The old woman was must be taking the piss. She was probably laughing at them. He didn't like the idea of leaving; it felt too much like running away. But just sitting here waiting for her to turn up again wasn't appealing, either. They just needed to bloody do something.

'Okay, we'll leave. We can call in somewhere on the way back and report this.' He turned to Charlotte. 'Let's get our things.'

'Wait.' Laura looked at Jack. 'What do you think?'

Jack paused. 'It might be a bit premature. We don't know what we're running away from.' He glanced between Laura and the others. 'But I suppose it would be good to let someone know about all this.'

'Agreed. And if we go, we can do just that,' said Alex.

Laura looked out the window. 'I think one of us at least should wait, to see if Martha comes back. I can do that.'

'You're not going to stay here by yourself?' Alex looked surprised.

'I could stay too.' Jack turned to Laura. 'That's no problem.'

Laura shook her head. 'It's fine. You can call in at the police station in Nanganook and send a cop out here; tell them about the weird message and the phone being cut and the fact that we can't find her. I'm sure they'll come take a look. If Martha's not back by then, we've done our duty and reported it, and then I can drive back myself.'

Hugh felt his conscience twinge at this, but Laura waved them off. 'It's fine. Really. Go, get your stuff.'

Fifteen minutes later, they were gathered on the front veranda with their luggage. One by one they hugged Laura. Jack turned to her and opened his mouth, but she just shook her head.

Hugh and Charlotte were first into their car. Hugh settled behind the wheel and turned the engine. 'We'll go straight to the cops, send them out here.' He waved back at Laura as the car started to move across the yard.

But it didn't get very far. After a few seconds, the engine started to sputter. Then it stopped, and the car rolled to a halt.

Hugh frowned. He turned the ignition, but the engine simply coughed and died again. He peered at the dashboard.

'Bugger! I'm out of petrol.' He turned to Charlotte and frowned. 'Didn't notice how low it had got. We might have to go with Alex.'

When Hugh got out again, Jack and Alex were looking at him questioningly. 'Empty tank.'

Bit embarrassing, but could happen to anyone. He turned to Alex. 'Mind if Charl and me go with you?'

Hugh took a moment to shift their bags, then they all got into Alex's car. Hugh felt better as the engine fired and they turned towards the gate.

But then that engine coughed and stopped too. It just whined when Alex turned the ignition again.

Hugh saw Alex peer at the dashboard.

Alex's face fell. 'No petrol.'

Hugh's stomach dropped. As one, Hugh and Alex turned to Jack and Charlotte in the back seat.

'You're joking.' Jack's face was drawn.

They all got out again slowly.

Laura was standing before the house, frowning, her arms folded.

Hugh said, 'Better get your keys, Laura.'

She returned quickly and went to her car. Sure enough, the engine fired but then stopped. She got out and nodded grimly.

Tension was gripping Hugh's throat. He felt his heart rate rising. This couldn't really be happening. 'She can't have done this. How would she do this?'

Alex was standing on the other side of Hugh's car. 'She siphoned the tanks.' At Laura's questioning look he said, 'Some of my clients have talked about it. Good trick for them to get free petrol.' He pointed to a crumpled petrol cap cover. 'Look – she's jemmied them open.'

'Bloody hell.' Hugh stared at the damage to his car, as Alex and Laura looked at their own cars and swore.

'Wait.' Jack's face shifted slowly. 'There are other cars on this property besides ours. There'll be the other green ute, for a start.'

'All the keys should be in that cabinet near the kitchen,' said Laura.

But after ten minutes spent trying the old green ute, and a station wagon whose engine wouldn't even kick over, it was clear they weren't going to be driving anywhere.

As they gathered back in the kitchen, Hugh felt the tension wash up his chest like a wave. 'Fuck!' He let his breath out noisily.

'Hey, mate,' said Jack. 'We're all stressed. But we need to settle down.'

'No, I won't bloody settle down, Mr Cool-calm-and-collected!' As Hugh turned, his toe caught the wooden edge of the dresser.

His throat opened. 'Christ!' he bellowed. The pain bit at him. He had to let the energy out. He picked up a plate from the table and before he could stop himself, hurled it against the wall with its awful message.

Everyone jumped as the plate splintered against the wall with a crash, shards clattering to the floor.

Silence.

He saw Alex and Jack move towards him, but he held up his hands. Then he dropped to a chair and rubbed his face. 'I'm sorry.' He raised his head. 'I – look, that was awful.'

He turned to Charlotte. 'Babe, I really am sorry. I scared you. Shouldn't have done that. I just feel so bloody frustrated.'

He reached out tentatively to Charlotte, hating her wary expression. He rubbed her arm.

'I'll clean that up.' He stood up. The silence went on, excruciatingly, as he made ineffectual sweeps at the broken crockery with a broom.

Laura got up and looked in the cupboard under the sink and found a dustpan. She laid it next to the mess on the floor.

Charlotte looked from face to face then let out a disbelieving laugh. 'We can't really be . . . stranded?'

'Of course we're not stranded.' Hugh looked up from his sweeping. 'We could always walk.'

Jack raised his eyebrows. 'Walk where?' He glanced outside. 'It's already really hot. Only going to get hotter. And there aren't any other farms here, remember? No neighbours.'

'Just walk out of the bloody valley,' Hugh went on. 'Back up the road.'

Charlotte shook her head. 'There's no way I can walk back out of here, even to the cafe.'

'Don't worry, Charlotte; there's no way any of us can possibly walk that far. It would take hours.' Jack was beginning to sound impatient. 'We'd have to get all the way back to the cafe, back up that winding road. It's too far, it's too steep, it's too hot.'

Everyone fell silent at the thought.

After a while, Alex said, 'I just don't understand why she's so convinced that there's something more to tell.' Seeing the others' expressions he said, 'I mean, why *she* seems so certain.'

'Perhaps she sensed something,' said Jack slowly. 'Before we even left. I mean, when you think back.' He took another breath. 'Really, the tension was there from the start.'

Chapter 17

Ten years previously

The group of hikers fell silent as they entered the forest. One moment they were walking away from the Fletcher house across the brightness of the paddocks, the sun lighting up the shimmering brown grasses. The next moment they pushed through a wall of trees, climbed up over a large rock and found themselves in another world.

'Oh wow.' Laura came to a halt, and they all stopped behind her.

Before them, tall gums reached up towards a canopy of leaves high above. Triangular fern trees curved out from the ground, their mighty arms reaching to points that curled backwards on themselves.

Jack saw Laura close her eyes and take several deep breaths.

All around him the loamy smell of the soil mingled with the background scent of gums. Leaves whispered together as the air shifted. Unseen birds dropped their notes into the warm air.

'It's a cathedral.' Laura let out a breath.

'It's the bush,' said Hugh. He wiped the back of his hand across his forehead. 'But it's a bit cooler in here, which is good. Come on.'

Laura lifted her chin. 'I'm taking a moment.' She reached out and touched the crinkly bark of a nearby tree.

Hugh sighed then glanced around. 'Yeah okay, it's quite nice.'

Jack was standing near Ed. 'It's great, eh?'

Ed nodded but was silent.

'I mean, getting out here, away from the city.'

'Yeah, right.'

'Anything wrong, mate?' Jack stuck an arm around his friend.

'Of course not! It's all good.'

Ed moved away and began to make his way further along the track.

Jack looked after him, puzzled. That was the second time in the last few days that he'd tried to strike up a conversation with Ed and been rebuffed. There was something weird going on. Why was it so hard for him and his best friend to talk? Had he done something to annoy Ed?

He shook his head. He was probably imagining things. A couple of days out in the bush, and they'd all be relaxed again.

He turned back to the group. They gathered themselves together and made their way along the path.

After a few paces Jack looked back.

The entrance to the forest had now totally vanished.

As his feet beat along the winding track, spiky leaves on either side pressed in against him. He stepped over rocks, his footsteps crunching dried leaves. He could hear his friends talking.

He knew there were ancient meanings in the landscape that he couldn't see or understand, but its physical presence was powerful enough. They were walking through a shallow canyon with rocks looming overhead on either side, sentinels that had stood for millennia. Behind the friendly chatter from the others lay a quiet that was full of potential. Life, all around them, pressing in.

As time went on the group fell silent. Jack felt himself give way to the rhythm of the walk, and the bush noises emerged around him. Tiny creatures hummed in the air, and rough bird calls tore across the canopy above.

Step after step, they made their way, into the forest.

The sun was now high above the line of hikers.

Charlotte took a deep breath. The forest was certainly very pretty. She made herself concentrate on the patterns of sunlight on the leaves, trying to distract herself from her left heel, which was already niggling.

The bloke in the shop had said these were the best boots, top of the range, waterproof, guaranteed comfort. Telling herself that was the reason, rather than their rather stylish red colour, she had plonked down the money. She knew she was channelling her uncertainty about a long hike into overspending on equipment, but it had soothed her at the time.

Looks like the bloke had lied.

But anyway – the fresh air. The beautiful gum trees. Being out here with the others. She hadn't mentioned it to anyone here, but at the last minute she'd been invited on a trip to the beach with another group of friends and had seriously considered it. Sitting by the ocean with a cocktail was perhaps more her style.

But this trip had been planned for such a while. And then there was the fact that the boys were going to be here. Things were always just that bit more fun with some boys around, in Charlotte's view.

'Hey, Charl.' The voice behind her was quiet.

She turned. How had Ed snuck up like that?

'Liking it so far?' he asked.

She made sure to give him a big smile. 'Yeah! It's great to get out here, isn't it?'

'So, look. I was just wondering.'

At his tone, Charlotte's face shifted.

'You know, what we were talking about the other week. Have you had a chance—?'

'Woo-hoo!' Hugh had come barrelling up behind Ed. 'Don't want to get left behind.' He looked between Ed and Charlotte. 'Oh wait. Sorry.' He made a pantomime of backing away. 'Don't let me interrupt your talk.'

'Don't be silly,' said Ed, but he did look annoyed. He turned back to the path ahead. 'Let's get a move on. I reckon there's a lookout just up here.' He brushed past her and headed up the path. Charlotte and Hugh followed.

Soon a narrow passage was visible to the right. Ed took the lead and they all clambered upwards. They had to press through the bush and pick their way over rocks.

Charlotte followed Ed up and found herself on a wide grey rock platform, the tree canopy a few metres below. Before her the bush stretched out, fold after fold of tree-furred ridges. The handful of clouds in the vast expanse of blue sky scattered tiny shadows across the ocean of green.

Charlotte put her pack down. 'This is a good place for a bit of morning tea, I reckon,' she said.

The others climbed across the rocks, laid down their packs and started rifling for food.

'Thought those rooftops I could see from my desk in the boarding house were going be imprinted on the back of my eyelids for ever.' Jack waved his arm at the trees. 'But this is more like it.'

It really was a stunning view. Charlotte screwed up the wrapper of her muesli bar and jumped up. 'I need a photo.'

'You won't be able to post anything,' said Hugh. 'No reception.'

'Ha ha. I don't post every photo, Hugh. Besides, I can do it when we get back. Now, squash up.' She held up the camera. 'Yes – got it!' Charlotte brought the camera down to look.

'Oh – crap!' With horror, she watched the little metal rectangle slip from her fingers and disappear between two rocks.

'I can see it.' Ed peered down. 'I reckon I can get that.'

'Bet I can get down there faster,' said Hugh. The next moment he and Ed both started slithering down.

'Bloody idiots.' But Jack was grinning.

'Are you guys okay?' called Alex after a minute.

Charlotte felt a twinge of worry. It would not be great if someone hurt themselves fetching her camera. 'Be careful!'

Ed's face appeared at the edge of the rock, and he waved the camera triumphantly above his head. Hugh appeared a moment later.

'Oh my god – thank you!' Charlotte beamed.

Ed gave a nod of satisfaction. Hugh turned away with an irritated look, and Charlotte couldn't help but smile to herself. She was relieved to be holding the camera again – but she could admit that it was also kind of nice having the boys fight over who could help her.

It wasn't too long before Ed stood again. 'Time to get going.'

They all gathered their bottles into their packs and made their way down to the main track.

As they settled into a rhythm, Charlotte thought it was getting warmer. Not too hot, not yet, but definitely warmer than when they started. They were following a thin dirt path and were now taking more frequent stops to drink from their water bottles. Far above them, sunlight lay in glossy pools on the treetops and glanced down between the tree trunks, spotlighting bushes and rocks.

As the path began to slope upwards the vegetation gradually shifted from rich thick leaves to a thinner, dryer scrub, and the palette of bush colours shifted from greens to greys among the spiky shrubs that grabbed at them as they pressed along the path. Charlotte could feel her muscles pulling against the slope.

They walked in silence now. She could hear leaves rustling, birds calling and the swish of their clothing as they strode the path.

Then Laura started. With a 'Shh', she stopped and pointed into the bushes.

'Look.' Laura spoke in a careful whisper. 'It's a wallaby.'

The furry grey creature was blending in well with the surrounding bush but, as its head twitched, they saw it. Charlotte felt a smile spread across her face. 'It's so tame.' She matched her voice to Laura's whisper. 'It's not afraid of us at all.' It really was adorable.

'Probably never sees people.' Laura still spoke softly. 'We're pretty far into the bush now.'

After a moment the wallaby twitched again and vanished.

They continued along the trail as it looped around boulders and wove through thin gullies. The chatter grew ever more sporadic as the sun moved overhead. Charlotte gave in to the rhythm of her stride and the hypnotic sounds of branches, birds and breeze.

It must have been at least another hour before the trail turned a corner and opened into a wider gully, boulders dotting the scrub, which stretched upwards on either side. Charlotte was relieved to see the bobbing backpacks ahead gather into a group. She caught up to them and felt air that was a little cooler from lying protected in the gully.

Ed turned. 'How about here for some lunch?'

'Sounds great,' Charlotte said with conviction. Everyone seemed happy enough to roll their packs down from their backs. There was not a lot of talk as they rummaged around for their food, but the meal brought a return of the conversational energy. Soon the birds had to compete with talk and hoots of laughter.

Hugh screwed up his sandwich paper, then reached over to his pack and ceremoniously drew out a can.

'Oh my god,' said Charlotte. 'You brought beer?' She gave Hugh a big smile and pushed his arm playfully.

Now Hugh held a can up to Ed, who shook his head, but he was grinning.

'What?' asked Hugh. 'I know you like a cleansing ale as much as I do, mate.'

'Sure,' Ed replied. 'It's just the weight of it, on a trek. You didn't want to carry some more water instead?' He waved his clear bottle at Hugh. 'And I've got my old faithful red platypus bottle as well.' He patted his pack.

'It's fine,' said Hugh. 'We can fill up at the camp. What's it called, Shepherd's View?'

'Stockman's Rest.'

'And I mean, Laura brought her bloody paint set.'

'Thanks for the reminder. I'm going to use it now.' Laura started to rummage in her pack.

The hikers lay back against tree trunks and rocks, and the chatter died away as the as the bush did its work, stilling their minds and relaxing their muscles. Curious birds hopped a little closer, and insects whirred in the warm air. They could hear the faint drone of an invisible plane far overhead, too tiny to see through the tree canopy.

Eventually Ed sat and surveyed the group. 'Hate to say it, but we should get going.'

Charlotte was pleased that the others groaned. She wasn't the only one who wanted to take it a bit easier.

Alex asked, 'How much longer do you think it will be?'

Ed twisted his face slightly. 'Few hours? It's not going to get dark until seven or so.'

He nudged Hugh with his foot. 'Get a move on, guys. I'm just going up ahead a little to check the map. Be back in a sec.'

Jack heaved himself to his feet. 'Pick that up,' he said to Hugh, giving the empty beer can a slight kick.

'Ah, leave it here,' said Hugh.

He was met by shrieks of 'No!'

'Joking! Just trying to get a rise out of you greenies. I wouldn't leave rubbish lying around this pristine wilderness. I'm not an animal.'

Charlotte stuffed her things in her pack and pulled the fastenings closed. She adjusted her shirt and smoothed down her hair.

Eventually, the whole group was standing, their bags hoisted on their backs.

'Hey, where's Laura?' asked Alex.

'She went off for a wee,' said Charlotte. 'That way.'

'Do you want to go hurry her up?' said Hugh.

Charlotte sighed. 'Okay. I'll go check.' She dropped her pack again and pressed her way between some bushes. There was a rock up ahead; no doubt Laura had used that for some privacy. She climbed the slope a little way and peered around. No Laura.

Taking the opportunity now she was away from everyone, she pulled out her lip gloss and applied it. Of course, she didn't have her eye on any of these boys, but that was no reason not to keep up her appearance.

She pushed through the bushes a little more and came out on another rock. She was just about to call Laura's name when she thought she heard a voice from below.

She looked down from the ledge.

Her face fell in shock.

Below she could see Laura, her arms wrapped tightly around someone else, one palm pressed against the back of his neck, the other gripping his bottom. But the boy with his face locked against her own was not Laura's boyfriend, Jack.

It was Ed.

Chapter 18

Charlotte nodded. Jack was right about the tension on the walk, right from the start, and they all knew it. But she wasn't convinced it was a great idea to talk about that. Especially right now.

Hugh turned to Jack. 'Forget the walk. We need to get out of here. Any bright ideas?'

Jack paused. 'We could look around outside the house.' Another pause. 'Perhaps there's another old ute in one of the sheds. Or a motorcycle.'

Charlotte didn't like the idea of climbing into some old truck. Presumably no one would suggest she should go on the back of a motorcycle. No – one of the others would ride it out and get the police in.

'Perhaps someone will come past?'

Alex turned to her. 'This farm's at a dead end. The road doesn't go any further. So, unless Martha gets some unexpected visitor . . .'

They all fell silent.

Hugh stood. 'Let's go check out the sheds, then. We'll have a good look this time.' He looked at Charlotte. 'You can stay here.'

'I don't want to wait here by myself.' It was broad daylight, so there really should be nothing to be nervous of, but Charlotte still didn't like the idea. 'What if Martha comes back all of a sudden? Who knows what she might do?'

'I'll wait with you,' said Alex.

She nodded reluctantly and Hugh, Jack and Laura headed outside.

Charlotte let a breath out slowly.

'I just feel stressed without a phone connection. It's a bit sad.' Charlotte managed a laugh, but she knew it wasn't convincing. She went to the kitchen window. The quiet of the countryside had seemed peaceful when they first got up. Now it felt ominous

Alex gave her a half-hearted smile. 'I know what you mean. We're so used to having them. Little lifelines.'

Alex stood and began to walk up and down the room. She wished he wouldn't. But she couldn't think of a thing to say that wasn't nervous babbling, and that wasn't going to help anyone. The minutes ticked past.

After about half an hour, Hugh, Jack and Laura returned, looking despondent.

'So much crap out in those sheds. But no handy vehicles,' said Jack slowly.

'No sign of Martha, either,' said Hugh.

Alex's throat was closing up and his blood was hammering in his ears. He reminded himself to breathe. 'So what the hell can we do? I mean, do we just wait here? Wait for Martha to reappear?'

Charlotte cleared her throat. 'Please can we get some breakfast while we think about it?' She looked a bit sheepish. 'I know this doesn't seem like the moment, but I'm actually starving.

It's already nine and normally I would have eaten about two hours ago.'

Laura nodded. 'Good idea. Help us think.'

Hugh stood. 'Dunno about you guys, but I need coffee before I can think any further.' Hugh looked across at the ancient coffee machine. 'Anyone know if that thing works?'

'We could all do with some caffeine.' Alex was relieved to have a distraction. 'I'll take a look.' He fiddled with the machine. It didn't seem too complicated. He opened some cupboards, looking for the coffee. The insides were a complete mess.

Alex pulled out some boxes of teabags. Right at the back of the shelf was a crinkled pack of coffee. He turned back to the coffee machine, but the water tank was empty so he went to the tap.

He turned the tap. A thin trickle of water came out.

Then stopped.

He turned the tap more. Nothing.

He tried the hot tap and discovered that it was already loose.

'Uh, guys.' He turned to the others. 'Small problem.'

Four faces looked up.

'There's no water.'

They looked back uncomprehendingly.

'What do you mean?'

'I mean, there's no water coming from the tap.' He twirled the handles to show them.

'Perhaps it's just that tap.' Jack heaved himself up. 'I'll try the sink in the pantry.' A muffled *crap* gave them their answer. He emerged with a serious face, said, 'Downstairs loo,' then went out again.

Then he reappeared, shaking his head.

Alex felt a nasty creeping sensation. He made himself take another breath.

'Better try the bathrooms upstairs,' said Hugh, and strode from the room, followed by Jack. But they reappeared in a few minutes with their faces heavy.

'Hang on,' said Charlotte. 'I used the loo when I got up. It definitely flushed.'

'Cisterns would have been full,' said Jack. 'Bet they won't flush now. And if the water ran in the tap . . .?'

'Actually it was just a trickle,' said Charlotte. 'I didn't think, at the time.'

Alex was trying desperately not to reach the conclusion that was screaming at him. But the tense expressions on the faces of his friends were not helping one little bit.

Alex felt his voice rising and getting louder as he struggled with a wave of panic. 'Oh god. You can see what she's doing, right?'

Chapter 19

Ten years previously

'I can't wait to refill my water bottle. There's not much left.' Alex fanned his face.

The group had come to a halt at a small rise in the track.

Ed was holding the map in both hands and looking around to scan the terrain.

Alex watched as Ed pulled out the compass that was hanging on a neck strap and checked it against the map.

The sun had dropped lower in the sky, sending shadows shooting across the path. But the air was still warm against Alex's skin.

'Not long now.' Ed's voice was confident.

Charlotte shifted from one foot to another and sighed. 'Thank goodness for that. Feels like we've been walking for ever.'

'Should be, yeah, just another twenty minutes along here.' Ed pointed.

Charlotte's face fell. 'Up that hill?'

'Yep.' Ed nodded. 'The campsite is on a bit of a ridge.'

Alex saw Charlotte's face. He said, 'Hey, there should be a good view when we get up there.'

As the ground sloped upwards more and more steeply, Alex felt his muscles straining against the hill, and his pack pulling at his shoulders. He took a breath and gazed around.

'Look at those colours.' Laura waved at the sky but her smile looked a bit forced. 'I have to try to remember that exact shade. I'll paint it later.'

Alex noticed some birds among the slender gum leaves up above. He also saw another wallaby but was too tired to point out the wildlife. Better they just keep going, no more stopping. He told himself there was nothing to be anxious about. They were well within their predicted time.

On they climbed, the only sounds the swishing of their arms and legs, and their breath as they hauled themselves up rock steps.

It felt like much longer than twenty minutes but finally Ed called, 'Here it is.'

'Thank god,' said Charlotte, swinging her pack onto the ground, and dropping to sit on a low rock.

They were standing at the edge of a wide area of flat earth surrounded by soaring gum trees. Rising ground on three sides protected it from the wind, and on the final side was an open view over endless miles of bushland.

They had a dress circle view of clouds that had lined up to reflect the western sun, as if just for their benefit. Even as they watched, the colours shifted and glowed. The pink and yellow light played across their faces.

Hugh dumped his pack on the ground. 'I think we're due a celebratory beverage. I might even share it with those who are keen.'

'I don't know if I want a sit down or a drink the most,' said Charlotte. 'Or to consume that chocolate bar that I've been thinking about for the last hour.'

'Perhaps we should get the tents up first,' said Jack.

'No. The first thing is filling our bottles.' Ed's voice was firm. 'Let's go find the creek before we do anything.'

They bent over their packs and extracted bottles, while Ed looked again at the map. 'There should be a decent creek in –' he swivelled slightly then pointed '– that direction.' He set off and the others followed.

The prospect of a rest and a meal had re-energised them, and they swung their bottles and chattered as they made their way through the trees.

'Yep, and it's . . . here,' said Ed as they rounded a rock.

Alex happened to be watching Ed's face, so he saw the exact moment when shock spread across his features.

They were looking down at a deep vein in the ground surrounded by bushes on either side. But there was no running liquid. There was no water at all. The line in the ground was filled with dry rocks and leaves.

'So, ah, where?' asked Jack.

'Not seeing any water,' said Hugh.

'No.' Ed's face was now frozen. 'It's dry.'

Alex felt his own face go still.

Charlotte's face was full of disbelief. 'How can it be dry?'

'It's dry.' The repeated syllable from Ed struck like a muffled drum.

Everyone fell silent. They turned to Ed.

Ed looked back at them blankly. Then he shook his head. 'Okay. So, we need to dig down.' He turned to Hugh. 'Run back and get that trowel that you brought to dig for a toilet. Everyone else, find a good big stick, or a nice pointy rock.'

In a few minutes, Alex located a heavy stick and crouched in the creek bed, pushed aside leaves and began to lever out the dirt. It was hard and dry.

He wiped the sweat from his forehead with the back of his hand and glanced at the others. They were all energetically clearing the earth.

The minutes passed. The soil became slightly damp as they dug down, but no liquid appeared.

Ed stood. His face was more strained now, but he rallied. 'Okay, even if we can't dig down to the water, there must be tributaries. So, we'll spread out and look.'

Alex nodded, along with the others. There would surely be water somewhere nearby.

Ed directed them to different places, and they spread out and began to scan the ground, with slow, careful steps. No one spoke.

Twenty minutes later they gathered. Everyone's face was drawn. The conclusion did not need to be stated.

Alex's heart was beating a little too fast as he tried very hard not to think about the implications of the landscape around their camp site being completely devoid of water.

Chapter 20

Jack stared at the kitchen tap along with Alex, Charlotte, Laura and Hugh. Just moments ago it had looked so innocuous.

'Oh god,' breathed Charlotte. Her hands flew to the top of her head.

'That woman is really messed up.' Hugh shook his head. 'That she would do this. After what we went through.'

The memory of exactly what they all went through rose between them.

Jack took a slow breath. 'Hang on. Let's not panic. We've all found the water cut off at home at some point. This may be a coincidence.' He didn't actually believe it, but it was possible. 'Let's check the mains tap. Anyone happen to know where it is?'

Four blank faces stared at him.

'At our place it's in the front yard near the fence,' said Charlotte. 'I guess so they can read the meter. But they wouldn't necessarily do it that way out here.'

'It'll be outside. Somewhere near the house,' said Hugh.

Jack nodded at Hugh. 'Right, come look with me?'

'I'll come too,' said Alex.

'Me too,' said Laura.

'Well, I'm not staying by myself.' Charlotte got up.

The five of them went out to the back veranda and made their way around the old building, looking for pipes and taps. Their first walk around the homestead yielded nothing. Halfway round the second circumnavigation, Alex spotted a loop of bronze piping with a tap. It was half concealed behind a small bush.

Alex's hands shook a little as he gave the knob a couple of twists.

Hugh disappeared back towards the kitchen to try the kitchen tap, but he soon reappeared, shaking his head.

Jack could see his dismay mirrored in the others' faces.

They stood, staring at the sunlit valley. Strange that it looked entirely unchanged.

'Hey. What's this?' There was a strange note in Charlotte's voice. She reached for the tap. Then she straightened up. She was staring at a small fold of blue paper. 'It says "Jack".' She turned to him with a puzzled expression.

Jack felt a creeping sensation across his skin. His hand reached for the little piece of paper as if of its own accord. Slowly he opened the note and took in the scribbled words. He could feel everyone looking at him.

He could hardly believe his eyes.

The others had crowded around, so there was no chance of keeping it to himself. Slowly he read out the words.

youre not really such a genius at school are you stop pretending

He felt his cheeks grow hot and heard a roaring sound in his ears as the others stared at him and he stared at the paper. Surely, she couldn't know? How the hell could she know? It was so long ago, and he certainly hadn't told Martha.

He dragged his gaze from the scribbled words. Three puzzled faces stared back.

Hugh gave a short laugh. 'Oh man, what new bullshit is this? We all know Jack *was* a genius at school – because he's a massive brain, and he worked bloody hard.'

Jack had in fact done very well at school since his first day at kindergarten. Anyone looking at his family would assume the familiar story, of immigrant parents pressuring their child to do well academically. But in fact, Jack's parents hadn't hothoused him at all. Quite the opposite.

Staring at the note, Jack forced a smile onto his face. He made himself laugh.

Hugh was shaking his head. '"Stop pretending"? Yeah, he just "pretended" to get into medicine.'

Jack remembered all the big family dinners; all the talk sitting around the table. The conversations all seemed to merge into one after a while.

'So, Jack, how are your studies going?' This would be from his grandma, or his aunt.

'Leave the kid alone, Mum. There's plenty of time.' Or, 'There's more to life than marks.' This from his dad.

His grandma would purse her lips, her eyes on the pastry below her hands forming effortlessly into folds, and then another aunt would say something like, 'Only if you want to be an *artist* like your father. Or an *actor* like your mother,' the emphasis ever so faint and ever so effective.

Then his dad would roll his eyes. 'I know you'll never understand. But there's more to life than earning money.'

If the conversation was very heated, an uncle might say something like, 'Sure, if someone else is paying your mortgage.

Or your school fees.' Then his grandmother would frown and shush them.

And in the car on the way home his parents would complain about their materialistic relatives, and how they didn't know how to enjoy their good fortune, and how much they both disliked having to go to those big gatherings where the rest of the family looked down on them.

Jack would stay silent in the back seat.

And as he grew older he began to understand with a growing admiration that his grandfather was the boss of the office supplies company that Jack had been taken to visit so many times as a small boy – the owner, in fact, and that there were actually Zhang Supplies stores all over the country. And that the house Jack lived in and the school he went to were well beyond the reach of an actor and a painter of moderate success, which was a fact that his parents never acknowledged.

Soon enough, his answer to the questions of how his studies were going was 'very well', and his answer to what he wanted to do at university was 'medicine'. The only response from his grandfather was a quiet nod, but it was worth more to Jack than any number of effusive hugs from his mother.

Now Alex said, 'What does the note mean, Jack?'

Jack looked back on his school-aged self with a protective kind of pity. How obsessed with his school marks he'd been. He had been so determined to be a success in the eyes of the world.

Well, he had fulfilled his goal very well. He had in fact often been described as a 'genius' at school.

Jack turned to Alex. He let out a breath and forced a surprised look across his face. 'No idea what she means. Like Hugh said. She must be nuts.'

Chapter 21

Ten years previously

'The fuck do we do now?' Hugh's gaze shifted from the dry creek bed to his friends' faces, as though something might change.

Alex stared again at the long line of dry leaves gathered in the dip in a mocking imitation of the stream they had wanted to find.

'We're okay.' Ed's words were positive, but his worried face contradicted them, and it was almost more alarming than the absence of water. He let out a long breath, then stared out into the bush for a moment. Then he turned to the others. 'Look, we're a bit dry, a bit thirsty. But no need to panic. First thing is to keep whatever water we have, keep it for tomorrow.'

'Okay.' Hugh turned to Ed. 'But then, tomorrow?'

Ed took a breath. 'Let's check the map.'

Alex could see the others' uncertain faces as they trailed behind Ed back to the camp.

Ed pulled the map from his pack, then sat with it spread out in front of him.

'We'd planned to hike out this way, via Nanganook.' Ed's gaze darted from face to face as he thought.

Jack looked over his shoulder. 'How about . . .' He paused. 'We walk down to the Nanganook river. There'll be water in that river, no question. Then we can head out along the other valley.'

Hugh looked over Ed's other shoulder. 'That's a longer way out.'

'It's a longer way out from the river.' Jack pointed to the paper. 'But the important thing is, it's not that far from here to the river. So, if we set out tomorrow morning straight down to the river, instead of the route we were going to take, it should be fine.'

Ed nodded slowly. 'I think you might be right, mate.'

The idea of the other river immediately lifted their mood a little.

'It'll be a thirsty night and a bit of a dry day tomorrow, but, if we pace ourselves, we'll be right.'

'Not sure.' Hugh looked unconvinced. 'It's a hell of a walk on no water.'

'Do you have a better idea?' Ed spread out his hands. 'Honestly, I'm open to anything.'

'Call for help?' said Charlotte.

Hugh had his phone in his hand and waved it. 'There's no signal.' He glanced up at the ridge behind him. 'Might be one from up there. Worth a try.'

'But if you did connect to someone, what are they going to do?' asked Ed.

'Chopper in some water. Get us out.'

Ed snorted. 'They're not going to send a helicopter in with a few bottles of water for us. They wouldn't even send the rangers in unless we were lost. Which we're not. And we're not injured, either.'

Alex thought that calling for help was actually a good idea, but he didn't want to disagree with Ed. Anyway, they could always try later if things got worse.

Ed spoke in a calmer tone. 'Look, it's not that bad. Six healthy people can walk the distance to the river. No one's going to chopper us out in this situation.' He began to pace a little from side to side. 'Jack's right. We'll bed down at the campsite as planned, get up early, get going while it's cool.' He waved back towards the empty creek bed. 'That isn't great, but we're not stuffed yet.' He even mustered up a bit of a smile. 'We're all right. We can still have some fun.'

And with Ed's calmer expression, Alex felt his own worry subside a little.

Ed stood and grinned around at his friends. His relief seemed to have given him a burst of energy.

'That's our smart Jack.' Hugh slapped Jack on the back. 'There's a reason why we brought you.'

'Ha!' Ed let out a laugh. He seemed to be in a better mood. 'Is he really that smart? Is it all just his brain power? Eh, Jack?' He gave Jack a wink.

Alex happened to be looking at Jack at that moment, and almost started back in shock at the furious glare that Jack returned Ed.

Chapter 22

It was obvious to Alex that Jack did know what the note near the mains tap referred to but that he clearly did not want to share it with the rest of them.

'So does this mean we've got you to blame for being stuck here?' Hugh looked at Jack. 'Why has Martha got some bee in her bonnet about you, of all people?' Hugh laughed, but there was a real question in his look.

Alex stole another glance at Jack, who still looked shaken, although he shrugged again and gave his own short laugh. 'Search me.'

Laura stood to one side, her face tense, her arms folded.

'Forget Jack.' Charlotte shook her head impatiently. 'This situation is not his fault. I'm more concerned about what it says about Martha. I mean, stranding us, cutting the water – it's bad; it's dangerous. But that message on the wall, and now, leaving that note – it's seriously weird. It's *deranged*.'

They all fell silent. Alex knew the others were thinking the same thing. What new, twisted angle to their predicament did this note represent?

'Let's not try to guess how Martha's brain works just now. She's trying to get inside our heads. But we really need to sort out the water.' Jack shoved the note in his pocket and turned back to the house. 'So, the mains water is off.'

'But there's also the tank water,' said Hugh.

'That's right,' said Laura. 'The big tank is at the back, past the old laundry.'

Alex thought Laura was looking pretty worried. But he probably had the same expression on his own face.

Without a word they all set off to the back of the house.

The tank was a large corrugated iron structure, once silver, now almost entirely covered in rust. It looked pretty dodgy, but if it held water Alex wouldn't be fussy. He already felt thirsty.

A tap was protruding from the base of the tank. Jack reached for the knob, but it wouldn't budge.

Alex realised he was holding his breath.

'Out of the way.' Hugh stepped forward, and Jack managed a smile as he stepped back and waved Hugh forward.

It looked like Hugh had to put a bit of muscle into it, but eventually the knob moved, and they all cheered softly. Best of all, liquid started to run out. Alex fell a burst of relief.

'Okay let's grab a container,' said Jack.

But then the trickle stopped. Jack banged the side of the tank, and it gave a metallic echo. He walked slowly around to the other side of the tank.

'Bloody hell.' At Jack's voice, Hugh, Alex, Laura and Charlotte followed him around.

Jack poked his foot at the muddy ground. 'Look. This is a swamp. And there.' He pointed at another tap protruding from the tank, a larger one than the first. He reached forward and

120

twiddled it and his voice rose. 'She left it open. She's fucking emptied the thing.'

Alex felt his throat closing. So this water situation really was deliberate. He saw the stress written on the others' faces as they each swore.

Then Alex spotted something else. He didn't want to believe it. He pointed. 'Look.'

It was a small blue square of folded paper.

Another silence as they all stared disbelievingly.

'Holy crap.' Hugh reached for the paper. 'Another fun message from Mental Health Martha?' His voice was light but Alex could hear a waver. 'Let's see what this one says.'

Hugh opened the note. But then his smile dropped away.

'What?' demanded Charlotte.

Hugh went to screw up the paper, but she put her hand out onto his arm.

'What does it say?'

Hugh forced a laugh. 'Okay, this time she's going for me.'

With a look of dread on her face, Charlotte leaned over and read out the scribble on the little blue piece of paper.

you really cant control your own strength can you

Chapter 23

Ten years previously

The colours in the bush were shifting and softening as the sun dropped below the horizon. The camp clearing was busy, but there was no talking.

Jack was unfolding a tent with Charlotte and Laura. Ed and Hugh had another one already laid out and were sticking poles together.

'You two going to share a tent?' Hugh looked at Jack, then glanced over at Laura. Jack opened his mouth. He assumed the answer was yes.

'I'll need to share with Charlotte,' said Laura quickly. 'So, she doesn't have to share with any of you farting boys.' She grinned.

Jack saw Hugh raise his eyebrows. A sinking feeling pulled at Jack's stomach. He told himself that Laura was being considerate. Charlotte probably wouldn't be too keen on sharing with any of the boys. Jack shrugged at Hugh and went back to fiddling with the folds of canvas.

Hugh turned back to his tent, pole in hand, then stuck his head inside. A moment later the canvas bulged suddenly, with a large Hugh-shaped outline. Jack heard a loud, 'Bugger,' then the canvas lurched sideways, and Hugh backed out, straight into Ed.

'Watch it, Dumbo.' Ed put out a hand to steady Hugh.

But Hugh turned on Ed and leaned in. 'What did you call me?' Hugh's face was so angry that Jack himself felt a spurt of adrenaline. He sensed Laura and Charlotte go still beside him.

Ed raised his eyebrows. 'Easy, tiger.' He raised his palms. 'I wasn't referring to your brains. Just your size. You almost knocked me over.'

Hugh's face was tense for a moment but then eased, and he stepped backwards. 'Yeah, fine,' he said gruffly, and turned back to the tent, sticking his head inside. Ed also turned away and began to sort ground pegs.

Jack let out a breath. Bloody Hugh and his temper. A fight was all they needed right now.

Jack saw Charlotte turn to him and Laura. 'Whoa,' she mouthed.

The silence felt awkward, but Jack couldn't think of anything to break it, and it stretched on for a long time as the six of them continued to work at their tents.

A little later Jack saw Ed leaning over his pack, a little way from the rest of the group.

The atmosphere had certainly changed since they'd found the dry creek bed. Less talk. A shade of anxiety across all their faces. But even before they'd got to the creek bed, ever since the start of the walk, Jack had got the sense that Ed was avoiding him somehow. Certainly, he and Ed hadn't talked much on the trip so far. It felt uncomfortable, and Jack was keen to clear that feeling away.

Jack walked to Ed. 'Hey. Bit awkward before, with Hugh.' Jack nodded back towards the others. 'Guess we're all a bit on edge, with the water situation.'

'Yeah, doesn't help.' Ed stood up. 'It's okay. I didn't think he was really going to go for me or anything.'

Jack nodded.

'But perhaps don't annoy Hugh too much,' Ed said.

Jack looked closely at Ed. 'What do you mean?'

Ed looked away. 'Oh, nothing.'

'Come on. It's clearly not nothing.'

'No, look, I shouldn't have said anything. I promised I wouldn't.'

'But . . .?'

Ed paused. 'I'll just say. Hugh can be dangerous if he's really angry.'

Chapter 24

Charlotte looked at Hugh carefully as he glanced from face to face, shook his head and raised his palms. 'I've got no idea what she's talking about,' he said.

Charlotte's stomach lurched. She could not take her eyes off him. The words of the little blue note kept echoing in her mind.

you really cant control your own strength can you

'Hugh.' Her voice was wavering. 'What does that mean?'

He looked at her and said, 'Babe, it's nothing, really.' But then his eyes shifted away.

Charlotte knew that her husband was no sensitive reconstructed male, and she was fine with that. She actually found his physical strength attractive. While she would never say it to any of her friends, she thought of Hugh as a real man; she wasn't interested in all that feminism stuff. She liked the idea of a powerful protector, and he certainly had never directed any of his aggression at her. But lurking at the back of her mind had always been the niggling possibility that Hugh's physical strength might get out of control. Charlotte had always told herself that she had never seen him be really violent, that Hugh was a nice guy with a bit of a temper. But what if something serious had happened that she didn't know about? The others might not have wanted to say anything to her. Or perhaps they thought she already knew.

Hugh turned to Jack, Laura and Alex. 'Guys, we know Martha's not right in the head, okay? I mean she's already implied that our resident genius, Jack, is not very smart. So, she thinks I'm some kind of gangster. Whatever. Who cares what she thinks?'

Charlotte could tell that Hugh was not being straight with them. But she nodded slowly, along with Alex and Jack.

'Like Jack said, right now, more important than Martha's opinion of us is the bloody water,' said Hugh.

'Well, what can we do now?' Charlotte was really hoping there was something obvious that she somehow hadn't thought of. It was irrational, but the fact of the water being cut off seemed to be making her feel thirstier than usual. She tried not to think about how this might be affecting the baby.

'There must be other water around the place.' Laura was frowning. 'The hot water tank, for a start.'

Alex looked dubious. 'The hot water tap in the kitchen was already on. There was nothing coming out.'

'We should at least try to find the hot tank and check it.'

Jack turned towards the house. Hugh and Alex were on his heels, and Charlotte and Laura followed after.

They soon found the hot-water unit inside a cabinet in the laundry. The tall metal cylinder was slightly rusted. Jack whacked the side of it and a hollow sound echoed.

'She must have left the hot tap on in the kitchen and emptied this.' Jack shook his head. 'And now it can't refill.'

Charlotte fought against an urge to yell in despair. She focused instead on her stomach. 'How about we have that breakfast I suggested? We're not going to sort this out on empty stomachs.'

Back in the kitchen, Alex fossicked in the cupboards and found some bread and a half-filled jar of jam. Laura cut the brown spots from some ageing apples and shared them out. The friends sat at the table and ate in silence. Consciously or not, they had all sat so as not to be looking at that terrible word 'confess' splashed on the wall in red paint.

The others were probably also trying to convince themselves this was all some strange dream, Charlotte thought, but the table top beneath her hand felt all too real, and the air in the kitchen all too warm.

Then Jack pushed his empty plate away, frowning. 'Okay, now let's just think this through.' Charlotte looked at him. He seemed a little more energised now. Perhaps having a problem to solve was firing up his legendary brain. 'No need to panic. There has to be other water somewhere.'

There was a moment's silence. Charlotte looked out at the yellowing paddocks. It was already noticeably hotter, even inside the house, than when they had first woken up. She decided it wouldn't be helpful to check the thermometer near the door. 'I don't suppose there'd be any little pools of water out there collected between rocks or trees. It's too hot.'

'I don't remember any dams, either – none near the house, anyway,' said Laura.

Then Jack's face cleared. 'Hey, remember when Martha was showing us around yesterday? She said they kept water cartons in the pantry.'

'That's true.' Charlotte could picture her saying it.

In the pantry they were confronted by shelf on shelf of disorder; tins speckled with rust piled against plastic boxes of grains, cleaning products, ancient pickle jars.

They all began pushing the jars and tins aside, necks craning towards the back of shelves.

Jack heaved himself down to crouch near the floor. 'I reckon they'd be down low.'

'Here they are!' Alex turned with a triumphant look. 'I can see some cartons, behind this box. Give me a hand to move it.'

Hugh each took one side of the box and gave a yank.

Then Alex said, 'Oh no.'

'What?'

'Look.' Alex reached in and pulled out a large plastic water carton. He could do it with one hand, because it was empty. He pulled another out, then another.

'They're all bloody empty.'

Could this really be happening? Charlotte blinked, hoping she might wake up. But it was all still there in front of her, terrifyingly real.

She saw the others' faces go flat. She felt her own tension rise. This was a step up. Had these cartons always been empty? Or had Martha actually gone to the trouble of emptying them? The latter was a particularly nasty idea.

Then Jack said. 'Hate to say this, but . . .'

They turned to him.

He reached behind the empty cartons and drew his hand back.

They all stared at the little blue note sitting on his palm.

Jack said, 'This one is for Alex.'

Charlotte saw Alex's face drop. He laughed shakily. He held out his hand. 'Okay, so what's she got for me then? Let's have it.' His tone was light, but Charlotte saw the tremor in his hand.

His expression dropped still further when he opened the note. Hugh leaned over his shoulder and read it out.

tell them what you did at the party you liar

Chapter 25

Ten years previously

Eventually they got the tents standing. The dim light hanging between the gum leaves was beginning to deepen and dissolve into darkness. The soft colours of the sky were draining away, leaving a glowing dome that was fading from dark blue into black.

Charlotte sat with the others, resting after their work with the tents. She was near Ed and Alex. Laura was on the ground a little further away, stretching, Jack and Hugh near her.

'I'm going to get a fire started.' Ed got up and began to search in the bushes surrounding the clearing.

'Won't that, like, dry us out more?' asked Laura.

'It'll get cool pretty soon. We'll just have a small one and we'll keep a close eye on it.' Ed picked up some more sticks and added them to his pile. 'Besides, it will cheer us up.'

'You're right,' said Hugh. 'But you'll have to collect the sticks yourself. I'm buggered.'

'I just want to finish my stretches,' said Laura.

'I'll give you a hand.' Alex stood.

'Ah, Alex, you're always so helpful,' said Charlotte.

Ed turned. Charlotte heard him give a brief snort. Ed said, very quietly, 'Alex isn't as saintly as he seems.'

Hugh, Laura and Jack were probably sitting too far from Ed to hear what he said. They were also facing away from Alex at that moment, but Charlotte was looking right at him. So Charlotte and Ed were the only ones to see the look of horror on Alex's face.

Charlotte looked again. That was strange. Surely Ed was just joking? Why was Alex so concerned?

Alex turned away and began to fiddle with the stones near his feet. Ed moved off into the bush to gather wood. As Charlotte watched she saw Alex glance after Ed, then get up and follow him.

Charlotte decided that she might as well go and gather some sticks too, and there was no reason why that shouldn't be near the two boys. She moved carefully through the bush. Every so often she bent down and grabbed some sticks for kindling.

She could just hear their faint voices. She edged a little closer.

'. . . You said you wouldn't say anything!' Alex's voice was low and urgent.

Their voices faded away. Charlotte pushed a little closer, her head at an angle.

What on earth were they talking about? 'Saintly' might not be exactly the word she'd use to describe Alex, but it wasn't wildly incorrect. Alex was always helpful; he was the nice guy. Occasionally, it got a bit annoying, sure, but there was nothing wrong with being the nice guy. What did Ed have against Alex?

Eventually, Charlotte got close enough to hear what they were saying.

'No, they don't know – not from me, anyway.' Ed sounded impatient.

'So why did you . . .?'

The voices faded again.

'Yes, I know I was lucky that no one else saw. And I'm grateful that you didn't say anything.' Alex's voice was strained. 'But I thought—'

Ed cut him off. 'Don't worry, Alex, I'm not going to tell anyone. Your little secret is safe with me.'

Ed suddenly turned, so Charlotte crouched and began to gather more twigs, but Ed strode back towards the camp without a sideways glance.

Out of the corner of her eye, Charlotte could see Alex moving after Ed more slowly, his concern still clearly evident on his face.

Chapter 26

Charlotte watched Alex's frozen face as he stared at the message on the little blue note.

Finally, he looked up. His jaw worked. Then he croaked. 'Nothing.' A pause. 'I don't know what she means.' He turned away. 'Like Hugh said. Martha's clearly unbalanced.' When he turned back his voice was stronger. 'She's clearly just making up crap about all of us.' His laugh sounded forced also.

Jack nodded but didn't look convinced.

Hugh slapped Alex on the shoulder. 'What party does she mean? The infamous country party? What were you up to then, Alex? Did Martha see you disappear off with some girl, eh?' But his laugh sounded forced, and when Alex just shook his head, Hugh didn't persist.

Charlotte bet Jack and Hugh felt the same sense of creeping horror that she did. But they were all in the same boat – there was no way they could press Alex without suggesting their own messages might be true.

The notes were disturbing enough, with their vague accusations. But even more disturbing was this rigmarole; the trouble Martha had gone to in scattering them about where she knew they would look. The sense of some crazy plan being laid out.

Hugh smiled grimly. He said to Charlotte, 'So, babe, what's your message going to be?'

'Ha. Nothing. You know I'm such a good girl.' Mentally Charlotte tried to canvass anything dodgy that she might have kept to herself over the years. If she were honest, there were a few transgressions that Martha could pick from. But Charlotte reassured herself that Martha didn't know any of that stuff.

Jack said, 'Forget these crazy notes. We need to find some water soon. I think we should split up. Alex, Laura and I can search through the kitchen cupboards.'

'You and I could do the cellar,' said Hugh to Charlotte.

'Right.' Jack nodded. 'Then we'll try the rest of this floor before we go upstairs.' He turned to the kitchen cupboards.

'I'll start with these ones.' Laura knelt down to the lower cabinets.

Hugh pulled open the small door to the cellar. Charlotte ducked her head and crept carefully down the brick stairs.

'Wonder what we'll find down here.' Hugh let out a ghostly cry.

Charlotte felt his fingers on her neck and yelped. 'Piss off. Not funny.'

Hugh grinned. 'Do you reckon it's going to be Martha's chamber of horrors?'

As they reached the bottom of the stairs, Charlotte immediately felt the cooler air against her skin.

Small, high windows cast a dim light. Hugh felt around on the wall near the stairs, then a light bulb flared and Charlotte blinked a little.

Glancing around, she took in dusty shelves with even dustier wine bottles. Other shelves held cardboard boxes, tins and pickle jars. Everything was covered in a fine grey film. Charlotte let out a breath. Obviously, she hadn't actually expected to find any skeletons or corpses. But the tension of the morning had put her on edge.

Hugh began to push aside the paraphernalia on the nearest shelf.

Charlotte moved away a little and began poking behind some boxes. They worked in silence for a few minutes. Charlotte tried not to think about what would happen if they didn't find water. She rubbed at her stomach. Her doctor had told her to stay well hydrated. Could dehydration bring on a miscarriage? Surely that would take a long time. She tried not to think about that, either.

Then Hugh gave a cry, and Charlotte turned.

'Water cartons,' said Hugh.

'Yay!' Charlotte felt a rush of relief.

But her face fell when Hugh turned to face her.

'But they're empty too,' he said. 'Of course they are. Christ.'

He kicked at a nearby box and Charlotte blinked as a rush of disappointment threatened to overwhelm her.

'Got something?' At the sound of Jack's voice Charlotte turned. Jack was making his way down the stairs, followed by Alex and Laura.

Their faces fell when they saw Hugh shake his head.

Charlotte looked around the cellar then sighed. 'Anyway, doesn't look like there's anything else here. She turned towards the stairs.

'Hang on.'

Charlotte turned back at the sound of Hugh's voice and saw him holding a little blue piece of paper. Her heart sank. She was really hoping it had Laura's name on it, but she could see by the expression on Hugh's face that it didn't.

'Hey babe, it's your lucky turn.' Hugh gave her a light smile.

He went to open the note, but Charlotte strode across the room and snatched it from him.

Her fingers shook slightly as she opened the paper.

why didnt you help him it was no big deal

How the hell did Martha know about that?

Chapter 27

Ten years previously

The fire crackled and spat, sending flickers of light across the faces of the six friends and out into the dark bushland. Its hiss and snap expanded to fill the silence.

Charlotte watched the skipping flames. Ed had been right. Despite the shock of the dry water source and the anxiety that had provoked, the bright warmth had cheered them a little.

'Eat up.' Ed picked up his spoon and began to tuck in. 'There's no shortage of food.'

'I think it might just make me more thirsty.' Laura frowned at her plate.

'It'll give you strength,' Ed replied. 'It's just until we get to the river tomorrow morning, which won't take that long.'

Later, after the meal was finished and the plates stacked away, Jack looked around the group. Alex was gazing into the fire. Ed was scribbling in some sort of notebook. Hugh was trying to snap a stick, staring moodily at it, then trying again.

Jack looked across at Laura. 'You don't feel like painting?'

She shook her head. 'Too hard to see in this light.' A pause. 'But you don't need light for music.' Her low voice began to fill the silence, spinning out into a meandering melody.

Charlotte felt an old hesitation, then looked around at the fire-lit faces. She took a breath and began to pitch her own voice in harmony. She wavered but then grew stronger. Laura smiled at her as she sang.

When they stopped, Alex, Ed and Jack clapped. Charlotte felt better than she had since they had seen the dry creek bed, and she could see that the others' faces had lightened.

After a moment Jack grinned at Ed. 'Whatcha thinkin', Captain Ed?'

'Thinking about school.' Ed looked thoughtful. 'Bit sad it's over. We complained, but it was all right, even if it was full of rich people. Like this bastard.' He gave Hugh's leg a soft kick.

Hugh leaned back and stuck his hands behind his head. 'Yeah, yeah. Didn't stop any of you lefties taking advantage of the beach house.'

'I'm looking forward to travelling,' said Charlotte.

'India's top of my list,' said Laura.

'I'm actually looking forward to uni,' said Jack.

'Medical school doesn't sound too fun,' said Hugh. 'But Doctor Zhang will be out of there, earning the big bucks, before we know it.'

'If I get in.' Jack's voice was wary.

They all groaned. 'Of course, you'll get in.'

Hugh turned to Ed. 'Business for you, still?'

'Sure is.'

'What, no farm? Your dad won't be happy.'

Ed glanced at Charlotte. 'You could say that. He's just so set on passing the place on in the family. 'But I'll be near you, Hugh. Finance, wasn't it?'

'Well, I'll be far away from the money faculties, at art school.' Laura smiled.

'They won't know what hit them.' Jack leaned towards her.

Laura met his eyes, and give him a quick smile, but then turned to Charlotte.

'And what did you decide on?'

'Oh, it was tough. How the hell am I supposed to know what I want to do with my life? Marketing in the end. I think.' She sighed. 'I guess we'll all be splitting up, from the sounds of it.'

Laura shook her head. 'But we'll stay in touch.' Her face shifted with the shadows and orange light as the flames danced. 'I'm sure of it.'

Charlotte wasn't so sure. They'd gotten to know each other so well at boarding school, thrown together for bonding activities as part of the same house group on retreats and hikes just like this one. But they had grown into a bunch of people with pretty diverse interests, as was obvious in their different choices for uni courses. Charlotte still wasn't sure that she wouldn't rather be on that beach holiday with her other friends – especially now they had a water shortage on this one.

They were all silent for a moment. Then Hugh leaned across and began talking to Jack. Laura turned to Alex.

Ed closed his book and looked at Charlotte. 'So, talking of uni. I've been meaning to ask you. Have you had a chance to talk to your father yet? About the internship?'

'Your dad really isn't going to like that.' Charlotte stalled while her thoughts tumbled. Ed had first made this request a couple of weeks ago. And it had felt nice, having Ed Fletcher asking her a favour. Ed, the school captain, son of the fancy Fletcher family, who had their name on one of the school buildings.

It felt more than nice – it was reassuring.

It would surface in her memory, more often than she wanted it to, the grim morning when her father had stood in the hall with a suitcase, shaking off the arm of her weeping mother. Charlotte and her sister had peered through the stair railings. There was something very upsetting happening below; they just didn't know what. But she had been old enough to understand the contempt on her father's face as he gave his parting remark. 'And what's more, you've just bloody let yourself go.'

Charlotte's mother had gone on to take this as an instruction and had 'let herself go' further and faster, using the Martini glass as an instrument.

Charlotte was determined she would never feel the desolation that was written across her mother's face as she stared into her empty cocktail glass. Charlotte was never going to allow herself to be disregarded, abandoned by men, in that humiliating fashion.

She knew she put a bit too much effort into her appearance. She knew she flirted and sought attention a little more than many other girls. It's just that it felt so good, so comforting. So safe, to know that she could field those admiring glances.

So, when Ed had first asked his favour, she had smiled, and tipped her head to one side. Then she said she wasn't sure; she didn't think her dad would be keen on the idea.

Ed had looked rather surprised. Then disappointed. So she had told him she would ask her father anyway.

Now, sitting in the firelight, Ed laughed, but his face held an uncomfortable tension. 'Yeah, Dad's pretty pissed off actually. He hardly looked at me this morning when we left.'

'Ouch.'

'But, I'm sure. I want to run something other than a bunch of cattle; I like people. Dad just doesn't get it. Can't see why someone would want to go live in the city and work in an office tower.' Ed was gazing into the flames. 'Shouldn't have sent me to boarding school in Sydney if that's how he felt.'

He turned back to Charlotte. 'Like I said when we spoke the other week. At the moment, I wouldn't put it past Dad to say that he won't pay for uni unless it's agriculture. But, if I had an internship at a big firm, I'd have a bit of cash and that would mean I wouldn't have to rely on Mum and Dad.' Ed was talking quickly, and he put his hand on Charlotte's arm.

Charlotte looked down at the hand on her arm. The sensation of his warm skin on hers was far from unpleasant. She looked again at his face, bathed in the light of the fire and a smile spread across her face of its own volition.

'So, yeah,' said Ed. 'Have you asked him?'

She looked up across the fire at Laura, thinking about the memory of her and Ed entwined in an embrace. It brought up a much darker feeling. When it came to boys, the rules of the game weren't always simple. She paused. 'There are lots of schemes you can apply for. Doesn't have to be at my dad's firm.'

'I know, but they're all so competitive now. My marks are fine, but they're not brilliant, not like Jack's. I think all these places want a Jack Zhang. But your dad's the CEO. If he wants to bring a family friend into the business, that can happen.' Ed was looking at her expectantly. 'Anyway, it would really help me out if you could put in a word for me.'

'Yeah, so, actually I did ask him.'

'And?'

She looked down. She traced a line in the dirt with the point of her hiking boot, her head tilted to one side. She remembered her discussion with her dad and his enthusiastic response. *Of course, I'd love to have Ed on board. He's a fine young man. School captain, right?* She looked across at Laura again, and her dark feeling strengthened.

She turned again to Ed's eager face. God, having him on tenterhooks like this actually felt so good. It made that dark feeling fade right away.

'And I'm afraid he said no.'

Chapter 28

Jack watched Charlotte as she stared at the little blue note. No doubt she was feeling the same horrified disbelief that had washed over him when he read his own note.

Jack could sense that, with each new question, the tension had tightened around the friends. It was clear that each of them was not being honest in their disavowal of the suspicions that Martha had thrown – and that had lent its own dynamic to the stress of the situation.

But Jack was wondering, perhaps more urgently, how on earth Martha knew, or thought she knew, these things about each of them, and he was sure his friends were wondering the same thing.

Hugh was looking over Charlotte's shoulder. He was frowning. 'Who's "him"? Is that Ed? And what "help"?'

Charlotte closed her eyes then opened them. Took a breath and looked up.

'No idea. She's mad. Clearly.' Then, the lightest of mocking tones in her voice, 'Like you all said.'

Jack almost smiled. Touché. They all knew. None of them could be openly suspicious of the others without bringing suspicion down on themselves. No one could enquire too closely without risking the interrogation turning to their own note.

'Of course,' said Hugh in a sardonic tone. Then his face shifted, and he turned away. 'Anyway, who cares what this madwoman thinks? We need to work out how to get the hell out of here.'

Charlotte had been standing very still, but now she jerked into motion and headed for the stairs. 'Starting with getting out of this bloody cellar.'

Back in the kitchen, Jack said, 'Look, we don't know what's going on. Martha could come back any moment really. Perhaps she just went out for a bit, wanted to give us a bit of a scare. Perhaps she'll turn up and put on a spread for lunch, laughing at how upset we are. But, in case she doesn't. If we assume we've got . . . a little while before Martha reappears.'

Jack could sense Hugh, Alex, Laura and Charlotte responding, turning to him. He remembered what it was like, back in the classroom at school, when he put his hand up to explain the answer and everyone turned to him because they knew he would have it right. It had been a good feeling. And his friends' responses now were giving him just a little more energy than he had felt lately. He pushed his glasses up his nose and infused a note of confidence into his voice that he really wasn't feeling. 'We should search the house. Find out what's here. What we have to work with.'

'What, a morse code set? Some carrier pigeons?' Hugh's tone was light, but his face was tense.

Jack waved his hands vaguely. 'I don't know what exactly, but it's worth looking. Checking what little bits of water there are. I mean, like what's in the kettle? Any glasses of water upstairs? Even a vase of flowers or something.'

'We could turn all the taps, collect the last dribbles from the pipes,' said Laura.

The sense of purpose lightened their expressions a little as they began opening cupboards and sorting through the clutter on the bench tops, calling to each other as they worked.

Twenty minutes later they stood around the kitchen table, staring at their collection. It looked very paltry. A half-filled kettle. A small amount of water that was in the old coffee maker. Some tinned fruit in juice. A few plastic water bottles that they'd brought with them.

Their disappointment was all the worse for following a brief feeling of hope.

'There are bottles of ancient wine down in the cellar, but even I'm not sure they count,' said Hugh. 'Do we want to be thirsty or drunk?'

'I don't know,' said Laura. 'Alcohol might be more dehydrating.'

Charlotte sat on one of the kitchen chairs and put her face in her hands. Hugh patted her shoulder vaguely.

'Come on, Charl,' said Alex. 'At least there's no shortage of food. That stack of tin cans down in the cellar would feed an army.'

Jack saw Charlotte try to muster up a smile. 'I would suggest a cuppa,' she said. 'But perhaps that's not a great idea. Can we go outside for a bit? I think I need some fresh air.'

They moved to the back veranda. Jack looked out across the valley. It was still so quiet. No breath of breeze to disturb the heat. It all looked so normal.

Suddenly, a voice crackled forth.

'Have you remembered anything yet?'

Jack jumped, felt adrenaline thudding through his veins. The four friends looked about wildly, but there was no one. The voice had sounded out of thin air.

Chapter 29

Alex heard the sudden voice and, almost at the same moment, saw Jack jump and turn his head. His heart hammered, and he looked desperately around the veranda and the yard.

Charlotte's and Hugh's eyes were wide, and they too were twisting their heads. Laura looked very tense as she scanned the yard.

'Martha!' Hugh's face twisted. 'Where the hell is she? Has she been in the house this whole time?' He wrenched open the kitchen door and strode inside. Jack and Laura followed on his heels.

Charlotte clutched at Alex. 'I don't want to see her! Stay with me.'

Alex automatically gave her arm a reassuring squeeze, but his breath was coming fast. It was impossible to tell where that voice had come from. He jumped down onto the lawn and checked around the side of the house. There was no one there.

After a few minutes Jack, Laura and Hugh returned to the veranda, shaking their heads.

Then, the voice sounded again. 'You must have something to tell me by now!'

Jack's expression shifted, and he darted forward. He reached behind one of the wicker chairs on the veranda and held up a black rectangular device.

A radio.

'It's a two-way,' said Jack. He pressed at some buttons, saying, 'Martha! Hello? Martha?'

But there was no answering voice.

'Anyone know how to work this thing?' asked Jack.

'I do.' Alex stepped forward and put out his hand.

'You do?' asked Hugh, with a note of surprise.

'We use them at work. When there's a couple of us at a big site with our clients.' He pressed the send button. 'Martha? Is that you?'

There was a pause. 'Alex.' A cracking silence. 'Dear Alex. Have you got your friends with you?' Martha's voice had a mocking tone.

'Yes, we're all here.' Alex took a breath. This felt like dealing with one of his clients when they were very upset, so he reminded himself of the need for a steady, calm voice. 'Martha, where are you? We've had a bit of an odd morning.'

'Is that right?'

'Martha, what's going on? The water's disconnected. Our cars aren't working. And we can't call anyone – the modem's missing.'

A pause. 'Really?'

Jack said, 'Martha, whatever the issue is, how about you come back? We'll sort it out.'

'NO!' Martha shouted, and they all jumped. 'The discussion is over. Just tell me. *What really happened?*'

The radio fell silent.

Alex looked at the others. 'She can't hear us until I press this button.'

'No way in hell do we say anything.' Hugh was shaking his head. 'Last night we thought it was a bad idea because she seemed a little unbalanced.'

'And she's clearly way more volatile than we thought.' Jack looked stressed.

Laura looked mutinous. 'Wait, guys, perhaps . . .'

'No.' Charlotte laughed wildly. 'We definitely cannot tell her now. What will she do next? Perhaps she's got some dynamite set up and she'll blow the house away.' She looked at the others. 'Joking. I mean, surely not. But you take my point.'

Alex paused. 'Martha. Please come back here; we can sort out whatever is concerning you.' He set the radio to receive and took a breath.

'Right. So that's the way it is.' Martha's voice was short. 'One piece of advice. You should start with being more honest with each other. Then you can be honest with me.' Another bitter laugh. 'Over and out.'

'Martha. Wait. Don't go.'

But call as they might, there was no answer. The radio was now a lifeless black box.

Alex gave it a little shake, then felt a laugh bubbling up. Did he think Martha's voice could somehow be encouraged out of the box with a bit of movement?

'We should reconsider.' Laura's jaw was set. 'At dinner last night Martha asked us point blank what really happened. And now we can see that she's really serious. Like I said, I think we made the wrong call, all those years ago.'

Jack cleared his throat. He took a breath. 'We had good reasons, at the time. And given how Martha reacted after Ed was found, and everything that happened after that, I still think we were right.'

Chapter 30

Ten years previously

The park rangers from Flat Top Hill, the nearest operational centre, had been the first to arrive for the search for Ed. They gathered near the Fletcher house. They unloaded backpacks and smoothed out maps over the bonnets of their vehicles.

Jack sat with Hugh, Alex, Charlotte and Laura, watching the rangers. They looked so efficient and energetic. They conferred, briskly rubbing in sunscreen. They fastened hats and checked water bottles. Their radios scratched and jittered. It all seemed so unreal.

'I'll come,' Robert Fletcher was saying to them.

'It might be better—' began a ranger.

'I'm coming.'

'Me too.' Martha Fletcher stepped forward.

'No,' said Robert. 'You're needed here.' He nodded at the young hikers, huddled together. 'You've got a job to do.'

Martha opened her mouth. Then closed it and nodded. 'Right. I'll get some hot drinks going. I'm sure everyone could use one.' She strode quickly into the house.

A little later, the rescue coordinator headed towards the group of friends and introduced himself as Phil. 'Just need to confirm a few details with you guys,' he said.

Phil's voice seemed to Jack to be coming from a long way away. People were drifting around, as though in slow motion. Jack watched Martha directing other women as they assembled a trestle table and set out mugs and a large urn.

Hugh stood up. 'Anything we can do.'

Jack's legs felt so heavy, but, as Alex, Charlotte and Laura stood, he dragged himself to his feet.

Phil was smoothing out a map. 'So. You guys said you were heading down from Stockman's Rest, where you spent the night, right? And you were heading along this trail, when you last saw Ed.' Phil traced his finger along a line on the map.

They all peered at the map and nodded.

'And so.' The ranger looked from face to face. Jack could see the skin crinkling around his eyes. 'How was it that Ed got separated from the rest of you?'

Jack couldn't meet his friends' eyes. The silence went on. It was excruciating.

Finally, he looked up. The others were also stealing glances at each other.

Phil was waiting.

A man on the other side of the yard looked up and called, 'Hey, Phil.'

Phil turned. 'Excuse me, guys, I'll be back in a sec.'

Jack watched him walk across the yard.

'So . . .' Hugh's voice was slow. 'What are we going to say?'

Jack was looking at the ground at the exact moment the idea

was raised, so he couldn't say who had spoken first. But it seemed that everyone immediately agreed.

We can't tell . . . No, we can't . . . What's the point?

Jack took a breath. He felt guilt pulling at his stomach like a fist twisting a rag. He looked away, then back to the group.

'I'm sure it won't help.' Alex's voice was urgent. 'Don't you remember the school camp? And the food packs?'

Oh yes. It was all too vivid in Jack's memory.

All six of them had been on the school trip in year ten, together in their house grouping as usual. They were hiking a coastal path along with the other houses in their year at school. The equipment had been split between the different house groups, and their particular group had been tasked with carrying the key food staples.

The first part of the trip had gone well, everyone seemed to be having fun. Then they had finally arrived at a sandy lagoon after a long walk down a steep track. With loud whoops, all the students had stripped off T-shirts and leapt in, the water cool against their sweaty skin.

Unfortunately, they had left the food bags on nearby rocks, perilously close to the water line. And as they played, the tide seeped inexorably in, washing the bags into the water.

Laura had noticed first. 'Oh crap. Guys, look – the bags!'

They turned, their faces falling in horror as they saw the waterlogged backpacks bobbing in the lagoon water.

'I'll get them.' Hugh leapt across the water, Ed jumping after him.

The boys dragged the bags back to dry land, still laughing at that point. But the laughter had died away as they pulled out soggy food.

Jack could still remember, clear as day, the face of the year master, when he heard what had happened. The six of them had gone to the master to own up, nervous, but confident that it was the best course of action. The school placed a great deal of emphasis on honesty and responsibility for their actions. At the back of Jack's mind was the possibility that they might even be praised for owning up so readily. But instead, the teacher had totally lost it.

Spit flew from his mouth as he leered over them, shouting. 'That was unbelievably irresponsible! You shouldn't have been swimming. You've now put the whole camp in jeopardy. I can't believe your carelessness.' Probably he had been fuelled by anxiety about the welfare of a group of students who now had significantly reduced food supplies. Possibly also some guilt that the swimmers had not been properly supervised. Or even the wisdom of giving most of the food to one house group.

Then the ultimate blow. The six of them had been sent home early, to face parents who were also angry at their disgrace.

Now, outside the Fletchers' house, the friends looked at each other as they recalled the camp.

Hugh nodded at Alex. 'You're right. Fat lot of good owning up did then.'

'It just brought down a whole world of pain on us,' said Alex.

'And that was just some lost food.' Charlotte looked haunted. 'Not a lost person.'

They stared at each other.

'And this is just talking to the rangers.' Hugh nodded towards the other side of the yard. 'You feel like explaining everything to Martha?'

Martha had arranged a trestle table in the yard, and was bustling behind it, arranging equipment. Her movements were quick and jerky. Her face had a fixed, bright look.

They watched as she began to spoon out some tea. She put one, then two, then three teaspoons in the pot. The woman standing next to her looked sideways as more and more teaspoons went in.

As the friends watched from the other side of the yard, Martha stopped spooning tea and picked up one of the mugs and threw it hard against the ground.

One of the search administrators looked up, took several strides across the yard, put an arm around Martha and led her away.

'Oh my god,' breathed Charlotte.

Phil the ranger made his way back across the yard. He looked from face to face. 'Yeah, so, what were you saying? How did Ed get separated from the rest of you?'

A long pause.

Hugh went first. His voice had an odd tone. 'Ed decided he would go ahead and look for another water source.'

'Yeah – he was being responsible,' said Charlotte. 'As usual.' Her voice was fast, panicky.

'He was basically the leader of the walk,' Alex went on.

'It was a mistake,' said Hugh quickly.

'Of course, we can see that now,' said Laura.

Jack felt himself nodding.

'We waited and waited,' said Charlotte. Her voice was high and breathless. 'Went looking for him, shouted, for ages. He never came back. We decided we'd better go for help.'

'We should never have let him go off by himself.' Jack looked at his friends, and they all shook their heads together.

'Okay, got it.' The ranger nodded. 'Well, try not to stress too much. We'll find your friend.'

'How about we just go back into the scrub and look for ourselves?' said Laura. 'They can't actually hold us here.'

New search teams had arrived. Police rescue, their dark uniforms bringing a new seriousness. SES volunteers, with bright, helpful faces. More national park staff in their khaki.

The five friends were gathered in the living room of the Fletcher house. They had been shooed inside by the searchers. Told to rest. Like that was ever going to happen.

Charlotte turned to Laura. 'I don't know. They're the experts. What if we got lost? Or hurt?'

'Jack – you'll help?' Laura looked at him eagerly. 'Come on. We can't just leave him out there!' Her voice rose in pitch, and Jack felt a lurch of anxiety.

'Laura. Get a grip,' said Hugh. 'The searchers are onto it. They know what they're doing.'

For once, Jack was grateful for Hugh's assertiveness.

Charlotte was looking through a window. She started. 'They're coming back.'

Jack felt a stab of hope. He ran to the window, crowding in with the others.

'What? Is there any—?'

'No.'

Hugh said, 'It's too dark now.'

Charlotte said, 'But they'll be back at first light. Isn't that how they say it? "At first light."' She flopped on a chair. 'God, this is torture. I just wish there was something we could *do*.'

* * *

156

On the second day, the search teams grew larger still. A helicopter now groaned overhead.

Jack felt his own silence growing, as talk between the friends dried up. They slouched in the living room or on the veranda, wandered in the yard. Offered to help in the kitchen.

Alex brought a glass of water to his lips, looked at it, then put it down again.

'I know,' said Jack. 'Try not to think about it.'

Jack wandered outside. He could see Martha ferrying trays of mugs between the kitchen and new groups of rangers.

When Martha saw Jack, she came straight over. Her face was bright. 'They're very good, the rangers. They've found people before in these hills, you know. Three years ago, they got two German hikers out.' She nodded eagerly.

Jack could only nod in return. Martha hurried off again. Jack went to the others, who had emerged from the house and were sitting on the edge of the veranda.

He saw Phil, the rescue coordinator, staring at a map. He saw him feel for his radio, then bring it to his ear.

He saw the weight roll over the man's body and his shoulders slump, and at that moment, Jack knew. He felt a faint ringing noise in his ears.

He saw Phil move slowly over to Robert. He saw Robert call for Martha. Martha put down the urn she was carrying and hurried to her husband.

Jack could see Phil's face, twisted. He was speaking to them, his palms open.

Martha was shaking her head. She stepped backwards. She held up her hands. She pushed at the air. She shrieked, 'No!'

Everyone in the yard turned at the sudden yell.

Jack heard the word echo in his own mind, push up through his own throat, as he whispered to himself, 'No.'

He saw Robert start forward and grab Martha as she slumped.

Then a terrible cry burst forth from Martha's mouth. It went on and on, shifting from cry into scream, and Jack heard cries and sobs break out among his friends as his own throat closed up and a terrible heaviness spread within his chest.

His heart was hammering. A wave of horror was breaking over his body. He knew he would hear Martha's cry for the rest of his life.

Finally, finally, the terrible noise stopped and came to a halt in gasping sobs.

Jack thought the moment could not get any worse. But then Martha threw off Robert's arms. She turned to the group of friends and marched towards them.

Jack saw Robert's expression shift, as he started after Martha.

Martha halted before the group of friends. They stared at her, frozen. Martha's mouth was open, her face muscles were working.

'You!' Martha's chest was heaving; she was taking great gulps of air. 'This is your fault!' she screamed. 'You – you left him behind. You left him there to die!'

Chapter 31

Charlotte stood outside the kitchen. She could hear her parents within. As was so often the case these days, her mother sounded stressed; her father, irritated.

'I don't know, Geoff. Why invite more attention?'

'They have attention anyway. This is a way to for them to put their side.'

Charlotte stepped through the door. Her parents fell silent and looked at her with the false cheeriness that always overlaid their manner towards her these days.

'Darling, how are—'

'You want us to do it.' Charlotte cut across her mother.

Her father shifted on his feet. 'I think you all should have a chance to put your view.'

Charlotte took a breath. She and the others had discussed the request for an interview. Hugh and Jack had thought it might be a good idea. Laura and Alex were against it, Alex particularly so. Charlotte wasn't sure.

The call had come from an *Advocate* journalist, one Ainslee Blake. 'It will be a friendly interview. I know you're all grieving,' Ainslee had said. 'This will be a chance for you to give your story. After all you've been through.'

They had been through a lot, Charlotte thought – not just the walk and Ed's death, but the following media interest. It had been intense. Former schoolmates chased for comment via social media. Journalists camped outside their houses.

Just the other day, Charlotte had jumped and shrieked as a reporter with a microphone sprung out at her at the bottom of her driveway. She had to run back into the house.

'We'll do it over lunch,' Ainslee had said. 'We'll take some photos.'

Now Charlotte tipped her head on one side and regarded her father across the kitchen. 'Okay, maybe we should do it.'

A few days later, she met Ainslee at a nearby restaurant, over-looking the harbour. Ainslee had suggested that it might be easier if it were just Charlotte and her, rather than having the others come along.

The interview had started with what seemed to be a girly catch-up. Ainslee poured the wine generously. Charlotte felt herself relaxing as the water shimmered on the other side of the window.

'It's such a difficult time of life, isn't it?' Ainslee was looking at her with more sympathy than a lot of strangers had shown her lately. 'At the end of school, everyone with their different plans and ambitions.'

'Oh yes, that's so true,' Charlotte nodded.

'You had a few different personalities in that group, I think. Was it all good between you?'

'Oh yes, fine. Well, mostly fine.' Charlotte might have given a bit more detail at this point than she would have without the wine, but Ainslee seemed so nice and caring.

Charlotte had secretly enjoyed standing for the photographer, her hair and clothes adjusted just so, the water at her back and an appropriately serious expression on her face. She reminded herself that this was about Ed's memory.

'Was there any interest between you and Ed, by the way?' Ainslee smiled at her with a conspiratorial grin.

Charlotte shook her head but couldn't help a smile in return.

Ainslee nodded in a knowing fashion.

Really, they had gotten on like a house on fire. Charlotte was sure Ainslee would give them a great profile. And, as her parents had said, it might feed the media beast, help get all those reporters off the friends' backs.

That weekend, she eagerly opened the paper, keen to see how the picture would come out in print. She stared in shock at the newsprint.

Ainslee hadn't used that photo. In fact, she hadn't used any of the group photos they had given her. Instead, there was a photo that must have been grabbed from someone's Facebook page. Ed was standing to the side, while Charlotte, Hugh, Jack, Laura and Alex had their arms slung around each other. It seemed to subtly suggest Ed was other, somehow excluded.

A low knot of unease grew in Charlotte's stomach. She began to scan the article. The unease suddenly exploded.

Charlotte denies there was any interest between her and Ed but her smiling blush as she does so tells another story . . . She says they were all good friends, but alludes to tension that had grown between them over the past months . . .

She dropped the paper and covered her mouth. Then she heard her phone ring.

'Charlotte? Have you seen it?' It was Laura.

'Yes,' Charlotte croaked. 'It's wrong. I didn't say that stuff. She's completely misrepresented me. You've got to believe me.'

But bad as that experience with the print media had been, worse was building up for them.

A few months later, Charlotte was leaving a university lecture when Eloise, a young woman in her marketing tutorial, waved her over. Charlotte been hoping to meet a new crowd of people when she started uni. She avoided giving her full name in introductions, and no one had recognised her from media photos. But establishing her social life had taken longer than she'd thought it would. She'd felt a new kind of reserve keeping her restrained as she attended the round of social events that had come with the first semester. So she was pleased that Eloise had signalled to her. Perhaps she'd suggest a coffee.

Eloise's face was alive with a mixture of horror and excitement. She put her hand on Charlotte's arm. 'I guess you've seen. You poor thing.'

'Seen what?' An all-too-familiar sinking feeling.

Eloise composed her face. 'This webpage. It's a kind of Wiki. For the death of your friend.' She held out her phone to Charlotte.

The website was headed, 'What really happened to Edward Fletcher?' Charlotte scanned the text.

So the six of them went in and only five came out. And they say he just got lost by himself? Hahahahahaha

They say Ed was having an affair with one of the other boys. Theres a motive right there

Girls from that school are all total bitches and sluts.
My cousin went there. Miserable. Left after one term

The dark haired boy looks just like this guy who raped my
friend at a party. Wouldnt be surprised if he was the killer

Charlotte felt giddy. This was nuts. There was a whole set of
people out there who were devoting serious time to analysing
what had happened with her and her friends.

'Oh, I'm so sorry. I thought you'd seen it,' cooed Eloise as
Charlotte's face crumbled. Charlotte turned suddenly. She bent
over a shrub growing next to the path and vomited.

Now Eloise's look of shock was genuine. She put an arm
around Charlotte's shoulders. 'Oh, sweetheart! Here, have a sip
of my water. Do you need to sit down? Let's get a coffee. And
definitely don't look at Twitter.'

That evening Charlotte looked at Twitter.

The speculation was like the Wiki, but much worse. Charlotte
couldn't seem to tear her eyes away, but she finally stopped when
she got to '*That blond bitch is pretty hot Id still fuck her even if she
is a murderer. I would start by . . .*'

She squeezed her eyes closed and her face began to crumble.

Chapter 32

'I agree.' Charlotte's voice was emphatic. 'I do not believe that we made the wrong call. It was an awful time and there was absolutely nothing to be gained in giving all the complicated details.'

Alex nodded. He was very happy to back Charlotte up in that opinion. 'And definitely no reason to go into back into it all now.'

'Absolutely.' Hugh's voice was short. 'But, forget that for a sec. I want to know how Martha knew to activate that radio right then? Is she *watching* us?'

Alex looked around automatically, and all the others did too.

The valley stretched out in front of them, the gentle roll of the paddocks rising towards the bush at the base of the cliffs. Plenty of places for someone to hide.

'Let's go inside.'

At the kitchen table, Jack heaved himself into a seat. 'So this is not just Martha's idea of a funny prank.'

Hugh nodded. 'She's not going to come roaring up the drive in her ute and magic the water back on, cackling about how she really had us worried.'

Alex noticed Laura standing to one side, gazing outside. She looked frustrated.

'So let's take a moment. Calm down and think,' said Jack. 'There must be some way forward here. We've got no phone line, no internet. No transport. Not much water.'

Alex glanced out at the sun, which was by now high in the sky.

'And a madwoman out in the bush, possibly watching us with a telescope or something,' said Hugh.

Alex really wished Hugh wouldn't joke like that.

Jack cut in. 'We really can't use this to call for help?' He pushed his glasses up his nose and picked up the radio handset. 'Seems so crazy that we've got it here but it's no use.'

They had tried fiddling with the frequency but had found nothing. Alex had pointed out that the range wouldn't be very extensive, and the cliffs around the valley would be acting as a natural barrier.

'There must be something in the house that's useful,' said Alex.

'We've had a pretty good look,' said Charlotte. Frustration twisted her forehead.

'Actually . . .' At the new note in Jack's voice the others turned to him.

Jack sat forward. 'We haven't quite been everywhere. There's Martha's study. I tried the door when we were upstairs just now. Still locked. But we should have a look in there.'

'What, break the door down?' asked Laura.

'Laura, the woman's destroyed the phone line, trashed our cars and cut the bloody water. I don't think we should be too shy about breaking into her little lair.'

'Hey, there's that set of key hooks in the pantry.' Alex disappeared into the next room then reappeared with some small brass keys. 'Dunno if these are even the right sort, but we can try.'

Upstairs, Alex's fingers shook slightly as he tried each key. Three wouldn't fit in the lock. Two slotted in, but neither of them turned.

'I'll shoulder it.' Hugh eyed the door. Alex pressed his lips together. Even in this situation, Hugh had to show off his physical prowess. Well, good luck to him. The door seemed pretty solid.

'Don't hurt yourself.' Charlotte put her hand on his arm.

Hugh took a few steps back and ran sideways at the door.

'Christ!' He stepped backwards, rubbing at his shoulder. 'Didn't budge an inch.'

'How about we try to lever it?' Jack looked thoughtful. 'We could see if there's anything in the sheds outside.'

Alex followed Jack out to the corrugated iron shed closest to the house. The door was creaky but opened easily enough. Inside, it looked like a timber and metal storage warehouse that hadn't been touched for years. Everything was covered in dust and cobwebs. Alex was careful where he stood. There were probably whole families of spiders in here. Not to mention snakes.

Jack rooted around and picked out a large screwdriver. He weighed it in one hand. 'This should do it.'

Upstairs again, Hugh inserted the fine end between the door and the door frame and shoved against the other end.

There was a loud splintering crack as the wood split, and they all gave a soft cheer.

The door swung open with a faint creak.

But at the sight of the room within there was a long silence.

Chapter 33

It was the messiest room in the entire house. One of the messiest rooms Hugh had ever seen, which was saying something.

On every surface, across the desk and shelves, a filing cabinet, two easy chairs, and on the floor, sat piles of papers and books. Cardigans, shoes, sunhats. Balls of wool, crochet needles. Stacks of cardboard boxes filled the corners. The blinds hung crookedly from the window frame. And everything was layered with a fine film of dust. Balls of the grey stuff lined the edges of the carpet.

But that wasn't the most striking part.

Every inch of every surface was covered in photo frames containing the face that none of them would ever forget. Pinned to the walls, holes pressed carelessly into the wallpaper, were yet more – unframed – photos. Ed, frozen in time, in every conceivable life stage.

There was Ed as a baby lying on a rug. As a toddler, dragging a small elephant on wheels. Here was Ed in a school polo-neck shirt, proudly holding up a sport ribbon. There was Ed with Martha and Robert, the Opera House in the background.

And other ageing papers were pinned between the photos. Hugh stepped closer. A Mother's Day card. A set of lined papers covered in a rough scrawl, a primary school creative writing assignment. More of the same childish ephemera were tacked up on the other walls too.

'Well, now we know why there aren't any photos in the rest of the house.' Hugh found he couldn't muster a smile.

The others were still staring, silently.

Finally, Charlotte spoke. 'I was shocked by the state of this place,' she said, still gazing around the room. 'Considering how house proud she was, back in the day. But this room is next level.'

Laura just shook her head slowly.

'It's like this is the heart of it – all the mess, the decay.' Jack was peering at more school assignments pinned to the wall. 'As if it all radiates out from here to the rest of the house and the farm.'

'Let's get on with it,' Hugh said gruffly. He didn't think of himself as an emotional person, but he was also feeling disturbed by the state of the room. 'Going to take a while to sort through all this crap. I'll start on this.' He yanked open the top drawer of the filing cabinet.

Charlotte moved a couple of blankets then sat at the desk chair. 'I'll go through these drawers.'

'There's so much stuff here.' Laura looked from face to face. 'How about I go grab some of those cardboard boxes from downstairs? We can empty drawers into them as we go, which will make it easier to put everything back.' No one replied and she slipped out the door.

There was quiet as they began lifting papers and moving books aside.

168

Jack was the first to speak. 'Look at this.' He held up a little cardboard box. This is a pretty serious antidepressant. It's dated two years ago.' He fished out a foil blister pack. 'None of these have been taken.'

'She must have stopped taking them,' said Hugh. 'Makes sense.' The room was quiet as they searched, except for occasional comments about the impressive array of ancient documents and knick-knacks that had been kept.

'I can't believe there is every edition of *Knitting World* back to 2005,' said Jack. 'Shoved in logically next to this set of old building records. Looks like house plans and old maps.' He flicked through a pile of large sheets of paper.

'And here's a box with every rubber band that has ever entered the house,' said Alex. 'But all mixed up with every paper clip they've ever found.'

'A set of souvenir teaspoons.' Charlotte held up a piece of wood with spoons hanging between sets of tiny nails. 'They must have made a trip through far north Queensland. And rural Victoria. But where the hell is Patchewollock?'

Hugh wiped his forehead from time to time. It was hot in the little study.

The papers in the cabinet were in a complete mess. He looked past bills and certificates. He pulled out a shoebox and found it was full of letters and cards. They looked pretty old. He shoved the drawer in and moved to the next one. Another shoebox.

'Hey.' The others turned to look at him. 'These ones are from Laura.' They crowded around as Hugh pulled out the papers. There were Christmas cards, birthday cards, postcards. 'They really kept in touch.'

Hugh automatically looked at Jack.

Jack glanced away, but then he said, 'I saw them talking after dinner last night. They did seem . . . close.' Jack looked unhappy.

Charlotte looked up from sorting through a rubbish bin overflowing with papers. 'Hey . . . where *is* Laura?'

Hugh looked blankly between Jack, Charlotte and Alex.

'She's been a while getting those boxes,' Charlotte persisted.

Jack got up laboriously from where he was sitting on the floor. 'Might just go down and take a look. Perhaps she's found something.'

After about ten minutes, Hugh saw Jack's bulky figure in the doorway.

'I can't see her.' Jack's breathing was heavy and his voice held a tense note.

Hugh waved a hand at him. 'She must be down there somewhere.'

'No, I've been through the whole house. I really can't see her.'

'Don't be bloody ridiculous, of course she's there.' Hugh stood and headed to the door. 'Let me look.'

'Let's all go.' Charlotte laboured to her feet. 'It's too hot up here anyway.' She glanced at the bin she had been looking through. 'I can take this downstairs to finish.'

Downstairs was very quiet. It didn't take long to look in each room and be clear Laura wasn't there.

'She must have gone outside – perhaps she's taking another look in the sheds.' Hugh felt a spurt of irritation towards Laura.

'It's pretty warm out there,' said Charlotte. 'I might wait here.'

'I'll wait with you,' said Alex.

It was so damn hot outside. Hugh shook his head again. What the hell was Laura up to, out here in the heat?

Hugh and Jack spent ten minutes looking around the yards and through the outbuildings, but there was no Laura. They headed back to the house.

Hugh now felt a trickle of worry, which only increased his irritation. He turned to Alex. 'We could check the ground floor again.' He didn't really believe Laura had snuck in the front door and was hiding in the living room, but could she have hit her head somehow and fallen over?

The four remaining friends roamed distractedly through the dining room and living room, looking behind doors and sofas.

Twenty minutes later they all stood in the kitchen, staring at each other. There was no other conclusion.

Laura had disappeared.

Chapter 34

Jack turned away from his friends, pulled out a chair at the kitchen table and sat. He rubbed at his temples, hearing the others' confused outbursts.

'Where the hell has she gone?'

Jack turned to face them again. He pushed his glasses up his nose. He didn't know if he should voice the ideas that were warring within him. And he didn't even know which was the most disturbing.

Then Charlotte gave voice to one of them. She cast a worried glance out the window. 'Did Martha somehow . . . *grab* Laura? Is Martha, like, out there? Waiting to pounce on us?'

Jack rose with the others, and they all peered outside.

'We didn't see anyone – no sign of Laura or Martha – when we were looking outside.' Hugh's voice was still definite, but slightly less belligerent than it was. 'We didn't hear anything, either.'

'Well, you wouldn't, if she was hiding.' Alex's voice was tense.

Charlotte moaned softly. 'God, what's Martha up to? Poor Laura.'

Hugh glanced at Charlotte's worried face then said, 'There is another possibility.'

Everyone turned to him.

Jack knew what was coming.

'Maybe Laura is part of this crazy shit. Along with Martha.'

'Whoa.' Alex's eyebrows shot up. 'Why would you say that?'

Jack was pleased that at least someone else had doubts. 'Yeah, why on earth would Laura do this?'

Hugh raised his chin. 'Last night, remember, she wanted us to, you know, be more "honest" with Martha. She kept on about it.'

'So what?'

'So, she's not exactly in lockstep with the rest of us on that one,' Hugh went on. 'Also, I don't know about you lot, but I reckon she's seemed different on this trip. Detached, or something.'

Jack had to agree with Hugh. Laura had seemed a bit cooler than normal. Jack had thought it might just have been directed at him, but if the others had noticed then it might be something bigger. He felt a tiny lift in his spirits, despite his concern for her. Perhaps her distant manner wasn't personal to him.

'Perhaps she's been planning this, with Martha, all along,' Hugh went on.

'Hold on.' Jack made himself take a breath. He had to remind himself that defending Laura was neither his duty nor his right. 'It was pretty clear, yesterday, that Martha isn't exactly calm and stable at the moment.'

'She's batshit,' said Hugh.

'Laura might have been a bit distracted, but she hasn't been unbalanced.' Jack knew he was trying to convince himself at least as much as the others. 'If she seems a bit different, it might be her diagnosis. That's big news. That would shake anyone up.'

'Sure. That's part of my point. Perhaps it shook her up enough to come up with some crazy plan with Martha.'

'Hugh, you've got no reason to say that.' Jack tried to keep the edge out of his tone, to say it like he was calmly analysing the situation.

'Martha lost her son.' Charlotte rubbed her stomach. 'And then there's Robert's death. Two big traumas. I know a cancer diagnosis is no fun, but it's not the same kind of thing.'

'But Laura lost . . .' Alex glanced at Jack, then his voice trailed away.

'He wasn't her boyfriend.' The words rose in Jack's throat despite himself. He hated how he sounded. 'They didn't have long enough . . .' His voice died.

He saw the others' careful glances at him and looked down. They were filled with pity for him. It was hard to stomach.

Charlotte's voice was soft. 'I know you won't want to hear this, Jack. But I think Laura really loved Ed.'

Chapter 35

Ten years previously

'Hey, wait up for a second.'

Laura turned at the sound of Charlotte's voice, then grinned. 'What? You want to come with me for a wee?'

Charlotte picked her way quickly through the dim light across the uneven ground. 'Forget that for a moment.' She glanced back at the boys sitting around the fire and then turned again to Laura. 'First chance I've had to talk to you. So, this morning. What the hell?'

'What do you mean?'

'I saw you. You and Ed. Snogging like your lives depended on it.'

Laura felt a sharp stab of dismay. 'Did Jack . . .?'

'No, it was just me. I went to find you. Couldn't believe my eyes.' Charlotte had a gossipy smile on her face.

Laura turned away, her mind churning. What could she possibly say?

'So, what's the story?' Charlotte took a step closer. 'I mean, are you just bored?'

'No!' The idea was offensive. 'Obviously, I wouldn't fool around with someone else just for something to do.'

Charlotte let the silence go on for a moment. 'Well?'

'It's – it's serious, Charlotte.' Laura could feel a smile at her mouth, despite her words.

She could still just make out the gossipy look on Charlotte's face, but now there was something else playing behind it.

'Hmm. So how long's this been going on, then?'

'Not long.'

That was in fact true, although for a while now thoughts of Ed had been working their way into Laura's mind, sneaking up on her repeatedly until she'd had to acknowledge their presence. She'd firmly dismissed them, but they had persisted.

Then, more recently, the thoughts had shifted from curiosity into hope, as she admitted to herself that Ed Fletcher was far more interesting to her than was really right, given her relationship with Jack. And was Ed, perhaps, looking at her more than was normal? What did his expression mean? She had told herself not to be silly. Popular, good-looking Ed Fletcher, school captain, interested in her, Laura?

She remembered the exact moment when that hope had shifted wordlessly into certainty. It was just days ago but it felt like she had lived an age since then.

She and Ed had emerged from the same exam room into a school corridor with its ordinary smell of carpet and sweat. They had stood together, going over the paper with relieved laughter.

Then she noticed that everyone else had left the corridor. She turned to find those bright eyes of his resting on hers with such a tender look, his face unbearably softened. And she had grasped her courage and held that gaze. His hand was warm as it took hers. Nothing had been said. Approaching footsteps made him drop her hand, and afterwards she had walked away, glancing down to check that the floor was still there because she felt like she was floating a foot above it.

They hadn't said much at their next meeting, either. They were too busy to talk.

And since then, Laura had felt an expansive joy she hadn't known was possible, rising within her and hijacking all her thoughts. A joy tempered only by the rapidly increasing dismay about the need to tell Jack.

'So it's clear you haven't told Jack,' said Charlotte.

'No. I know we have to. Obviously. But we decided we'd tell him after the trip.' Laura knew there was a defensive note in her voice. 'Look, this hike has been planned for so long. We'd all been looking forward to being together, out here. We thought, let everyone enjoy it, before we all go off in different directions for uni.'

'I guess.' Charlotte raised her eyebrows. 'But, I mean, it's not just any bloke. Ed is basically Jack's best friend.'

'I know, I know.' Laura felt the awful guilt rise again. The only thing that made it bearable was the thought of Ed. It was love, Laura was sure of it She had never felt this way before. 'Look, this is not some fling, Charlotte. I wouldn't be doing this if it wasn't serious. The thought of telling Jack makes me feel physically sick.' Actually, she could feel it right now. 'You can't say anything to him. And don't tell the others, either.'

'Of course, I wouldn't do that.' Charlotte was tracing a line on the ground with her shoe. There was a strange expression on her face.

'Promise me.'

'Okay, okay, I promise.'

'What is it?' Laura looked more closely. She paused. 'Can't you believe Ed's really interested in me?'

'Don't be silly.' Charlotte laughed. 'You're gorgeous. Always have been.'

'But I'm not one of the beautiful people. Like you and your other friends.'

'What even is that?' Charlotte laughed again. 'Look, Ed's great. He's also pretty hot, so good for you. It's just hard to get my head around it. With him and Jack being, like, best mates and all.'

Laura winced again.

'It must be serious.' Charlotte glanced again at the campfire. 'Just give the rest of us a heads up, so we can be well out of the way when Jack finds out.'

Chapter 36

Hugh couldn't bear the worry written across the others' faces.

He looked away. Hugh liked to think of himself as strong and confident, but the feeling that was building in his own chest was very far from confidence.

This whole situation was outrageous. Unbelievable. Being stuck out here on this isolated farm. And with every hour that passed, with Martha not showing up, crazy smile or no crazy smile, it became more unbelievable.

When they first discovered the modem was missing and the petrol tanks were empty, he'd been frustrated. Then the water being cut off had shifted things; it suggested something a bit more ominous than an inconvenience. But at that point Hugh had told himself that Martha was probably just trying to give them a scare; no doubt she would be back in an hour or so, with her trademark grimace.

But then that bloody series of notes, which was possibly even more of a worry than the water. It was all so mad. The others hadn't believed him when he said he didn't understand what his note had been referring to; but neither did he believe any of the others' denials. He wondered again about Charlotte. How had she been meant to be helping Ed? And why hadn't she helped him?

And now – bloody Laura disappearing. Hugh told himself she was definitely up to something. It was better than thinking that Martha had somehow taken her.

Alex had started pacing. The guy looked more worried than any of them. Hugh could see Alex's chest working.

And behind him on the kitchen wall, that bloody message Martha had painted, like it was constantly screaming at them: *CONFESS*.

'Settle down, mate. You're stressing us all out.' Hugh met Alex's eye and inclined his head towards Charlotte.

Alex dropped to a chair. 'Sorry.' He stared out the kitchen window then started drumming his fingers.

Charlotte burst out, 'I'm worried about Laura. But I'm so damn thirsty too!' Her face was creased with stress.

Hugh's concern rose too, and with it his habitual irritation. He knew it was wrong, but he just felt so restricted by Charlotte.

'I'm sorry, guys, I know we're all thirsty. But I'm also worried about the baby.' She rubbed her stomach.

'Of course,' said Alex. He looked at Jack and Hugh. 'How about we take a break and all have a bit of a drink?'

They gathered around the kitchen table and measured out four glasses. 'You can have extra,' said Alex, pushing a glass towards Charlotte, and she managed a small smile.

Hugh tried not to gulp his glass of water down, but it was hard.

Charlotte stood. 'I don't know about you, and it may not be the right moment, but I have to eat. It feels like I ate that toast several days ago and I don't have to be hungry as well as stressed.' She gave her stomach a rub as she went into the pantry.

'I'll give you a hand.' Jack followed Charlotte into the little room.

Hugh could hear them opening cupboards and murmuring.

Then he heard Charlotte gasp.

'Ah, guys.' Jack's voice held a warning note.

Hugh's eyes met Alex's and they strode into the pantry.

Jack was standing next to the gun cupboard, holding the door open. Two long black rifles stood there. Next to them, where another weapon had been the previous afternoon, was an ominous space.

Chapter 37

'They were all there yesterday.' Jack's face was grim.

Charlotte was standing perfectly still, her fingers pressed against her mouth.

Alex felt the panic rise within him. 'Oh, god,' he whispered.

'Holy shit.' Hugh looked incredulous. Then his face shifted. 'Well, two can play at that game.' He reached out and pulled one of the remaining guns from the cupboard.

'Put that thing down,' cried Charlotte.

'Actually, you won't be able to play at that game.' Jack stepped forward. 'Look.'

They followed his hand as it pointed at the empty shelf above the rifles.

'All the ammo's gone.'

Alex let out a whimper.

His chest was working, his blood was thundering in his ears. The awful panic, which had been lurking within him all morning, jumped higher and higher. 'She's going to kill us!' The words leapt out of his mouth involuntarily. He gasped for breath again.

Jack took a step forward and Alex felt his grip on his arms. But he threw him off and looked about wildly. There was only one thing to do. Where was it?

He dashed out to the veranda and spotted it: the two-way radio.

With shaking fingers, he picked it up. Pressed the transmit button.

'Martha!' he cried. 'Martha, are you listening? I'll tell you, I'll admit it. About the bloody country party.'

Jack, Hugh and Charlotte went still.

'I stole Hugh's money. It was me, I took it! There. Are you happy now, Martha? I've told my goddamn secret, and now you can let us go.

'Martha! Martha are you there?'

But the radio lay silent in his hands.

Soon afterwards, they were all sitting at the table. They had made him sit, and Jack had insisted Alex drink a little more of their precious water supply. Charlotte had looked into his eyes and urged him to take slow breaths.

The panic had retreated to a more manageable level, and his breathing had slowed.

Three faces were looking at him with concern. But also curiosity.

He mustered up a wobbly smile. 'I've done it now, haven't I? Can't put that genie back in the bottle.' He turned to Hugh. 'It's true. I did steal your money. You remember – the three hundred bucks that went missing at Ed's country party.'

Alex stood in the sitting room, surrounded by the bags of the party guests. He watched Hugh and Jack barrel out into the hallway.

Someone had called to them, and they had immediately dashed out, laughing. The ceiling was so high above Alex, it seemed to disappear into darkness. Light shone through the long drapes. It illuminated Mr Fletcher's desk.

Alex could see the envelope that Hugh had just shoved behind a pile of papers; they looked like plans and maps.

An envelope that Hugh had filled full of money.

Alex thought of the other students at school. They all had so much cash to spend on clothes and gadgets. Always so free with the money on excursions to the movies and theme parks. They were obviously getting big allowances. Alex had never had access to that kind of money.

I need that money, he thought. I need it, and no one else is going to give it to me.

When Alex thought back to his childhood, a dim series of rooms always came to mind, himself a small boy looking up at a mother and father who were always facing away from him. There were so many memories to choose from, so many times when he'd found himself alone, no one seeming to care what he needed.

Like at the wake after his grandfather's funeral. He had been too young to understand what was happening, but not too young to feel the sadness seeping off the adults. He'd waited patiently through the church service, growing hungrier. When they arrived at his aunt's house he'd been delighted to see the plates of food being carried out of the kitchen.

He stood near his mother. The food was being passed around, but it was all at adult height; he couldn't reach. As the hunger pangs grew, he tugged at his mother's skirt. She was smiling and nodding at the man standing near. She didn't respond. He tugged harder.

Then her angry face was staring down at him. 'Don't interrupt me!' She glared furiously. 'You're a rude little boy.'

The man also glared at him.

Alex had hidden himself behind his mother's skirts, tears pricking at his eyes. He tried to ignore the twisting in his stomach.

Finally, he spied a plate of patty cakes sitting on a side table. He sidled across the room, reached up, grabbed two precious cakes. He snuck from the room, ran up the hallway and into a bedroom, where he slid down behind a dressing table, stuffing the food in his mouth.

But although his hunger was sated, and the cakes exploded in his mouth with a delicious burst of sugar, he still found himself with tears rolling down his cheeks, his throat swelling. Alex realised at that moment that, really, he was on his own. No one else was keeping an eye out for him. He would have to look after himself.

And it had been true. He'd had to look after himself. All his life.

Now he stared, fixated, at the desk with that tempting envelope. It was practically glowing in front of him, almost begging to be taken.

Hugh would hardly miss it. His family was so wealthy. Alex had seen the cars that Hugh had been dropped off at school in. His family's beach house was enormous; their regular house even larger.

Alex thought about all the trips to the movies and meals out that he'd declined, pretending to be too busy studying, when the reality was he had no cash to pay for his ticket. He thought about all the sidelong glances at his uncool old clothes.

He'd tried asking his parents for more pocket money, but it was very hard to get them to understand; it was difficult even to get their attention. They would just nod vaguely or go back to whatever it was they had been talking about. They were so wrapped up in each other, always together, always talking; Alex always the unwelcome interruption.

When he pressed them, his mother would become angry, accuse him of being a spendthrift. It was not like his parents couldn't spare the money; they bought all sorts of unnecessary things. But they just didn't think it was an issue for Alex, and when forced to confront the topic, they seemed to think it was good for him to have a tight budget. His father would make a comment about how his own allowance at boarding school had been twenty cents a week or something, and how it was important for Alex to learn to live within his means.

There were a lot of notes in the envelope. They would keep him going for months. He might even be able to buy a few clothes, help him fit in with the others.

Alex imagined himself wearing the same trainers and track jumpers that the other boys wore.

He reached his hand out. He grabbed the envelope. It was in his hand. He heard voices. He quickly shoved the envelope in his pocket, sure he was about to be found out. But it was just another bunch of kids dropping bags in the sitting room.

He turned and hurried out of the room.

Now, in the kitchen, Hugh looked more mystified than angry.

'Yeah, I remember, but what the hell? I mean, why?'

Alex laughed mirthlessly. 'Why do you think? I needed the money. I couldn't keep up with you guys.'

Hugh still looked puzzled. 'But how did you even know it was there? I didn't leave the cash in my bag, in case any of those kids from other schools decided to have a rummage around in people's things. You remember, some money had gone missing at the previous party, that one out near Wagga. I figured no one was going to go through Robert's desk.'

Alex nodded miserably. 'I saw you. When we were dropping off our bags in the sitting room. I saw you take a wad of notes out and shove them in the envelope, and you put them on Robert's desk behind a pile of maps and plans.'

'And then there was that big fuss when you discovered it was missing, and I was too scared to own up. I told myself it would blow over. And the longer I left it, the harder it got. So, I didn't tell. And, you've got to believe me, I've been ashamed of what I did ever since.'

Hugh stood up. Alex looked at the floor. If Hugh hit him, it would hurt, but he'd understand.

There was a long, horrible silence.

Out of the corner of his eye Alex saw Hugh sit again. He risked a glance at Hugh's face.

Hugh shook his head. 'Man, that was a bit of a low move.'

'I know it was. I'm so sorry.' Alex choked back a sob. He just could not, he could not cry in front of them all.

Then Hugh sighed. 'Okay, it was shitty thing to do. But it was so many years ago. We were kids.'

Alex shook his head. That was irrelevant. He'd stolen from his friend.

'Mate. Settle down. Look, if it helps, I forgive you.'

Alex looked up. Hugh had his hands spread wide. 'Really. I mean, we all do things we're not proud of.'

Was Hugh for real? His expression seemed sincere enough.

'Yeah, obviously I was pretty angry at the time. But no one's perfect.' Hugh grinned. 'Not even me.'

Alex glanced at Charlotte and Jack. They didn't look as horrified as he thought they might. Charlotte even gave him a sympathetic smile.

Alex had dreaded this moment. He'd thought that one day, he would be found out, somehow, and that moment would be filled with the endless disgust of those around him. He was sure they would basically disown him.

Now Alex's brow felt lighter. His breath came a little easier. Perhaps it would be okay after all.

Hugh said, 'It was ten years ago. We've got much bigger problems on our hands. Like dealing with the madwoman. We've got to stick together.'

Jack looked thoughtful. 'For me, the most interesting question coming from what you just said, Alex, is how the hell Martha knew.'

Alex went quiet.

'Well?'

'Ed knew.' Alex paused. 'On the walk, it was something I was stressed about. You won't remember, but he made this remark, "Alex isn't as saintly as he seems."'

Hugh and Jack looked puzzled and shook their heads. But Charlotte narrowed her eyes. 'Yes, actually, I remember him saying that. Seemed pretty odd; it stuck in my mind.'

'Well, that's what he was referring to. The money that I took.'

'But how did Ed know?'

'He guessed.'

The changing room smelt of adolescent boys, as they shouted and laughed and unzipped their bags.

Alex was one of the last to leave. He pulled his trainers off and placed them carefully on the floor then rooted around in his PE bag for his school shoes.

'Nice trainers.'

Alex looked up. Ed was staring at him, his eyes flicking between his trainers and his face.

'Nikes, huh?'

Alex's mouth went dry. He nodded.

'Pretty fancy.' Ed put his head on one side. 'Those things cost a fortune. How did you buy them? You don't normally have cash like that.'

Alex's throat was so dry he couldn't speak. He shrugged.

Ed's eyes narrowed. The silence stretched out. 'You took Hugh's money, didn't you? It was you, at the country party.'

Alex shook his head. 'Of course not.'

But Ed didn't believe him. 'You did. You look guilty as sin. Bloody hell. You little thief.'

Alex saw the look of disgust on Ed's face and felt his own grow hot.

'I didn't.' But then his throat closed up again, and to his further shame, a sob burst out, and then another. He turned to Ed. 'Please don't say anything. Please. Hugh doesn't need the money.'

'That's not the point.' Ed looked shocked.

'I know, I know. Look, I can't take them back to the shop now; I've worn them.'

'Why on earth wouldn't I tell Hugh?'

'Please, Ed, please. I'm really sorry, I wish I'd never done it, you've got no idea.'

Alex looked out the kitchen window, remembering. 'Eventually he agreed not to tell. But he would keep mentioning it to me when no one else was around, and I was so stressed. And when he made that remark on the walk, about me not being so saintly – he did it deliberately, so that you guys could hear, and I was convinced he was going to come out with the whole story.'

Jack shook his head. 'Maybe he told Martha.'

Charlotte looked puzzled. 'I wouldn't have thought they were that close. But I guess he must have said something to her.'

'Well, she found out somehow.'

As Charlotte, Jack and Hugh continued to debate this point, Alex took a breath. It occurred to him that they would now have to discuss the notes Martha had written to them. The implication was pretty clear – if Martha's accusation to Alex was true, then the other accusations were probably true as well.

The discussion went on, without any of them making this point, but Alex felt too relieved at the surprisingly kind response he'd received to bother pressing the others. He felt so much lighter, he almost laughed. So what if the others had things they regretted? Let them keep their little secrets.

'Are you thinking the same thing I am?' asked Hugh.

Alex started. Perhaps Hugh was going to bring it up after all.

'I'm thinking, Laura still hasn't turned up.' Hugh looked from face to face. 'And haven't you noticed? We've had a pretty bloody good look around this house now. And there's no little blue note for Laura.'

Chapter 38

One hour earlier

Laura went downstairs and paused in the kitchen. There would never be a better moment. She left the house, then turned and looked back. There didn't seem to be anyone at any of the windows. No doubt they were still all upstairs going through all the crap in that crazy study. Quickly she moved around the side of the house and out of view.

She swallowed her rising nervousness and made herself keep walking.

As the events of the morning had unfolded, Laura had watched with mounting horror. The awful message on the kitchen wall had shocked her almost as much as it had shocked her friends.

But not quite as much.

The others didn't know the extent to which she had kept in touch with Martha. Soon after Ed's death, Martha had confronted her. Were you and Ed just friends, really? At first Laura hadn't wanted to tell; after all, with her involvement with Ed, she had been betraying Jack, even though there hadn't really been much of an overlap. But Martha had kept at it. She could tell, said Martha, that there was something between them. She said that she saw the way Ed had looked at Laura when he thought no one was watching. *A mother always knows*, Martha said.

That thought had been unexpectedly intoxicating. Yes, Ed really had loved her, and she had loved him. It was such a real bond that it was even visible to others.

'I knew it. You loved him too.' Martha had clasped Laura against her chest, and the two women, the younger and the older, had cried together.

Gradually, Martha had become a confidante who seemed to understand better than anyone else what Laura had gone through. Laura's own mother had been sympathetic, of course. Had held her hand throughout the awful months of the inquest and the relentless media interest in the case of the young people who had left their friend behind in the bush. But in the end, her mother's sympathy had a limit. One day she said, 'I mean, you and Ed never actually officially went out together, did you?'

Whereas Laura knew that Martha shared her feelings. The others were grieving, obviously, but she and Martha really suffered more; Laura knew it.

As the years had gone on, perhaps it had got a bit weird. Martha had seemed to need more than she could really give. Martha would get in touch a bit too often, suggesting coffee. But the bond remained. So when Martha had pulled her aside after that awful dinner in the house last night, Laura was unsurprised.

Martha had put her hand on Laura's arm. Leaned in and spoken quietly and urgently. She was so close that Laura had noticed a bit of lipstick that had congealed along the edge of Martha's mouth. 'The others are obviously not going to say anything. But you're different.' The older woman's eyes seemed to be boring through into her mind.

Laura had stayed silent.

'I just need to understand. I *need* to.'

Staring at the older woman, Laura had paused.

Over the years, Laura been torn. She had worried at the situation, analysing her response this way and that. Was it the right decision, morally speaking? On the one side she really wanted to tell Martha what had happened, to relieve herself of the awful burden of knowledge. Perhaps that really would be the right thing to do.

So many years had now passed. What's more, the cancer diagnosis had made Laura think anew about lots of things, had made her really question whether she was living the right way. Sure, she was not in immediate danger, but perhaps she didn't have as long on this earth as she had assumed. She shouldn't be wasting it, living a lie.

But on the other side was the loyalty Laura believed she owed her friends. They had all shared the terrible experience together, and they had made their decision together. Telling Martha would be betraying them. In the end, in that moment in the dining room, her belief that it was rightly a group decision had won over.

She had said, haltingly, 'Martha – I. The thing is. It's not just my story to tell.'

Then Jack had come into the dining room and interrupted her and Martha at just that moment. Martha had pulled away, but not before Laura had seen the fire in her expression.

Still, Laura had not expected the message, the violence of the message, they had discovered in the morning. And then the modem being removed, and their petrol siphoned. And then the shock of the water being cut.

Laura had planned to wait for the others to come around to confessing, but now it was clear that Martha was going to keep them at the house, stranded, until she got what she wanted.

It really was her duty to tell Martha the truth before someone was hurt. She had the connection to Martha. She understood Martha better than the others did.

She hadn't bothered trying to persuade anyone else to come with her because it was clear none of them would agree. In fact, they might have tried to stop her. So she had just slipped away during the search of the study.

Now she pulled out of view from the house and made her way across the paddock. She wiped her forehead. The day was warm and getting warmer. It was not helping her trepidation about the upcoming conversation.

She had an idea about where she might find Martha. The older woman had mentioned it from time to time as a place she went to escape, particularly when Robert had still been alive. Martha had said he filled the house with his own unbearable melancholy, and when she had felt unable to keep herself afloat in the face of his grief, she had taken herself off there. It was worth a look. If Martha wasn't there, Laura could return to the house; she might not even have been missed.

As she stepped across the grassy paddock, Laura rehearsed the coming conversation. She would need to be very careful about how she approached it. Martha was obviously disturbed. There was no knowing how she would react. It was possible that, rather than gratitude for knowing, Martha would lash out at Laura for her silence over the past ten years.

She was approaching Martha's hideout. She took a breath.

Ah, there she was. A slight, thin figure, walking to and fro. Something about her jerky movements made Laura halt. Her stomach clenched again.

She saw Martha turn Laura's way. Martha stopped her pacing. She stared at Laura.

Laura's dread ratcheted up. But there was no turning back now.

Laura held up her hand in greeting, and forced herself to walk towards the older woman

Chapter 39

One hour earlier

Martha saw Laura approaching and felt a mixture of frustration and pleasure. Laura turning up like this was a bit of a complication. But it was hard to be angry at Laura, this young woman whom her Ed had loved. She knew Laura was on her side, underneath it all.

She could see Laura's expression was pained. No doubt she had argued with the others before coming out here. They had probably tried to stop her.

'Martha.' Laura raised her hand slowly.

'My dear.'

They embraced, then Laura pulled back.

'Martha, what on earth is going on? You've got us all really scared.'

'Good.' Martha pursed her lips.

'Martha, you can't do this. It's really upsetting. It's – mad.'

Martha couldn't look at her. 'It's your fault, you kids. You've driven me to this.' She turned back. 'You won't be honest. And I need to know what really happened. I *need* to.'

She did need to know. It was her right.

That question constantly haunted her: how was it that those other five children had survived, when her son, her dear Edward, had not? She had listened to the inquest, to all the evidence given.

In the months after the hike, she had studied the five of them, trying to understand what it was about them that had meant they had survived. Why had they been spared? How had it happened, that she had been left alone, with no one left to mother; her child gone?

Ed's birth had changed her so completely, had sucked her into a new way of being with such a wrench that, at the time, she'd hardly been able to register the sad news that had trailed in its wake. The birth had been drawn out, with complications, ending in surgery. Martha was still in shock, still dealing with her astonishment that such an experience could happen to her, when the doctor explained that she would not be able to have any more children. At the time, the idea of having another baby, of going through birth another time, seemed so impossible that she dismissed it. The idea of another child was completely unreal.

But Ed grew and thrived, and Martha came out of the fug of new motherhood to understand that another child would in fact be wanted and loved. Only at that point had its impossibility really struck home.

Everyone kept telling her how lucky she was to have a beautiful little boy, so healthy, so good-looking. Such a good baby. So she told herself not to be ungrateful, to get on with it, to concentrate on loving him.

And loved him she had. On occasion she had been frightened at how much she loved him, as if from a presentiment that a horror, in proportion to all that love, would one day be exacted as a necessary corrective.

And so, when the final blow had fallen, when his body was found and all hope was gone, and the anguish had crashed around her, it felt like the arrival of a long-expected fate. Of course, of course, she would not be allowed to keep him, her dear, perfect boy.

She had grieved, as if grieving might relieve her pain. But nothing had helped, not even time. The torment had instead grown over the years, like a strengthening vine, twisting into new forms, fresh varieties of pain.

And Ed's friends were lying to her. She could sense it. She knew it. She knew they were lying to her, and that was because they were somehow to blame for her son's death. And only when that blame had been properly allocated, had found its rightful home, could she herself be free.

Martha knew that lesson about blame; knew it in her very bones, because she had absorbed it along with her earliest childhood memories.

Whenever any infraction occurred in the large house that she had grown up in, she and her five siblings were lined up by their nanny, all made to stand with their toes along the edge of the rug in the kitchen, to endure her interrogation. Everyone who was capable of standing had to line up, from the teenagers to the toddlers.

Nanny Parsons would walk slowly up and down the line, frowning and quizzing each child, tapping her palm with a wooden spoon, before pronouncing her judgement as to who had really caused the disruption or the injury or the damage, and that child would then have to stand forward to be rapped over the knuckles with that same horrible spoon.

Martha had been a dutiful child and, unlike her brothers and sisters, had not felt her knuckles sing, but she had never forgotten the occasion when Nanny had turned her piercing stare on Martha and pronounced her responsible for breaking the green mixing bowl that lay in pieces right in front of them on the kitchen floor. Martha had been the last child to hold it and must have placed it too close to the edge of the table.

The experience of being blamed was a whole new kind of horror for young Martha. She realised that, although she always tried to be good, this horrible feeling could still find her, with no warning or logic. She would always remember the sensation of her insides churning and the roaring in her ears, as she contemplated the spoon and her imminent humiliation.

But then her sister Susan had pointed to the cat, whose face still held a tell-tale line of the milk that had been in the bowl before the accident, and Susan had cried out that Misty must have knocked the bowl off the table.

And the feeling of vindication, at seeing blame and responsibility allocated elsewhere, was seared onto Martha's memory as the sweetest of reliefs.

Now, here in the paddock, she had to find out the real story behind this most horrendous of events. Knowing what really happened to Ed, where blame should be rightly allocated, might be the one thing that could ease her terrible pain.

Laura stood before her, the heat rising from the yellowing grass.

The young woman took a breath. 'Let's sit down. Perhaps I can help you.'

Martha led Laura to a large rock. Her hands were trembling. The two of them sat. She saw the younger woman's chest rise as she took another breath. A kind of horrified excitement began to grow within Martha. Was this to be the real story, after all this time?

'Martha, first you have to understand the situation we were in.'

In a wavering voice, Laura began to tell the story Martha had been waiting to hear.

Chapter 40

One hour earlier

Laura stopped. Her gaze had been fixed in the distance, far across the paddock, as she told her story. Now she finally looked up at Martha. They both had tears in their eyes.

Martha stared at her, waiting. Eventually, she said, 'And?'

Laura shook her head. 'And what? That's it. I've told you everything.' What was Martha waiting for?

A frown creased Martha's face.

'You're still lying to me.'

Laura shook her head. 'I'm not. Martha, I've told you everything.'

'Wait here. Just wait.' Martha turned. She walked to the small brick structure that stood nearby at the top of the rise and disappeared inside. In a moment she reappeared, carrying a bundle of canvas and marched back to Laura. She unfolded the bundle.

'Look what I found. Behind one of the walls in the laundry.' She spat the words out. Held out the object inside.

It was a red drink bottle with a platypus sticker.

Laura's face dropped. She recognised it instantly. It was the second water bottle that Ed had taken with him on the walk from which he had never returned. The red bottle that had never been located.

'It wasn't in the backpack they found in the bush.' Martha pressed her lips together. 'All his other things were – his jacket, his beanie, his journal, his sleeping bag. But not this bottle.'

'Someone else brought it back from the walk.' Martha's voice was tight. 'Someone hid it in the wall in the laundry. Someone who had taken it from my boy; his water, which he needed to survive.'

Laura's throat was completely dry. Her blood thudded in her ears. She could feel a ringing sensation. She drew in a sharp breath. The words wouldn't come.

Finally, she croaked, 'I don't know how that got there.' She made herself meet Martha's furious gaze.

'Stop lying to me!' Martha shouted. Then the older woman turned and stalked away. She crossed the grass and disappeared into the brick hut.

Laura stared after her, her mind whirling. A deep discomfort was growing in her stomach.

She could picture the bottle, even now, in Ed's hand. It was his second bottle. She could see him, packing it away into his day bag after one of their refreshment stops.

After they had returned, when the search for Ed was underway, the friends had told the rangers about Ed's water supplies on the walk. When his body had been found, the bushland had been closely searched, all his possessions eventually located. Except this second bottle, which had never been found.

Later, the five friends had told the coroner about the second bottle, and they had all denied knowledge of where it was.

Laura felt a tightness in her throat. Someone, one of her friends, might have – must have – taken it from Ed. Secreted it in their own bag. Brought it back from the walk and, amid the activity of the search, dumped it in the building works for the laundry. It was an awful thought.

But still more awful was Laura's suspicion of who that person was.

A memory had returned to her, of the walk, and one of her friends, the morning after they had discovered the dry water source. Someone fiddling with Ed's bag, someone with an all too obvious reason to override any scruples about depriving Ed of the precious water they all needed so much.

Laura gazed wildly about, her chest working. She forced herself to breathe slowly. She told herself that she didn't know, not really, what had happened.

And meanwhile, Alex, Jack, Hugh and Charlotte were back at the house. And now Martha had even more reason for fury and vengeance.

She had to persuade Martha to let them all go. It was a harder job than she first thought, now Martha had this damning evidence. But she had to try.

She took another breath and stumbled after Martha towards the brick hut. The white ute was parked behind it. Laura drew near the door and cautiously gazed in. Martha was seated on a bench at the far side, her arms folded.

Laura looked around. It was a small hut, mostly filled with old, rusted machinery whose purpose wasn't quite obvious.

'Look, Martha . . .'

But Laura's words dried in her mouth. She saw, leaning against the wall of the hut, not far from where Martha sat, a long, thin, black shape. A shape that was, unmistakably, a gun.

'Laura. I'm disappointed. I really expected so much better of you.' Martha shook her head and rose to her feet.

Chapter 41

'You really still think Laura is setting all this up with Martha?' Charlotte turned to Hugh.

'I don't know, obviously – but it looks pretty damn suspicious, doesn't it?' Hugh's face was tense. 'She's disappeared. Martha hasn't written a little blue note for her. And—'

'Well?'

'I'm wondering how Martha knew about the money at the country party. Ed knew. Perhaps he confided in darling Laura about what Alex did. And then Laura told Martha. It's becoming more and more clear how close those two are. Sorry, Jack. But it seems pretty obvious.'

Jack threw up his hands. 'You don't have to apologise to me.'

Charlotte felt for Jack. Clearly, he was still attached to Laura, but had no official reason to still be interested – their breakup was ten years in the past. Charlotte's personal opinion was that Laura definitely wasn't interested in Jack any more and that Jack needed to move on. But no doubt that was easier said than done.

'Anyway, we don't know, and I don't see how it helps us if we did.' Jack spoke more calmly. 'We really need to work on getting out of here.'

'Let's think about that while we eat lunch,' said Charlotte.

Soon they were seated at the table. They had found some canned baked beans in the pantry and warmed them on the stove, then ladled them onto a bit more of the bread.

As she ate, Charlotte made sure to keep her eyes averted from the hideous message painted on the kitchen wall. She fanned herself with a tea towel. It wasn't just because she was pregnant; the others looked hot too. And pretty soon the heat alone would be really unsafe, even without the lack of water.

Hugh cleared his throat. 'I reckon we need to walk out. Just get the hell out away from this ridiculous crap.'

There was a silence, and Hugh pressed on. 'I know you said before it was too far, but I think one or two of us will have to.'

Alex looked uncertain. 'I dunno, Hugh, it's even hotter than this morning.' He strode across to the thermometer. 'Twenty-nine degrees; that's just inside. Must be at least ten more outside.'

'The cafe is the closest contact, right?' Charlotte screwed up her face. She couldn't remember any other building or house. 'Could we make it back there? It felt like such a long drive. And all uphill. Quite a big hill.'

'I think it really is too far. It would take hours.' Alex's voice was sharper. 'I actually wonder if we'd even make it. I mean, I hate to say it but . . .' Alex pressed on. 'Well, we know what happens when you try to walk without enough water.'

Charlotte could see her own shock written on the others' faces too. But Alex really did have a point.

After a moment Jack turned to Alex. 'Something you said,

when you were telling us about the money, at the country party. Something snagged my brain, but I can't quite remember.'

Alex screwed up his face. 'Uh, the bags? In the sitting room? My allowance? The shoes?'

There was a moment's quiet, then Jack's face cleared. 'The sitting room – with the plans and maps.' His voice rose with excitement. 'Remember, there was that pile of house plans in Martha's study. So, let's check them. Perhaps there's something nearby, something in the valley that we don't know about.'

'Like what?' asked Hugh.

'I don't know.' Jack frowned. 'But it's worth checking. I'm going to go grab them.'

He arrived back in the kitchen carrying the unwieldy sheets of yellowing paper and spread them on the table. He shuffled through, scanning them. There were building plans that appeared to be the drawings for the Fletcher homestead.

'Jeez, these must be over a hundred years old,' said Alex, fingering the thick paper.

Jack pulled a larger sheet out from under the one Alex was touching. 'This is what we're after. It's a survey of the valley.'

He took the map out to the veranda and scanned across the sheet, looking up periodically at the landscape. 'Look, there's the ravine, on the other side of the valley.'

He then rotated the paper and leaned in.

'We did a couple of hikes out there, back in the day,' said Hugh.

'Do you reckon we could walk there now? Get water from the river?' asked Alex.

Jack stood calculating. 'I would love to say yes. But a long walk with no water, in this heat . . .' His voice trailed off and he shook his head.

'I remember those walks we did out there,' said Charlotte. 'But we never climbed down the ravine to the river. Well, I certainly didn't, and I don't think you guys did either.'

Jack shook his head. 'You're right. The cliffs were too steep, too high.'

Hugh hesitated, then nodded agreement.

'There must be something else.' Charlotte's anxiety was building again. She took the map off Jack and bent over it.

'What? Some secret stream, near the house, that we've never known about?' But Hugh sounded despondent rather than sarcastic.

'I don't know, Hugh, but—'

'Wait.' Alex held his hand up. 'What's that noise?'

A deep droning noise was gradually getting louder.

'That's a plane,' said Jack.

They all took a few steps out into the yard and scanned the sky, turning this way and that, until Alex cried, 'There!'

The plane was small, a little twin-engine propeller craft. It was reasonably high up, but approaching the house.

Charlotte started shouting and waving, and the three others immediately joined in. For a moment she thought the plane was going to fly directly overhead, but then it began to curve away to the south. They cried more loudly and waved more vigorously. But the plane shrank inexorably into a tiny dot, and the noise died away.

Disappointment washing over her, Charlotte stood in silence, her shoulders dropped.

But then she stood a little straighter. 'Hey, I've thought of something.' She turned to the others. 'That plane was never going to see us. So, we'll make a big sign, lay it out on the grass. For any other planes that might go overhead.'

'Make a sign out of what?'

Charlotte thought for a moment. 'Got it.'

Charlotte brought the pile of white sheets down from the linen cupboard, along with needles and thread that she found in Martha's sewing room.

Hugh had thought they could use paint from the cans that were still sitting outside the back door of the kitchen. But when they prised off the lids they found that it had dried into unusable chunks. It had been red. Martha must have used the last of it to daub her awful message on the kitchen wall. So Hugh and Alex had gone to the outhouses to see if they could find more paint to use for the sign.

Charlotte unfolded a sheet across the table. 'I think we'll need a few of these, to make it big enough. We can stitch them together.'

Together they opened the fabric across the floorboards of the kitchen and lined up the edges. Using the thread, Charlotte began to tack two sheets together roughly, while Jack worked on the other two.

Charlotte tried not to think about the thirst that was tightening her throat. They needed to ration out what water they had. She tried not to think about what lack of water might be doing to her baby. And now they had to worry about Laura too. Was she okay? And if she was okay, what on earth was she up to? Her fingers felt a little jittery as she pushed the needle through the cotton as quick as she could. It didn't need to be perfect; it just needed to stay together.

She tried to breathe more slowly, but the tension kept rising. Her fingers kept shaking.

'Crap!' she cried. She had stabbed herself in the finger with the needle. With the tiny sharp pain, suddenly the stress of the morning overwhelmed her, and she let out a sob. God, were they going to die here in this bloody house? Their bodies found after they failed to return home, and someone decided they should sound an alarm? Her thoughts began to boil, ever faster.

Then there was a firm hand on her shoulder.

'Here.' Jack was holding out a mug. 'Drink.'

Charlotte looked at it. 'I can't—'

'Yes, you can. We're not on our last drop yet.' His voice was gentle, which made Charlotte sob again.

Jack rubbed her shoulder, and gradually she felt calmer.

He sat down next to her. 'It's awful. But we'll get out of this.'

Charlotte knew he couldn't be sure of that, but his confident voice helped.

'Let's just concentrate on getting this together. One thing at a time.'

She nodded and turned again to the sewing. After a time, she noticed that she felt calmer. The regular action of the needle through the fabric, the satisfaction of the rough tacking marching down the sheets, the sound of insects ratcheting in the shimmering haze outside; it was somehow comforting, despite their situation. A good distraction from the heat of the afternoon, which had just sent a trickle of sweat down her back.

Charlotte quashed the thought that she really couldn't afford to lose that drop of water and glanced at Jack, who looked absorbed in his work.

'What are you going to do when we get out of here?' It was better to think positive.

'Good question.' Jack managed a smile. 'Appreciate running water, for a start. Appreciate being able to just walk out of the house and down to the shops.'

'And you and – was it Jesse . . .?'

'Julie. We're having a break.'

'So . . .' Charlotte hesitated but decided that relationship confidences were going to be a better distraction than small talk. 'What happened with you two?'

Jack screwed up his face and stared out the window into the paddocks. 'She says I "won't let her in". She's probably right.' He turned to Charlotte. 'I've found it hard to really confide in other people, all these years, since the walk. You know?'

Charlotte did know. 'And . . . Laura?'

'I'm not interested in Laura.'

Charlotte nodded, her eyes on her sewing.

'Okay, that's not quite true. I suppose I have still been thinking about Laura. She's just *there*, in my head.' A pause. 'The thing is, we never really ended it properly. With Ed, and all that stuff that followed, she just wouldn't talk to me, and it eventually became clear we weren't going out any more. As the years went on, I saw other girls. But it's hard, when you don't talk about it.'

'No closure.' Charlotte nodded again.

There was a short silence, then Jack turned to her. 'Okay, your turn. Obviously, we're all used to you and Hugh now. But I think a lot of people were surprised when you got together. It was pretty soon after with walk with Ed, right?'

Charlotte thought back across the years to the time after Ed's death. The grief at his death was huge and the public commentary was awful but, surprisingly, those weren't the most difficult parts. It was the loneliness, the sheer bloody loneliness. Everyone treating her with kid gloves. Expressions changing when people saw her. Stilted words. Like there was a force field around her, keeping everyone away.

She had felt the urge to strike out, away from all that weirdness. So she spent too many nights hanging out at clubs where she wouldn't see anyone she knew, downing vodka tonics and throwing herself on the dance floor. She went home with boys. She even went out with some of them.

But then, they'd begin to know her enough to want to see her friends. Or worse, they'd start wanting to know her, properly, as a person. So, the shutter would come down. *No. You can't go there.* It had been completely clear in her mind that no one could be allowed in.

'It was at that picnic, wasn't it, near the harbour?' Jack looked up at her from his sewing.

'You've got a good memory.' Charlotte remembered how the glittering sunlight on the water had become more and more crazed as the wine bottles were emptied. Soon there had been spangles all through the air around her.

She had been sitting next to Hugh. Then their legs had touched, then their arms. And then, somehow, they were snogging, ignoring the catcalls around them. She surfaced, not so drunk that she couldn't notice some surprised expressions, but drunk enough that she didn't care.

They left without a word and went back to his apartment. They woke the next day, exchanging sheepish expressions across the crumpled sheets. But then they met again. And again. Then moved in together. And there had never been a reason for it to end.

Charlotte turned to Jack. 'The thing was, I didn't have to explain myself to him.'

Jack nodded.

'We both understood,' she said. 'I mean, about Ed.' *We both felt as guilty as the other*, she thought. It was a thought that had diminished in frequency over the years, but it hadn't gone away. Actually, she didn't know for sure whether Hugh felt guilty, because they had never discussed the question of guilt, but there was an opacity in him that she recognised from herself.

'I get it.' Jack looked thoughtful. 'It's only with you guys, from the walk, that I feel I can – it's not let my guard down, exactly. But, kind of, just be myself.'

After a moment Jack went on. 'And you and Hugh went out for ages, right, before you got engaged? But then it was a pretty quick engagement.'

'Yeah.' Charlotte paused. Damn it, why shouldn't she tell Jack? They might not even make it out of here. Saying it out loud would be a relief. 'I haven't told many people this. But the quick engagement was because I found out I was pregnant. It was an – it wasn't intentional. But once I was pregnant, I wanted to do things properly. *We* wanted to do things properly. Make it all official.' Charlotte knew the first-person plural should be more natural. But the fact was, it had been her driving the engagement, not Hugh. And that fact continued to hang over her much more than she had thought it would.

Jack was looking puzzled.

'I know; you're thinking about the dates. Why am I still pregnant, more than nine months after the engagement was announced? Well, as it turned out I – we . . . lost that one.'

Lost. Like they'd just mislaid the baby somehow. One little syllable that could in no way encompass the pain of that awful episode. That too had been surprising; that such a tiny life form, hardly big enough to change her appearance, could cause such emotion because it was no longer there inside her, growing.

Her face twisted a little, but she hurried on. 'And then after that, I couldn't get pregnant again fast enough. That's all I wanted. And I was happy that it happened quickly. So here we are. We're lucky really.'

She started to cry again. She was surprised. Where had this come from?

Jack got up and put his arm around her.

Her words came tumbling out, shocking her. 'But sometimes I think . . . I think Hugh doesn't really want this baby.' She definitely had not meant to tell Jack this. These were thoughts she kept locked inside herself. Too dangerous to let out into the light of day.

She managed not to say the rest of the words that were rushing up in her mind. *Sometimes I think Hugh doesn't really want me. That we got together in the shitstorm after Ed's death when no one knew which way was up. We stayed together out of inertia. And then there was going to be a baby, so then there was a wedding.*

'Hey, I'm sure everyone feels uncertain with a baby on the way.' Jack rubbed her shoulder. 'You guys will work it out.' He kept patting her shoulder.

It was actually rather comforting.

Chapter 42

'Look what we found.'

As Hugh's booming voice sounded, Alex saw Jack and Charlotte look up from their work.

Hugh held up a couple of battered paint cans, and Alex waved a set of brushes.

'You guys finished?' Hugh dumped his on the kitchen floor and rubbed his hands where the wire handles had cut in. 'Okay, let's get this sign going.'

Hugh levered open the cans. 'What are we going to say?'

'A simple "Help" would do it,' said Jack. 'Straight to the point.'

Hugh stepped across the cloth, roughing out the letters, then began to layer on the thick black paint. Jack picked up the other brush and worked backwards from the 'p'.

'Pretty good,' said Charlotte when it was done. She looked outside. 'Just need to get it out there. And then get back inside fast.'

'Okay, I'll take this corner.' Hugh nodded at Jack. 'You take that one. And Alex can grab the other.'

Outside, they quickly stretched the sheet out next to the house, far enough from trees that it wouldn't be obscured from above.

'Now we just need a squadron of low-flying aircraft. Or even one would do.' Hugh wiped the back of his hand across his forehead.

Alex noticed Jack staring back at the house. 'What is it?'

Jack paused, his head tilted.

'Come on, out with it.'

'I was just thinking.' Jack's voice was slow. 'That laundry building looks bigger from the outside than the laundry room seemed on the inside.

Alex regarded the tumbling-down laundry extension. Jack was right.

'Uh . . . so what?' Hugh looked puzzled.

Jack looked at Hugh. 'Maybe it's a sort of secret room, or even a hidden cupboard.'

'You reckon that's where Martha keeps the skeletons of her previous victims?' asked Hugh.

Jack managed a grin. 'Perhaps not skeletons. But maybe she hid the modem there?'

The three men looked at each other then hurried inside.

Charlotte gave them a questioning look when she saw them striding across the room purposefully, but Hugh just called, 'Follow us.'

In the laundry, they stepped carefully around the material from the ceiling and wall lining that had fallen across the floor. Pushing aside pieces of plasterboard, they made their way to the far end.

Jack pushed his glasses up his nose. He reached out and tapped at a wall. 'Look, it's lighter,' he said. 'Whereas that's the outside wall and it's heavier wood.'

Hugh gave the inner wall a heavy thump and they could all see it wobble.

216

Hugh tapped at it. 'Yep, that's light as a feather.'

'Wait.' Jack was peering behind a dusty set of shelves. 'I think I can see a door behind this thing.'

Hugh pushed at the shelf. 'Shouldn't be too hard to shift it. You take the other side.'

As Hugh and Jack shuffled the shelf, Alex felt his excitement rise.

After a bit of huffing, the shelf was away from the wall, revealing a small, lightweight door.

Hugh pushed at the door, but it wouldn't open fully. He peered through the crack. 'It's just a sort of walk-in cupboard. Not really a room. Seems to be a whole set of shelves and stuff in there.'

He grinned at the others then manoeuvred his way through.

Alex peered after him. 'What can you see?'

Hugh's voice came out of the dark space. 'Seems pretty empty.'

Alex looked at Jack and Charlotte, who raised their eyebrows. Then he heard Hugh give a low whistle.

'Looks like someone used this place as his hideout. Oh, Ed, you dirty boy.' Hugh leaned back into the room and waved a set of dusty magazines at them. 'Ed's porn stash. Well, unless it was Robert's. Or Martha's.'

Ugh. Alex remembered that Hugh always took the joke too far.

'Please.' Charlotte wrinkled her nose.

Hugh grinned. 'Look, cigarette packets too.'

'Let us take a look.' Alex shuffled in. Then Jack and Charlotte squeezed in after him.

'And what's this?' Hugh unfolded a piece of paper. 'It's dope.' He sniffed at the leaves. 'Probably too old to use now.' His face softened a little. 'So, Ed must have come here to get away from Martha and Robert.'

There was a silence. Alex remembered Ed telling one of his stories, rolling his eyes at his parents.

Jack's voice was thoughtful. 'I've been wondering what Ed would make of all this.' He waved his arm at the rest of the house. 'This crazy situation.'

'Yeah, me too actually.' Hugh let out a slight laugh. 'Bet he'd have been taking charge, jollying us along.'

'Cracking jokes to keep our spirits up.'

'Cool, calm and collected,' Alex added.

'Well, maybe.' Jack paused. 'Or he might have lost it. It's hard to say. Most of the time Ed was, you know, the calm leader. But he had his moments.'

'Like on the walk.'

They all paused for a moment, as the events of the walk came back to them.

'Yeah, that, obviously. But, if you think about it, that wasn't entirely unexpected, really.' Jack turned to the others. 'He did a pretty good job of being Mr Responsible, but occasionally it all got a bit too much for him and he'd snap. Like, do you remember getting the hall ready for the year eleven dance?'

'Oh, yeah.' Hugh smiled. 'God, Mr Delaney went apeshit, didn't he?'

'I don't think I heard about that,' said Charlotte.

'A whole bunch of us were in the school hall, trying to get it set up for the dance. We were running late. And Delaney had told us that if we didn't organise it properly, then it'd be unlikely we'd be allowed to hold the house dances the following month.'

'Ed was in charge, as usual,' said Jack.

'And a bunch of kids – I think it was Peter Mackay and his mates – started dicking around with the decorations.' Hugh shook his head.

'Yeah, for once it wasn't you.' Jack smiled. 'Anyway, Ed kept trying to get them to do the work, but they kept mucking around.'

'And then he finally lost it.'

'Started bellowing at them. Then turned and shoved a stack of drinks cans over onto the floor.'

'There was this almighty crash.'

'Peter and his mates froze. Couldn't believe it.'

'And Ed stormed out.'

'Delaney didn't see what Ed did, but he went off when he saw the mess.'

Alex looked surprised. Hugh and Jack fell silent, remembering.

'Did we even tell Delaney that Ed tipped the stack over?'

'Teachers wouldn't have believed us.'

'Hey, I wonder what else he kept here. Some kind of diary maybe?' Hugh looked around some more. 'You remember he used to write in that notebook?'

Alex noticed some rough scrawl on the wall. 'Looks like he was writing secret messages on the wall.'

'What the hell does that say?' Hugh leaned in. 'It's just collections of letters. 'AD . . . PW . . . SG . . . CD . . . LW. Huh?'

'Some sort of private code?' Alex wondered.

Jack was staring at the letters. His face was set. 'They're initials.'

'Initials of what?' Hugh's brow was furrowed.

Jack spoke slowly. 'People's initials.' He paused. 'I bet they're girls' initials.' Another pause. 'And the last one, LW, will be Laura Walcott.' He pressed his lips together.

Bloody hell. This was really awkward.

'The cheeky bastard. It's Ed's notches on the bedpost. Hidden away in this lair.'

Alex wasn't sure whether Hugh sounded disgusted or admiring. He saw Jack turn to Charlotte, who looked away. What was going on?

Then Hugh said, 'What is it?'

But she shrugged, her eyes fixed on the floor. An obvious blush spread over her face.

Realisation was dawning in Alex as to the source of Charlotte's embarrassment.

'Charl?' Hugh raised his eyebrows.

After a moment, she burst out, '"CD". It's Charlotte Davies, okay? Happy now?' She turned, squeezed through the cupboard opening and ran from the laundry.

Chapter 43

Charlotte ran into the kitchen. Her first urge was to dash out the door and away from everyone – but Martha was out there somewhere, watching them. With that rifle. Charlotte threw herself down on a chair and buried her head in her arms.

After a moment she heard footsteps.

Eventually she looked up to see the three boys gazing at her warily.

'So now you know. I slept with Ed,' Charlotte burst out.

Hugh was frowning.

'Ah, we can go out, if you like.' Alex started edging towards the door.

'Yeah, if you guys want to talk, we don't need to listen.' Jack made to follow him.

'Wait.' She sat up. 'There's nothing you two can't hear.'

She turned to Hugh. 'Obviously, it was before we got together.'

'When was it?' His voice was level.

'It was at the country party. That bloody country party.'

Charlotte spread her hands wide and spun around. 'Wheeeeee!' she called. She looked up at the stars spread across the black sky.

A wave of delight bubbled up inside her chest and she laughed as she staggered sideways.

The music was pounding, the firelight flicked against her friends' smiling faces. The alcohol in her veins gave everything a soft, distanced edge. Was there anything more wonderful than being here, quite pissed, at this party, right now?

She heard a shout and turned. There was Ed, climbing on top of a beer keg, a bunch of kids gathered around. She couldn't hear what he was saying, but then a cheer went up.

That boy. He was so damn popular, you almost hated him for it. And so damn good-looking. She regarded him now. She could see his lean physique against the light. Was he looking at her across the yard? That might have been a nod and a wave. She waved her hand back.

Lucy, standing next to her, nudged her. 'He's been looking at you all night.'

Charlotte turned and stifled a smile. 'Nah. Not Ed Fletcher.'

Lucy grinned. 'Yes he has. Reckon you're in with a chance there.'

Charlotte tossed her hair. 'Whatever. I don't care about him. You know it's Kieran I like.'

Kieran Patterson, with his broad rugby shoulders and his dark wavy hair. His was indeed the face that filled Charlotte's daydreams, perhaps all the more vividly because he never seemed to have much time for her.

'But Kieran's not here, is he?' Lucy downed the rest of her beer. 'And Ed is.'

The crowd that had gathered in front of Ed began to split off in different directions.

'Hide and seek. Ed's in,' a boy running past called to the two girls.

Lucy laughed and pulled at her arm. 'Let's do it.' She took off towards the bottom of the home paddock.

Why not? Charlotte cast a glance back at Ed, who seemed to meet her eye again. Charlotte tossed her hair and smiled, then turned and ran after Lucy. She stumbled slightly on the rough ground of the paddock, her balance addled by beer.

'Behind there.' Lucy grabbed her arm and nodded at a stand of gum trees.

'No; the shed,' said Charlotte. A laugh bubbled up in her throat 'We won't be seen if we go in there.'

But Lucy had already stumbled off behind the trees.

Charlotte glanced behind her again. There was Ed, heading down the paddock, looking behind trees. Coming closer and closer.

That old thrill of hide and seek. It was obvious why kids liked it.

Charlotte pushed open the door of the shed and stood back against the wall. Lights from the party shone dimly through the window, just enough for her to see the outline of the room. She smiled to herself then put her hand over her mouth to stifle another laugh. This was so silly. But so fun!

She heard footsteps outside and held her breath. Her eyes adjusted to the gloom. The door opened and she drew in a sharp breath. A figure appeared. It was Ed. She saw him smile.

'I know someone's in here.'

He moved towards her, his hands out.

'I'm going to find you.'

A giggle escaped her, despite her best efforts.

'That sounds like a giggle to me. A Charlotte Davies giggle.'

He really was flirting with her. A smile broke her face. A warm wave of satisfaction washed over her. Nothing else felt this good.

Then Ed was right in front of her.

'Got you.'

He was smiling. She was smiling. He moved closer.

Was he really? Was he going to . . .?

He took another step. Those blue eyes, staring deep into hers. He really was so hot.

'I'm so pleased I found you in here.'

She laughed again. The room was shifting slightly.

He was close enough that she could feel the heat coming off his chest, off his face.

Then his hands were on her waist. His lips were on hers.

Looks like Lucy was right after all.

'We were drunk. We were all playing some game. I ran into the shed, that one near Robert's radio aerial, down the hill from the house. Ed followed me in there. And . . . and it happened.'

Of that night, she couldn't remember too many details. There had been a lot of beer drunk. But she didn't need to remember the event itself to know why she had slept with Ed.

Charlotte didn't just like male attention; she needed male attention. With the years she had come to understand and admit it to herself. Without that attention, she felt lost. Unseen. Unloved. In danger of ending up like her mother, abandoned and alone.

The problem was, as she had also discovered over the years, was that the need to always look good, to be appealing, to attract that attention, was never assuaged. No amount of attention was enough to make her feel seen, loved and secure.

Her expanding pregnancy bump had only opened up a new front of insecurity. What about her bloated body and her stretch marks? Would Hugh still want her if she couldn't lose the weight after the baby arrived? At the heart of it all, would he still love her when, as must happen eventually, she was old and wrinkly?

She turned to Hugh. 'It was just the once. Honestly. And it was ages before you and me got together.'

'It's fine. Before my time.' He threw up his hands. 'But why did you never say? It's nothing to be embarrassed about. We were kids. That stuff happened.'

'I didn't set out to hide it. It was just a one-off; there was nothing to tell. And then, he – he died. And when it all came out about him and Laura, do you think she would have appreciated hearing that he and I had gotten together? Laura was sure that with Ed and her it was true love.' She glanced at Jack. 'Sorry, but she was. And so I didn't think she needed to know about Ed and me.'

A long pause.

'No, that's not what I'm embarrassed about.' Charlotte opened her mouth. Then she closed it again. Turned away for a moment, then back to face the others. She blinked. 'Ed asked me for a favour. Before we even went on the walk. He wanted me to ask my father to give him an internship at his company.'

Hugh looked puzzled. 'Why did he want one of those?'

'Remember he wanted to study finance?' Charlotte looked between her friends. 'And Robert hated that idea, wanted him to do agriculture? Ed wanted to get some independence from them, financially, while he went to uni. And he didn't think he'd get an internship on his own, didn't think he'd be competitive enough to win one of those things. So, he asked me to ask Dad.'

'But you wouldn't help him?' Jack looked at her closely. 'That's what Martha's note for you meant, wasn't it? "Why didn't you help him?"'

She turned to Hugh. 'I didn't really want Ed for myself, as a boyfriend. I was fine with it when he didn't want anything more after the thing at the party. But then later, on the walk, when I found out about him and Laura . . .' Charlotte's face twisted. 'He had chosen her and not me. Clearly some girls made him want more than a one-night stand. I thought, why her; why not me?

'He saw straight through me, too, when he asked me about it again, that night we sat around the fire on our walk.'

Ed leaned back. 'You serious? Just – no?'

Charlotte snuck a glance at his handsome face, his shock clearly visible in the firelight. Ed Fletcher wasn't used to being told no. It was hard to keep the smile from her own face.

He must have noticed. His eyes narrowed. 'Wait a second. Is this because of what happened with us, at the country party? Did you even ask your dad about a job?'

She laughed. 'Of course I did. What is it? Can't you even imagine that someone wouldn't want to employ you?'

Ed shook his head. 'I can tell you're lying. You're just bitter because I didn't pick you.'

'But, the thing is, it was more than just feeling overlooked.' Charlotte's face shifted. 'The way Laura spoke about her and Ed;

226

she thought she was in love. She made it sound so intoxicating. I didn't want a relationship with Ed – but I didn't have that kind of connection with anyone else.'

A long pause.

'It made me feel . . . lonely. What was wrong with me, that no one wanted me like that?'

Charlotte forced herself to look at Hugh. She saw him blink.

'I was jealous, but I was also hurt and sad, and so I – I told Ed that my dad had said no to the internship. I lied. Dad would have been glad to have him.'

Her face crumpled. 'It's awful, I know it was awful. Just petty and mean.' A sob burst forth. 'And now you all think I'm a complete bitch. But, really, I've been ashamed of myself ever since. I mean, he died. And pretty much the last thing between us was me lying and being mean.'

Hugh's face softened. He took a step towards her, then put an arm around her shoulders.

'Babe. It's okay. Hey, you were just a kid. It was ten years ago.'

She turned to him and saw his face soften.

'I don't think you're a bitch. And if it makes you feel any better, I don't think there was much need to worry too much about Ed's feelings,' he said gruffly. 'I mean, the bloke was keeping a fuck tally on the wall in his secret hangout. I know I'm not some sensitive metrosexual, but even I never did that.'

He put his arms out, and Charlotte rose and stepped into them.

She pressed her face against his chest. It was too much to hope for that he really didn't care about how she'd behaved, but he was being much nicer about it than she had imagined he might be.

She let herself relax against him, felt the strength of his arms about her back.

She heard Hugh say, 'What is it, Jack?' She pulled back and turned to Jack. He looked more animated than a moment ago.

'It was when Charlotte mentioned the shed, down the hill. Where she and Ed . . . We haven't looked in there.'

Jack's voice took on a note of excitement. 'Don't you remember? Robert used that shed. He'd hang out there, listening to the cricket on the radio. Probably wanted to get away from everyone.'

'And . . .?'

'But remember what he also had. There was that high aerial – because he had a radio transmitter. He was a radio ham.'

Charlotte felt a little glimmer of excitement. Was it too much to hope that the transmitter was still there?

The four friends immediately stood.

Charlotte noticed that, on their way out the door, Hugh kept his arm around her.

Chapter 44

Robert Fletcher's shed lay a little way from the house, in a dip between the high point of the homestead and where the ground began to rise again up towards the bush and the cliffs.

Jack led the way out the back of the house, across the yard, through a gate and out into the paddock. He felt the long grasses twitching against his legs as he walked, faster than usual and puffing a little. Maybe, just maybe, the radio was still there. And maybe Martha had forgotten about it because it wasn't in the main house.

The shed was small, made from corrugated iron that, like most other metal on the Fletcher property, was largely covered in rust. Jack peered through one of the windows, but the glass was so grubby he couldn't see anything.

Hugh tried the door. The knob moved but the door seemed stuck, so he shouldered it, and it gave way with a loud creak.

They all crowded through.

There was a strong musty smell rising from the earth floor. Dim light filtered through the dirty windows, showing a small workroom. A desk and old chair stood beneath one window. Shelving lined a couple of walls. Everything was dusty.

Jack shivered. He could picture Robert sitting at the desk, had seen him there on several occasions when he had visited the farm with Ed as a schoolboy. And now the man was dead. By his own hand. What thoughts had gone through his mind as he'd sat there, alone in this lonely valley? The room was creepy, its silence melancholy.

Alex stepped forward. He walked to one of the shelves, pushed aside a pile of books. 'Here's his radio. The one he used for the cricket.'

'But that's just a receiver,' said Jack. 'The transmitter set was bigger.'

For five minutes the quiet in the shed was interrupted only by the occasional comment, as the friends searched the shelves and boxes.

'A-ha!'

Jack turned to see Hugh peering into a cardboard box. 'I reckon this is it.'

Hugh took the box to the desk and began to pull out pieces of black plastic circled with wires.

Jack's heart sank.

As they turned the pieces over, it was clear the instrument was definitely not in working order. And from the look of the largest pieces, with their back panels removed and wires hanging loose, they had been placed in the box after an unsuccessful attempt at examination and repair.

Jack saw Charlotte's face crease up. 'Damn it.' She turned to Jack. 'It was another good idea from you. Shame Robert seems to have dismantled this for us.'

Alex loaded the pieces back in the box. 'We could have a fiddle with this later.' When he saw the others' expressions, he said, 'Yeah, okay, I'm not too hopeful.'

Jack was the last out of the door. He shoved a box out of the way with his foot and turned to go, but then he froze and yelled.

A strong, sharp pain was shooting up his leg.

The others turned back to him.

He looked down and immediately felt a visceral jolt of fear that was even stronger than the pain.

Streaking out the door, away from his foot was the long, sinuous form of a snake.

Chapter 45

Jack heard Hugh, Charlotte and Alex yell. The others jumped backwards, away from the slithering shape.

But Jack stood, frozen with fear.

'Oh my god, oh my god!' Charlotte gasped.

'Did it get you?' Alex's voice was urgent.

Jack nodded. He couldn't take his eyes off the two small puncture marks on his lower leg. The pain was getting stronger.

'Holy fuck, mate,' Hugh breathed.

'Does it hurt?' Alex tried to catch Jack's eye.

Jack just nodded again, his lips pressed together. He glanced sideways, but the snake had disappeared into the grass.

'What sort was it?' asked Alex.

'I don't know; I didn't get a good enough look.' Jack forced the words out, his voice tight. 'It was kind of thin, and black.'

Alex spoke quickly. 'Okay, that's good. Doesn't sound like a brown. Now, just stay still. Here, can you sit on this rock? Right. I'm going to bind it.' He was almost babbling. He took off his shirt and tried to tear it. When that didn't work, he tied the whole shirt around Jack's leg. 'Really you shouldn't move, but we can't leave you out here.'

The unwelcome thought pushed itself into Jack's mind: because it's not like we'll be calling an ambulance.

Alex turned to Hugh. 'Give me a hand, and we'll get him up to the house. We can check the medicine cabinet, might be something there for a bite.'

They stumbled across the paddock towards the house as quickly as they could, Hugh and Alex on either side of Jack, who limped awkwardly, keeping his weight off one leg.

'Hurry, guys.' Charlotte glanced between Jack's face and the house.

'Give it a rest, Charl, we're going as fast as we can,' Hugh snapped.

The bite was really throbbing now, and the skin around it was stinging. Jack could feel his breath coming in short bursts.

The trip back to the house seemed to take for ever, but eventually they were back in the kitchen. Hugh and Alex sat Jack down on one of the chairs. Charlotte stayed with him, hovering anxiously while the two other men ran upstairs to search the medicine cabinet. They dashed back down, carrying boxes piled with bandages.

'It's a total mess up there.' Alex dumped his boxes on the table. 'So, we just brought these down. We can look through them here.'

Alex unwrapped his shirt from Jack's leg, removed his shoe and sock, then took a roll of bandage and started to work his way up from Jack's foot. His hands shook but he bound the cloth tightly.

Jack tried not to wince. He was starting to feel faint but whether it was from poison or stress he couldn't tell.

'Where'd you learn how to do that, Alex?' asked Hugh.

'First aid course for work. Need to be able to treat the clients, if anyone gets injured.' Alex leaned back on his heels. 'Never done it on an actual wound before. Looks a bit wonky.'

Charlotte had opened the boxes and was sorting through them with sharp, impatient movements. 'There's so much crap in here. A lot of it isn't even medicine.' She removed a pile of photo frames from one box, then a set of moth-eaten tea towels, rummaged at the bottom then snatched up a box. 'Here! Some paracetamol.' She turned to Alex. 'He could have that for the pain, surely?'

Jack downed the pills with a precious few mouthfuls of water. He leaned back while Alex finished binding his leg and closed his eyes to shut out Charlotte and Hugh's concerned expressions. They were only adding to his own anxiety. This bite was the last thing everyone needed. He tried not to think about what on earth they'd all do if his condition went downhill.

Alex looked up at him. 'How does that feel?'

'Okay.' In fact, it felt awful. His leg was throbbing around the bandage Alex had fashioned. And now his head was aching. He closed his eyes.

'Do you feel faint, Jack?' Charlotte's voice was tense. 'You look very pale. Keep taking deep breaths.'

Hugh said, 'Shame you never finished medicine, Jack. You might know how to save yourself.'

'Yeah thanks, mate. Wasn't smart enough.' Jack's teeth were clenched. He knew Hugh was trying to lighten a tense situation with his trademark humour, but it wasn't helping.

'Oh, come on. You always used to say that. But you were always top at school. And obviously, if you hadn't – I mean, if you weren't, like, coping with what happened with Ed, you would have sailed through the rest of the course.'

'Not necessarily.' His head was really hurting now. He really wished Hugh would shut up. If Hugh didn't stop, Jack was going to say something he'd regret.

Hugh laughed again. 'Yeah, yeah, yeah. Heard it all before. You did so well at school, Jack—'

'Because I was taking drugs!' The words burst out of his mouth before he could think, and he smacked his hand against the table in frustration, dislodging boxes and papers, which all hit the floor with a crash.

Finally, Hugh was silent. And so was everyone else.

Jack opened his eyes and looked at their shocked faces. 'It's true.'

'Drugs?' Alex looked bemused. 'Huh?'

'Study drugs,' said Jack. 'Ritalin. Adderall. They help you concentrate, supposedly. I was taking them all through years eleven and twelve.'

'But I don't understand, Jack.' Charlotte's voice was slow. 'Why on earth would you need help to concentrate? You always did better than any of us at school, right from year seven.'

Jack knew it wouldn't make sense to them. It hardly made sense to him, as he looked back. But there was no backing out of the admission now. He'd have to try to explain.

'I just – I thought I needed it. At first – year seven, year eight – it was easy to get good marks but, later on, I suppose I lost my confidence.

'Then, in about year ten, I read this article about how these "study drugs" were used by some kids to help you concentrate. It sounded convincing; scientific.'

Jack remembered how appealing it had seemed. He'd be able to concentrate better, stay up later, learn more.

Now Hugh was looking at him closely. 'So that's what your little note from Martha meant.'

Jack nodded. 'I assume so.'

'But how did Martha know about these study drugs?'

'Dunno how she knew. But Ed knew.'

Alex's eyes narrowed. 'Oh. Is that what Ed meant, on the walk?

Jack looked at him. 'What do you mean?'

Alex looked embarrassed. 'Oh, just, someone mentioned how brainy you are, then Ed made some comment, asking whether you were really that smart, whether it was all just your brain power. And you didn't look happy.'

'That sounds about right.'

'I just couldn't work out why you were so horrified by Ed's comment.' Alex gave Jack a sidelong look. 'You looked really stressed.'

Jack let out a breath. 'Well, for a start, it might have become a bit of a thing with some students, but it was still illegal. Buying these drugs that you're meant to get from a doctor, and taking them when they're not prescribed for you. So I didn't want it getting out that that's what I was up to.'

'But taking a few pills?' Hugh looked sceptical. 'It's not that bad, really.'

'The thing is, I wasn't just taking them.' Jack took another breath. Might as well give them the whole story. At least it was a distraction from the damn snakebite. 'I was also supplying them.' He saw the expressions on his friends' faces shift again.

'You were running a drug ring?' Hugh looked incredulous. Then he let out a hoot of laughter. 'Jack Zhang? Ha!'

236

'Just to fund my own supplies; I wasn't trying to make a profit. I know it doesn't make it okay. But Ed knew, and he would keep bringing it up. He always talked about it as if he were concerned for me. But honestly.' Jack paused, then rushed on. 'I think he kind of enjoyed holding it over me. That I was doing something that could really get me into trouble.' Jack couldn't keep the bitterness from his voice.

Alex said, 'Why didn't you stop? Just give it all up?'

Jack shook his head, miserably. 'At the time I was convinced I needed them; that if I stopped taking them, I wouldn't be able to study as well, then my marks would go downhill and that would have been a disaster. My life ruined, et cetera. I wanted to make my grandpa proud.' Jack's voice cracked. 'Prove I was different from my parents, who were happy to live off his money.'

He took another breath. 'And I was in this chain of supplying them and had people at me from both sides, supplying and buying, and it all seemed too hard to back out. I really just wanted to get through the year twelve exams, get into uni, move away. Then I was going to step away from all that. Obviously, it was a stupid thing to do. And wrong. Making money off other kids like that.'

It was now also clear that it had been kind of a fork in the road; it was the first time he'd stepped off the straight and narrow. When things went wrong, it meant he already thought of drugs as an answer.

And they really did go wrong.

They'd all struggled, in those difficult years after Ed's death. They'd all had their different ways of coping that were more or less destructive, and his way was outside assistance for his brain chemistry.

He'd since weaned himself off the harder drugs, but the pot was still a habit, and he knew it was getting worse rather than better. He kept telling himself that he'd finish once he'd worked his way through the current supply. Then the next. But there were always sharp feelings that needed to be dulled, and it was so useful in that way. It was remarkably effective, for example, at thinning out the black cloud of heaviness that seemed so omnipresent these days, which made it hard to think or move.

'Well, drugs or not, that comment from Martha didn't make any sense. You were – you're still – bloody smart, Jack,' said Charlotte. 'Don't reckon those pills would have made much difference to your marks.'

'Yeah, it's obvious,' said Alex. 'Always was obvious.'

'Thanks, guys. But I'm still ashamed of it. It felt like cheating to me. I never told anyone, and I was never going to.' Jack shook his head. Having to talk about it now was bringing back all that old guilt and shame. He preferred to keep it locked up at the back of his memories, to tell himself it was all over and forgotten.

When he'd failed his first year of medicine, it had seemed like such a disaster. He'd never amount to anything; he'd always be a loser. What he should have done was take a break, deal with his grief. Work out what he wanted to do with his life and then work out what career he'd aim for.

What he'd done instead was race back to the old comfort of being 'good at school'. University was a secure and protected enclave, its rules for success clear and simple. He'd transferred to a science degree. And then he'd just kept going, not wanting to engage with the messy outside world. He'd enrolled in a doctorate – a PhD would finally prove to himself and to everyone else that he really was intelligent, impressive, successful.

But Jack knew the study wasn't taking him anywhere, really; wasn't going to help him find his way in the world. And that only made it all the harder to face up and write the bloody thing. All he felt when he thought about the work he should be doing, when he yet again put off making the appointment to see his supervisor, was a big ball of unpleasantness sitting at the bottom of his stomach.

He noticed Charlotte looking at him closely. Then she said briskly, 'Anyway, we don't need to go over all that now. How's the leg?'

'It's okay.' His story had been a useful distraction, but his leg was actually hurting a lot.

'Your colour looks a bit better. But you need to stay calm.' Charlotte laid a hand on his arm then glared at Alex and Hugh. She turned to the things that had been knocked onto the floor and started to pick them up.

Hugh and Alex joined in. They piled up the stack of photo frames that had landed on the floor. One of them had broken. Jack watched as Alex went to the pantry, then returned with some newspapers and began to wrap the broken glass. Charlotte was looking through the photos, although her eyes kept flicking back to Jack's face.

He needed something else to take his mind off the throbbing in his leg and the queasiness in his stomach. He peered across at the pictures. They seemed to be old Fletcher family photos. Women in large hats and long pale dresses. Picnics with men wearing suits. Others of women in mid-century dresses. And then the faded colours of photos from the later twentieth century.

Jack picked up the photo that had come out of the broken frame.

'Hey, it's Martha and Robert.' The others turned to see. 'God, they look so young,' said Charlotte.

Two figures stood in a paddock next to a small brick structure. A picnic rug was spread on the grass, plates and cups laid out for a feast. The distinctive high cliffs of Lost Valley lay in the background.

'Wonder where that was taken? What's that building?' asked Alex.

Jack turned the photo over. In spidery letters was written, 'Old Pump House. August '70'.

'Obviously in the valley somewhere,' said Hugh.

'Yes, in the valley.' Jack's voice shifted up a note. A surge of excitement overrode the pain from his leg.

Hugh turned to him. 'What is it?'

'I'm wondering, what the "pump house" was for.' He looked between the other friends. 'I mean, you pump liquid, right?'

Chapter 46

A little glimmer of hope rose within Alex, and, as he looked around the group, he saw it reflected on his friends' faces.

'Could be water.' Hugh nodded slowly.

'What other liquid would be pumped here? It's not an oil pipeline.'

'And, if it's water . . .?'

'And if it's water, it could be about maintaining the pressure through to this farm, this house, from the mains supply. And so, maybe, just maybe, it's where the water supply for the house is controlled.'

'Like some kind of an on–off lever?' asked Charlotte.

'I don't want to get our hopes up.' Jack winced then shifted his weight. 'But it's worth a try, right? Depending on where it is.' He thought for a moment. 'Remember when we heard that plane – we were in the middle of looking at those.' He pointed to the maps they had brought down from the study, which were now sitting on one of the kitchen dressers.

'Let's find the one of the valley.' Alex went to the papers. 'That building looks pretty old. Might appear on one of them.'

He cleared a space on the table and spread out the map. 'This is the one we were looking at before.'

They all bent over the sheets. But even after a very close examination, there was no little structure marked on the map of the valley.

'Hang on. That one might be too old – see, it has the cottage that was here before this house. Remember, Martha mentioned that.' Jack leafed through the documents for a moment, then pulled out another sheet. 'Here's one that has the current house; must be a bit newer.'

Again, they studied the paper.

Then Alex felt a little thrill. 'There it is.' He pointed to a small rectangle with the words *pump house*.

'Yay!' Charlotte clapped. 'And look, it doesn't seem to be too far from here.'

'I don't remember that at all.' Hugh frowned. 'Never seen anything that looks like it.'

Jack rotated the paper then looked out the window. 'That's because it will be behind that hill over there. So, unless you walked over that way, you'd never see it.' He bent again to the paper.

'Not too far. Maybe a fifteen-minute walk, I reckon.' Hugh was frowning.

'Great, so we can go take a look,' said Jack.

'Hang on a second. Martha's out there.' Hugh's face was serious. 'And she's got that gun.'

At that word, Alex's stomach dropped. There was a long silence.

Jack looked outside and Alex followed his gaze. The late-afternoon sun was dropping. Their help sign still lay on the grass, beaming out its message, but it probably wasn't going to be spotted. Time was ticking on, and they were still stuck here.

'I'm getting more worried about our water situation.' Jack set his teeth. 'It could be pretty dire pretty soon. And this might be our best chance to find water.'

Alex just managed to stop himself saying, *and then there's your leg*. He felt torn. He was thirsty and anxious, and wanted a way forward. And although Jack's condition didn't seem to be deteriorating, Alex was very worried about him. But there was Martha with that bloody rifle. 'We don't know where she is. Could be miles away.' He looked from face to face. The hours were ticking past, and everyone looked pretty rough already.

'Or she could be waiting just out there, hiding in the trees with the gun.' Charlotte paused. 'But there's another thing. Should we be out looking for Laura? She's been gone for ages now. And it won't be too long until it's dark.'

Hugh said, 'It's the same problem as before. We just don't know whether Laura's in trouble or whether she's part of the trouble.'

Another pause.

Charlotte looked at Jack's leg. 'Can you even walk that far, to this pump house?'

'The painkillers have helped.' He stifled a grimace. 'It's not getting any worse. Hopefully it was a bite but with no venom.'

'But even so, you have to keep still,' Charlotte insisted.

Jack looked between his friends' faces. 'What do you think, Hugh?'

Hugh took a breath. He put his fists on his hips. He looked very uncomfortable. 'Yeah, I dunno. I mean, we've got to get some goddamn water.'

Alex turned from face to face, his opinion shifting this way and that as they debated.

Jack said, 'I know it's hot. But I think we need to take a look.'

Charlotte stared out the window. 'I'm not even sure I can walk that far.' She rubbed her stomach.

'You stay here,' said Jack.

'I'm not staying here by myself.'

Alex look a breath. It was clear what needed to happen. He looked at Jack. 'You stay here with Charlotte. You can't go with your leg like that.' He turned to Hugh. 'You and I can take a look. Keep an eye out for any sign of Laura while we're out there.'

Hugh frowned, then nodded seriously. 'Yeah. Okay. Okay. Makes sense.' He kept nodding slowly.

'It should be me and Hugh,' said Alex. Much as the idea made him feel a little faint, it was obvious.

Half an hour later they were in the kitchen, Alex and Hugh applying sunscreen. They had a bottle of water each, a fraction of their precious supply carefully meted out.

'Be careful.' Charlotte gave Hugh a hug and he patted her back.

'Good luck.' Jack was leaning against the kitchen table. His face was tight; Alex bet his leg was still hurting.

Alex turned to Hugh, who nodded. They left the kitchen, crossed the veranda, then made their way across the back yard. Without a word, they opened the gate and went out into the paddock.

Alex gazed around. His legs brushed against the yellowy grass, insects flicking against him. Ahead the folds of grassland simmered in the distance. Gum leaves hung motionless from the trees. The cliffs stared down on all sides. There was no sign of Martha. Or Laura. Hugh's face was grim.

Alex felt the pull in his leg muscles as the ground rose. The long droning cries of cicadas reverberated against his ears.

Then at the top of the rise Hugh stopped and pointed. 'There it is.'

Alex saw a small brick building, little more than a hut. A cockatoo swooped low over the building and its screech echoed back to them. The dipping land between them was dotted with stands of gum trees, motionless in the still air.

He nodded at Hugh. They set off with renewed energy.

They had travelled just a little way past the hill when it happened.

A sudden very sharp crack burst against his ears.

He turned in shock to Hugh. 'Was that—?'

Then a high-pitched ping ricocheted off one of the fence posts to the right, and another crack, and without even thinking he dropped to the ground.

He twisted his head and saw Hugh also lying on the ground, his face stunned with shock.

No doubt about it. Those were gunshots.

Chapter 47

Alex tried to move his legs, but they wouldn't budge. All he could hear was his heart hammering and his own breath.

He tried to focus, but the fear was overwhelming.

He lay still for a moment. There was no sound. He made himself take deep breaths. He craned his neck. They were not too far from a group of trees. He looked back. Also not too far from the rise from which they had first seen the pump house.

He took a few more breaths. Martha must have been in the pump house; she must have fired at them. And she could be coming at them right now.

He twisted again. Hugh looked petrified. Alex moved his head, signalling that they should run to the nearby gum trees. Hugh nodded, his eyes wide.

Alex held up three fingers. 'Count of three,' he said quietly.

Three fingers, two fingers. Would he be able to force his terrified limbs to move? One finger.

He leapt up, flew across the grass and dived behind the trees. In an instant, Hugh was next to him.

'Holy fucking shit.' Hugh breathed the words. His chest was heaving. His eyes were wide.

'We need to get back past the rise. Back towards the house.' Alex infused his voice with a certainty that he didn't feel.

The paddock was still silent, the cicadas' cries silenced by the shots.

'Come on. Longer we leave it, harder it gets. Again, count of three.'

They set off.

Alex couldn't feel the ground under his feet. He'd never run so fast in his life. He fixed the hilltop in his sights.

Closer now, and closer.

The ground rose, flattened, then began to drop again. The house was in front of them.

His breath was burning in his throat. He could hear Hugh's panting breath.

Then there was a sudden burning pain in his leg, and in an instant he stopped and fell to the ground.

Chapter 48

Jack sat at the kitchen table, trying to ignore the aching throb in his leg, when he heard the sharp cracking sounds from the paddock.

His eyes met Charlotte's.

'That's not . . .?'

'Sounded like . . .'

His pain forgotten, he leapt up and in a moment they were at the kitchen window.

The landscape was quiet and still.

Then they saw the two figures appear over the rise and run towards them. Charlotte clutched Jack's arm. 'Oh my god,' she breathed.

'They're both still running. It's okay.' Jack was talking to himself as much as to Charlotte.

He stared at Hugh and Alex, willing them on.

Then there was another crack, and Charlotte shrieked.

With horror, Jack saw Alex fall to the ground.

Hugh was still running towards the house. The gate was ahead of him. Now he was through it. Now across the yard.

Hugh took the steps at a run, dashed across the veranda and threw himself through the kitchen door. He lay on the floor, clutching the floorboards.

Charlotte dropped down beside Hugh and wrapped her arms around him. Then she breathed, 'Alex?'

Hugh stared up at Jack, his face a mask of horror. Jack stared back, speechless.

Jack turned again to the window.

There, between the yard fence and the top of the rise, he could see a prone figure lying on the grass of the paddock. He held his breath. When the figure lifted an arm and waved, he let the breath out. An unintelligible cry came to them.

'Oh my god. Oh my god,' Hugh was whispering to himself.

Still Alex did not rise.

'We can't leave him out there,' said Jack. It was simply a matter of fact. He winced, as he felt his leg aching again.

Hugh put one arm around Charlotte and wrapped the other around his own stomach.

Jack peered out the window again. 'It was a couple of shots. She's not in view now. We can make it to Alex.'

He looked back at Hugh. Hugh closed his eyes. His chest was still heaving.

Before he could think any further, before the terrified voice in his brain urging, *stay, stay*, could get any louder, before he could reason that his leg was too sore and he should wait here, Jack ran out the kitchen door.

He was across the yard. Through the gate. Faster than he had run for a very long time. His breath heaving, he shot across the paddock. Threw himself down next to Alex.

He let his breath subside, then turned to his friend.

'It's okay.' Alex spoke through gritted teeth. 'I'm not hit or anything. But I went down on my ankle. Bloody killing me.'

'Okay. It's okay.' Jack was talking to himself more than anything. He craned his head again. Still no sign of Martha.

'We'll go back together. I'm going to help you sit up. Then I'll help you stand. Then you can have an arm around me, and we'll get you back.'

Jack forced himself into a crouch and helped Alex to a sitting position. Alex put an arm around Jack's shoulders and Jack heaved them both up to standing.

It was the longest walk of his life, stumbling quickly over the uneven paddock, Alex's face twisted, his leg held up as he limped.

They were across the paddock. Through the gate. Across the yard. Then finally, finally on the veranda, and then in the house.

The two men collapsed into the chairs, their chests heaving.

'You really need to get this looked at,' Charlotte said, then bit her lip. That was a bloody unhelpful thing to say. At least Alex had the self-control not to respond.

They were all in the kitchen. Alex was directing her as she bound his ankle.

She stood back to examine the bandage. Then she dropped to a chair and turned to the others.

She could almost see the tension in the air.

Jack was sitting at the table, breathing slowly but heavily. Alex was playing with the packets of dressings. Hugh was staring at the floor, looking moody. He's really embarrassed, Charlotte thought. About Jack being the one to go rescue Alex, and not him.

God, she was thirsty. It was hot. She tried not to think about her thirst, and whether it was harming her baby. She tried not to think about Alex's ankle and Jack's leg. About Laura's absence, and why she might be gone. And Charlotte definitely did not want to recall those horrendous gunshots, and the anguished dash across the paddock.

'I can see why she chose the pump house.' Jack pointed at the map. 'We couldn't see her from the house but, look, from that position she has a view of everything between the house and the road back up the hill.' He traced his finger along the paper. 'So she'd be able to see anyone who tried to walk out.'

Jack looked up at the others and saw their expressions. 'Sorry. But it's best that we understand.'

Another silence fell.

That persistent pull, from her thirst, again. Charlotte reached automatically for the water bottles but stopped herself in time.

Then she saw Hugh reach for the same bottle, but he didn't stop. She watched him unscrew the lid. Bring it up to his mouth.

'Can I just ask how much of that have you had?' asked Jack.

Hugh stared at him belligerently. Slowly he lowered the bottle. 'Only my share.'

Jack raised his eyebrows.

Hugh leaned forward. 'What are you getting at?'

'I'm just saying we need to go easy.'

'Okay.' Hugh's voice was tense.

'And be fair about it.'

Hugh ostentatiously breathed out slowly. 'And I'm not being fair?'

'That's not what I said. But.'

'But what?' Hugh took a step towards Jack, his chin raised.

'Will you STOP!' Charlotte bellowed, and the men fell silent.

'God *damn* it!' Charlotte actually stamped her foot. 'Why do you have to keep pulling this shit?' She glared at Hugh. 'We have got to stop this. Look at us.' She stared at the other three. 'Hot. Thirsty. Injured. Angry. It's exactly like it was, on the walk. Exactly how we were feeling. Before it happened.'

Chapter 49

Ten years previously

The sharp pulse of a kookaburra's cry awoke Jack. For a second he forgot where he was, confused by the tent sheet hovering above his face. Then the events of the previous evening came back to him. The arrival at the camp site. The horrifying sight of the dry creek bed. He reached for his glasses, wriggled up out of his sleeping bag and gathered himself into a crouch, trying not to disturb the sleeping figure of Alex.

He stuck his head out of the tent. The air was clear and mild. Early morning sunshine caught the tops of the trees, lying glossy on the still leaves. It was a lovely morning. If only they didn't have the worry about the water. He stood, stretching.

Laura was perched on a rock. She turned when she saw him. 'It's beautiful, isn't it?'

He nodded and sat next to her. He kissed her cheek softly then pulled back. He couldn't read her look. Was it sadness? 'What's up?'

She shook her head. 'Nothing.'

'We'll be okay.'

They sat in silence and the minutes ticked past.

Soon the slow whine of zippers opening alerted them to their friends rising. Ed wandered over, hair askew and face creased. 'Can't believe this one got up before me.' He nudged Jack with a foot.

Then Charlotte appeared, her sleeping bag wrapped around her shoulders. 'I suppose coffee is out of the question?'

'I'd like nothing better,' Ed replied. 'But we'd better save the . . .'

'Water,' she finished.

Alex was next to appear. 'Anyone know where Hugh is?'

'Probably gone for a slash.'

Ed started rummaging in the pile of packs for breakfast. The others joined him, pottering with plates and packets. Leaves crunched under foot and bird calls echoed across the clearing. They were all seated, munching at their breakfast, when Hugh finally appeared.

'The hell have you been?' asked Ed.

Hugh waved his phone at them and looked sheepish. 'No luck with a signal. Went up to the ridge and back. Have to say I'd love a huge drink of water right now,' he said.

Groans all around.

'Just don't think about it,' said Ed.

Ed hurried them through their meal, then got up and started to pack the bags. The others struggled to life with scattered complaints, but Jack felt an undercurrent of tension, held at bay last night by the campfire and prospect of a plan for the new day, and his own movements quickened.

'Make sure you collect all the tent poles,' Ed called. 'Wait, there's one over there.'

'I've got them.' Charlotte handed the poles to Ed.

'Has anyone seen my small pack?' Ed frowned.

'Here you go.' Alex handed it over.

'Thanks. Hey, Jack, make sure you grab the rubbish near that rock.'

In another twenty minutes, Jack stood with his friends as they hoisted their packs onto their backs.

'Cheer up.' Ed looked around at the others. 'We need to preserve our water. But it's only a few hours to the bottom of Nanganook valley and there we can fill up.' He smiled. 'Go for a swim if we want. We're going to be fine.'

Jack followed Ed along the narrow track, stepping up and over rocks, pushing past bushes. The night's sleep, uncomfortable though it was, had given him more energy and he walked with a steady rhythm. He wanted to see that river as soon as possible. He didn't waste energy on gazing around. He ignored the sculptural flowers that glowed in bursts of colour among the dull greens and looked straight past the small gathering of kangaroos.

Ed and Jack were walking ahead of the group, when a loud cry from behind made them halt. Jack met Ed's eyes and, without a word, they hurried back.

They rounded a corner and stopped. Laura was on the ground, her face twisted. Hugh, Alex and Charlotte were crowded around her.

For a moment Jack froze, but then he rushed forward, dimly registering Ed's leap forward at the same time. Then Ed seemed to slow, so Jack reached Laura first.

Laura's face was tense and pale. Jack dropped his pack then crouched at Laura's side. 'What happened?'

'Twisted my ankle. Really bloody hurts.'

Gently he loosened her boot and rolled her sock down. 'Does look a bit swollen.'

After a few minutes, Hugh and Jack helped Laura to her feet. She tried to put her weight on the ankle but winced.

Ed kneeled near Laura's foot. 'Get the first aid kit.' Ed looked at Jack then pointed at his bag. 'We'll wrap it.'

Jack opened Ed's pack and rummaged past his lunch and bottles but couldn't see the kit. He turned to his own bag and opened it, but then remembered that his own kit was right at the bottom of the bag. He turned back to Ed's bag and searched again, finally pulling out the little white case with a red cross.

Soon Ed was feeding cloth around Laura's leg. 'Think you can stand now?' Jack noticed how gently Ed was winding the bandage.

Jack helped Laura to her feet again, and she tentatively stood on the sore ankle. 'Lean that arm on me,' said Jack. 'Then you don't have to put your weight on it.'

'You can't carry me out.'

'We can take turns with you leaning on us,' said Hugh, and Ed and Alex nodded. 'And we'll carry your pack too.'

'I'm so sorry, guys,' she said, shaking her head.

'It's okay. What else are we going to do?' said Alex.

Jack tried not to think about that.

Now, the group moved much more slowly, matching their pace to Laura's as she hobbled, an arm around one of the boys. They had to stop more frequently too.

Ed kept glancing between Laura's face and the path ahead. Seeing this, Jack said to him quietly, 'You worried about the time?'

Ed shook his head slightly. 'We'll be all right.'

They continued on, the bushes edging slowly past, the crowns of the trees moving slowly overhead. They strung out into a line along the narrow path, their packs bobbing in a row. The sun inched across the sky. The temperature rose slowly, and they fanned their faces.

'It's so bloody hot,' said Hugh, standing in the shadow of a large rock.

'Yes, okay, Hugh, thanks for reminding us.' Charlotte's voice was tight.

'Sor-ry.' Hugh put his hands up.

'Well, just don't. We're all hot.'

At the next stop, Charlotte put her pack down and pulled out her bottle. She looked at the others defiantly and took a swig.

At this, Hugh, Alex and Laura reached into their bags.

'Guys, you need to go easy.' Ed looked between them.

'We know. But we're bloody thirsty. Don't you need a drink?'

'I'm saving mine.' He patted his day pack. 'Made myself not touch it since first thing this morning.'

'Bully for you.'

'Are you sure this is the right way?' Charlotte looked at Ed.

'Yes, I'm sure.' Ed's voice was clipped.

Jack sensed Ed's rising irritation. He really wished Charlotte would be quiet.

'It's just—'

'You're welcome to take over, if you're such an expert.' Now Ed was glaring at her.

She raised her hands. 'Okay. It's just, it's getting hotter, and we're all—'

'I know. I fucking know, okay. I don't need you to tell me that.' Ed hoisted his pack on his back and set off, without a backward glance.

The alarm that had been sitting in Jack's stomach began to grow. Ed's obvious stress made it harder for him to keep his own worry under control. If Ed was concerned, then perhaps they really were in trouble.

Without a word, trying not to look at each other, Jack and the rest of the group set off after their leader.

Chapter 50

The buzzing adrenaline of the gunshots and the dash back to the house was gone. As the fact of their predicament pressed in again, their spirits followed the downward pull of the setting sun. Try as they might, they could think of nothing else that might help them escape.

And there was still no sign of Laura. Was she in trouble? Or was she somehow in league with Martha, causing their distress? But if so, then why were they still here? Surely Laura would have told Martha all about what had happened on the walk with Ed.

They scrabbled together some dinner from the pantry and ate it sitting in silence and sipping carefully at their allotted water. The last of the evening sun beamed through the kitchen window and tinted their faces with its golden light. A slight breeze shifted the trees outside.

Hugh leaned forward, his elbows on his knees. He stared at the floor, trying to picture how this situation was going to end. It would be dark soon, and still they were stuck here. It was a massive relief that Jack didn't seem to be getting any worse, but he was still quite pale and was clearly moving his leg very carefully. He definitely needed to have it checked properly. Hugh glanced over at Charlotte and he felt another twist of anxiety. She was also looking pretty rough. The others could say what they liked, but if nothing changed by morning, he was going to walk out and get help, somehow.

'So, Hugh. When are you going to tell us?'

Hugh looked up. Jack was leaning back in his chair, his head tilted sideways.

'Sorry?'

'What did Martha mean when she said "you can't control your own strength"?'

It took Hugh a moment to realise what Jack was referring to. Then he looked away.

'Might be time to explain it, Hugh,' Jack went on slowly. 'I mean, the rest of us have all 'fessed up about our little messages. You're not still going to claim you don't know what Martha meant?'

Hugh was quiet for a long time, remembering. The shame welled up, as it always did.

Hugh glanced at Charlotte. Her head was down, but he could see her lips pressed together with tension.

Alex was looking at the table, not meeting his eye.

'Come on, mate. Fair's fair.' Jack maintained a steady gaze. 'And if not now, then when?'

Hugh looked around at his friends, looked away. His instinct was to deny and deny, to keep at bay the shame of it all. Then he thought of the confessions his friends had offered up that day. They'd revealed some stuff they obviously felt bad about, but the world hadn't fallen apart. He realised his need to hide everything, at all costs, had somehow drifted away.

'What the hell does it matter now, anyway?' He sighed and sat forward. 'That bloody country party.'

The flickering light of the fire was combining in a very interesting way with the pulsating music and the large number of beers Hugh had put away. The face of the guy standing opposite him seemed to be advancing and receding, even though the bloke was standing still. Unfortunately, the beer wasn't blocking out the prick's voice.

'I know you won and all, mate, but I just didn't expect that you'd have so many shit tacklers on your team.' Another sly smile.

He'd come up to Hugh as he was coming back from taking a slash in a paddock and cornered him, away from the other kids. He said they'd played opposite each other at last weekend's rugby match. Hugh didn't recognise him, although he definitely remembered the comprehensive defeat that Hugh's team had dished out to the opposing school.

The guy was shorter than Hugh, but almost as broad across the shoulders. He was standing, legs apart, one hand holding a beer, the other on his hip. He was leaning too far in towards Hugh's face.

'I mean, when I tackled you, mate, you just went straight down.'

The guy's head was tipped back, a sneering smile on his face.

Hugh could tell the guy was sore about the loss and wanted to needle him. It happened sometimes. But he wouldn't just say his piece and move on. He wouldn't shut up. He was going on and on, his annoying voice in Hugh's ear, louder and louder.

261

Hugh took a huge gulp of beer, hoping it would sooth his irritation. He looked around for someone else to go and talk to, but the two of them were around the corner of the house, out of sight of the other kids.

'Yeah, mate, I really thought, the way you went down, you were just a complete pussy.'

It was possibly the worst thing the guy could have said. That old, unwelcome memory rose up.

Camping with his dad, two other friends and their fathers. He must have been about six or seven. The dads had rigged up a rope that the boys could use to swing across a creek.

The other two boys had taken their turns. Hugh had stood on the creek bank. He grasped the rope, rough under his fingers. The other boys looked across from the other bank, the excitement of the swing still alive on their faces. But Hugh didn't feel excited. He couldn't take his eyes off the water below, which seemed to be rushing very fast. It was such a long way down. He hesitated.

'Come on, Hugh,' one of the other dads had called. 'Don't be such a slow coach.'

Then his own father's voice, an angry whisper in his ear. 'Get on with it. Now.' He turned. His father's face was furious. He was embarrassed. His son was letting him down. 'You get across that water now,' his dad hissed. 'Don't be such a bloody girl.'

Now, in the firelight, at the party, the shame of that moment flooded over him as it had so many times before. And the next instant, the relief of a surge of rage.

Fast as lightning, he bunched his fist, pulled his arm back, channelling all his pent-up emotion, and swung it as hard as he could, as hard as he had ever hit anyone, at the side of the other guy's head.

And just for a second it felt wonderful. Such a release. So satisfying, to see the bloke's expression freeze, that sneering smile drop away. Then to see his whole body drop.

The guy fell to the ground, a dead weight.

Hugh looked at him, lying on the grass, and felt his rage drain away.

The yard around him seemed to swing a little.

Hugh waited for the bloke to stir, but he was still.

He bent down. 'Get up, you prick.'

But it seemed like he was out cold. Jesus, perhaps he really had whacked him too hard.

Hugh yelled at him, slapped the guy's face, but nothing.

Hugh really wished he could remember how angry he'd felt just moments ago, because now that energising rage had been entirely replaced by an even more unpleasant wave of guilt and regret.

He stood again and the ground seemed to lurch a little. He tried to marshal his thoughts. Better go get some help. Probably need to tell Pa Fletcher.

Hope this guy was all right.

'And you know the rest of it. The ambo came, took him away. Thank god he recovered.'

Thankfully, also, the boy had been too drunk to mount any kind of assault case against Hugh. Apparently, he couldn't remember what had happened.

Hugh thought the kid's parents probably hadn't bought the story Hugh had told everyone – that the kid had stumbled while drunk and hit his head. But if the parents had looked into it, they had probably realised that even if anyone else had

263

seen what had happened, they were all so drunk they'd make terrible witnesses.

Now Hugh sat in the kitchen, avoiding the others' eyes. No one said anything. Fair enough. Alex had stolen some money, and Jack took some drugs because he thought it might make him even smarter, and Charlotte once slept with Ed, then wouldn't help him out with a job. But he knew none of that was as bad as his assault on that boy.

'Felt so bad about it. Ever since.'

'Bloody hell.' It was Jack.

Hugh couldn't meet his eye. He nodded. 'I know. Awful.'

'That's not what I meant. All this time, it was you. When I thought it was me.'

'Huh?'

'The story was that he'd fallen and hit his head, right?'

Hugh nodded. 'I was pretty scared, when he didn't come to. When I told Ma and Pa Fletcher I just blurted out that he'd fallen, then when the ambos arrived I said the same thing, and it was too late to take it all back.'

Jack said, 'So, earlier in the party, before it happened, I'd been drinking with that same kid. I got pretty drunk myself that night, as you all remember. And I kept handing him shots, pushing him to down them. And all this time, all these bloody years, I thought he fell over and knocked himself out because he got so drunk with the alcohol I had plied him with. But actually it wasn't that at all. So that's a huge bloody weight off my mind!'

'Well, glad I've helped someone, I suppose.' Hugh managed a sardonic smile. He looked around at his friends. 'Guys, I know it was awful, I know I really messed up.'

Jack looked at him, and his eyes narrowed. 'Let me guess. This is something that Ed knew, right?'

'Yeah. Ed told me later that he actually saw it happen. Saw me deny all knowledge, too.'

Jack nodded.

'Bloody Ed.' It just burst forth from Hugh's mouth before he could stop himself. 'No, really. Just like with you and the drugs.' Hugh nodded at Jack. 'Ed kept giving me the impression that he might dob on me about attacking that kid. Never quite in so many words, just kind of subtly implying it. Well, I'll say it: I think he enjoyed the power trip.'

'It's true.' Jack nodded. 'With me, he gave me the impression he was just checking in, just wanting me to stop doing the drugs, he was sure they weren't good for me. But there was always an implication behind it.'

Charlotte looked at Alex. 'And with you too – sounds like he had the same thing going, teasing you about the money?'

Alex blew his cheeks out then let out a breath. 'I suppose that's what was going on. He was kind of dangling his knowledge in front of me. "Don't worry, Alex, I won't say anything." But always leaving me wondering if he actually would.'

Hugh shook his head again. 'So we were, each of us, thinking that it couldn't really be that Ed was being an arsehole to us, 'cause he was such a nice guy, so popular. But if we'd compared notes, we would have seen the pattern.'

Hugh paused. 'Actually, dear old Ed could be a bit of a prick.'

Chapter 51

Darkness crept around the house. Night creatures began their lonely cries. The moon brightened and began its inexorable drift across the sky.

The friends were gathered in the kitchen. Alex, Jack and Hugh were picking at the scraps of food they had gathered for dinner.

'I've been thinking.' Alex cleared his throat. 'It's a bit cooler now. Could we think about, maybe, trying to walk out?'

A long silence.

'It's not as hot now as it was today.' Jack was staring out the window. 'But it's still warm. And we have even less water than we did this morning.'

'Gotta say the idea of getting the hell out of here sounds pretty good.' Hugh looked through the window, up towards the valley cliff tops, dimly outlined against the night sky. He imagined being up there instead of down here, and almost ran out the door there and then.

The others followed his eyes.

'I dunno.' Charlotte looked uncertain. 'It's still just as far. I'm really not sure I could make it. And now we have two walking wounded.' Charlotte waved at the bandages on Jack's leg and Alex's ankle. 'Could you two even make it down the driveway?'

'There's less chance of Martha shooting at us – it would be harder to see us in the dark.' Alex had tipped his head on his side.

'But more scary to be out there in the dark, with her lurking somewhere.' Charlotte wrinkled her forehead.

Another pause.

'Let's get some rest tonight. Gather our energy.' Jack sounded more certain now. 'We can get up early, and it'll be light, but not yet really hot. Maybe Alex and I will feel better after a night's sleep.'

It wasn't much of a plan, but it would have to do.

Hugh turned to Charlotte. In the dim yellow light, her face was drawn. 'You do look exhausted. Might be an idea to rest first.'

He could see her face soften as she turned to him. 'I am. But I'm not sure I could go to sleep. And, I mean, should we even go to bed? I feel like we should wait to see if something happens. What new horror might she have in store?'

Hugh wanted to say, what might *they* have in store. But there didn't seem any point in questioning further what Laura's role in this might be. Like Jack kept saying, where would it get them?

'We could keep a lookout, from the roof terrace,' said Jack. 'Take it in turns.'

Hugh nodded along with the others.

'I like the idea of being out in the fresh air as long as we can,' said Charlotte.

'Let's all go up there, to start with. If no one can sleep just yet,' said Jack. 'Reckon I could hobble up there. What about you, Alex?'

Alex nodded. 'Sure. Be good to get some fresh air.'

Upstairs, out on the terrace behind the low parapet, Hugh looked across the moonlit valley. Just like the previous evening, it was silvery grey under the star-scattered sky, but Hugh thought the past twenty-four hours had given the scene before them a very different feel. Now the black shadows of the gum trees seemed ominous. Every shift of air made Hugh want to check over his shoulder. The only good thing was that it was a bit cooler than during the day.

'I'm still nervous,' said Charlotte. She shuffled closer into Hugh.

'We're okay,' said Hugh. He squeezed her shoulders.

Today, out in that paddock, after the first shock of the gunshots, his next thought had been of Charlotte, and the relief of knowing she was safe back at the house. And it had felt so good, like a hit from a drug.

Actually, it was kind of nice now, the feel of her beneath his arm. The look of comfort that stole over her face as she snuggled in against him. He wasn't feeling that old irritation at what he used to think of as her neediness.

'What an insane day. I just can't believe it,' said Charlotte. 'I mean, Martha seemed kind of wired when we arrived yesterday afternoon. But if we'd had any idea what she was up to – my god, we would have turned around and run a mile.'

'The whole thing's nuts. What I just can't believe are those notes,' said Hugh. 'That's an extra level of crazy. That she sat there and wrote them out, planted them around the place.'

'Well . . .'

At the hesitant note in Jack's voice, Hugh turned. Surely the guy wasn't going to suggest it was somehow okay?

'No, I agree, it's crazy, but I do have to say something.' Jack looked serious. 'Hugh, I for one am actually so glad that you told us about that guy you hit, at the country party. You really helped me. All this time I've been feeling bad, thinking he hurt himself because I gave him too much to drink. So, there's one little silver lining. You've really taken a weight off my mind.'

'Well, you're welcome, I guess.' Hugh turned to Jack. 'But that's just something else for me to feel bad about. When it happened, I was too scared to own up. Then afterwards I thought I should just keep quiet, wouldn't make any difference, telling anyone.'

The discomfort pulled at him. 'But if I'd owned up years ago, it would actually have helped. I would have spared you.'

And if I hadn't bloody hit that kid at all, it would have been better still, Hugh thought. He might as well face it. The reason why he had got so angry and lashed out so hard at the kid at the party was because he suspected that what the other boy had said was in fact true. He was a wimp. He hated pain. And his tough-guy act was just that – an act to compensate for the cowardice that he feared was actually his defining feature.

Look at today. The horror of those moments when he had finally arrived back in the house, then realised that Alex was still out there, came flooding back. Try as he might, he simply had not been able to get up and run back outside again, towards those terrible gunshots.

But Jack had faced up to them, even with his sore leg. Bookish Jack had shown him up.

'Hey mate.' Hugh turned to Jack, cleared his throat. 'Got to say again. So impressed at how you went back to collect Alex. I – I couldn't do it. You were really brave. Well done.'

Jack turned away.

'No, really. Braver man than me.' Hugh felt tears pricking, blinked them away furiously.

'Just ran out there without thinking,' Jack said gruffly.

'Well I was very pleased to see you.' Alex tapped Jack's arm.

Then Hugh heard Charlotte, next to him, whisper, 'Hughie. It's okay. I'm glad you didn't go. Because you were right there, next to me, looking after me.' She snuggled closer still, and Hugh felt his face soften and his heart lighten just a little.

Jack looked at his friends' familiar faces, grey in the moonlight.

The past day – was it really just one day? – had been unbelievable. One mad discovery after another, their situation more and more frightening, the pressure ratcheting up as time passed and the heat gathered and no one woke up from their nightmare. Martha had clearly thought her disturbing plan through carefully, designing it to exert maximum pressure.

And it had worked. The tension in the group had skyrocketed until, one by one, they had each snapped in their own particular way, losing their temper, or blurting out their secret, or displaying their lack of fortitude.

But Jack could see that the stress was also tempering them; bringing out strengths they didn't know they had and drawing them closer than they had been in a long time – possibly ever.

He saw Charlotte tip her head to one side. She looked at him.

'You know, I was actually kind of pleased to hear your story too,' she said. 'What did you call them? Study drugs? I mean, the rest of us did drugs, all sorts, so I don't think drugs are like, wrong, obviously. But the fact that you took something "bad". And even dealt them yourself.' She smiled. 'It's just good to know you're human, like the rest of us.'

Jack saw Hugh and Alex grinning to themselves.

'It's true!' She nodded. 'Honestly, I've always felt a bit intimidated by you; you've always been so smart and successful. But, that you did something dodgy. It's kind of . . . reassuring.'

Alex nodded. 'I agree.'

Jack felt his eyes stinging a little. He pushed his glasses up his nose. 'I thought you'd all be disgusted. That I, well, cheated.'

'Nope.' Hugh slung an arm around Jack. 'You keep suggesting those drugs somehow made a difference, but I just don't believe that. Drugs or no drugs, you can't get away from it: you're a big brain. Always have been. But what we know now is that you're really one of us. Less than perfect.'

Jack felt a smile creep across his face, and relaxation stealing through his limbs, despite his sore leg. The tension that had been locked away inside him loosened a little. It was nice, really nice, actually; he did feel that bit closer to his friends now he'd opened up to them. He wondered whether things with Julie might work out a bit better if he could do the same with her.

And then Jack thought of that awful time in the kitchen earlier that day, the way he'd ignored his leg and swallowed his fear, and had run out to get Alex, and felt a new kind of strength beginning to solidify inside him. The heavy black cloud dissipated just a little.

Charlotte felt Alex stir next to her.

'Well, while we're on this –' Alex chewed his lip '– I am also glad I owned up about your money, Hugh. It's actually been a weight off my mind. You saying you forgive me for that.'

Hugh reached out and slapped Alex on the back. 'No worries, mate.' Then he rummaged in his pockets and a look of horror crossed over his face. 'Hey, wait. Where's my wallet?'

271

Charlotte saw Alex turn to Hugh, his face filled with alarm. Then Hugh burst out laughing and Alex's face relaxed.

'Got you!' Hugh chortled.

Alex's smile was somewhat forced, but after a moment he leaned back, with a softer expression.

Charlotte couldn't help thinking of her own confession, about sleeping with Ed at the country party and the internship thing. She wasn't as sure as the others that her confession had done her any good.

She shook her head. 'It's good that you two feel better now, Alex, Jack. But I'm not so delighted to have my little thing with Ed ripped out into the open.' She glanced at Hugh, but his face was neutral.

She took a breath. 'That I was so mean and unhelpful to him.' Her voice was wobbly. 'No one likes admitting to being a bitch.' She stared at the silvery countryside.

'Wait, Charlotte.' Alex touched her arm. 'I should have said this before. You know what struck me most about that story? It wasn't that you were somehow mean to Ed. It's not like he had some right to an internship at your dad's company or anything. He actually put you in a bit of an awkward position. What I was thinking was how you kept quiet afterwards, about sleeping with Ed. You could have boasted about Ed, like, as a conquest or something. But you kept it to yourself. Because you were being considerate of Laura.'

Charlotte paused. 'Of course.'

Alex shook his head. 'Not everyone would have done that. You were thinking of how she'd feel.'

'Yeah, too right.' Hugh rubbed at her arm. 'Probably don't say this enough, babe, but you really are such a nice person and . . . I love you.'

Charlotte blinked quickly. She turned to Hugh and pressed her face into his arm. And despite the spooky moonlit night and the thirst pulling at her throat and the whole horrifying day they had just staggered through, she felt a wash of comforting warmth.

For a long time they sat in silence, staring at the stars, thinking back over the day.

Then Jack cried, 'Hey, that star's moving!' But the plane was so far up, such a tiny flashing dot, no one even pretended to yell.

'Okay, how are we going to do this?' Hugh asked. 'I reckon we'd better keep watch, right? Don't want the old girl surprising us in our beds with her rifle.'

Jack nodded. 'You and me and Alex can take turns.'

'I'd argue, but I'm just too tired,' said Charlotte.

'I'm happy to do a later shift if you like; you can come wake me,' Jack offered. 'It's not like I'm going to sleep very well; my leg's still a bit sore.'

'There's a clear view around the house from up here. Perhaps we should do it in pairs; one looking either way,' said Hugh. 'Keep each other awake.'

'Good idea.' Jack nodded.

Alex said, 'Surely someone is going to notice we haven't answered our phones, no texts, nothing. Raise the alarm.'

'They'll probably assume there's no signal,' said Hugh, gloomily. 'I don't know about you, but Charl and me were telling people how remote this place is.'

'And not hearing from someone on their weekend away is hardly enough to send out a search party,' said Charlotte. 'For all they know we're enjoying country cooking and soaking up the peace and quiet.'

'They'll notice when we don't turn up to work on Monday.'

They went quiet. No one wanted to be waiting at the house still by the time they were due back at work. The idea was unthinkable.

'We are getting out of here before then.' Jack stood up carefully. His voice was rigid with determination. 'We sleep; we'll be up early; things will look different tomorrow.'

Chapter 52

For a few seconds, after she woke and before she opened her eyes, Charlotte forgot where she was. She was back in her own place with Hugh. When he got up to open the curtains, she'd see the leaves in the tree just outside their bedroom window. She thought of the baby growing inside her and smiled.

But then the events of the previous day flooded in with all their dread and stress and her eyes flicked open. Sure enough, there was the diamond-pattern wallpaper of their room in the Fletcher house. They had now been stranded in this bloody place for a whole twenty-four hours.

Light was just starting to edge between the curtains. Charlotte became aware of the hard mattress and the musty smell of the sheets. And, try though she might to slip around the thought, she was also aware of how thirsty she was.

She looked at the side table. There were a few centimetres of water left in her glass next to the bed. She remembered the four of them sharing out the water last night. The others had insisted she take more than her share. She tried to resist drinking it now, knowing she should ration it out, but then she snatched up the glass before she could stop herself, and took a big sip.

Her head hurt a little. She put a hand to her stomach. Thirst was definitely not good for the baby. She tried not to think about that.

Hugh was still asleep. She sat up, swung her legs around, then stood. She needed to eat.

When she walked into the kitchen, she saw Alex standing near the toaster. He was frowning but, when he saw her, he summoned up a smile. 'You hungry too?'

'I'm always hungry these days.'

The toaster pinged and ejected two slices. Alex started spreading jam.

Jack appeared at the doorway, rubbing his face. He looked exhausted. He limped across to the table, took a seat and winced slightly.

'Your leg hurting?'

'It's okay. It must have been just a puncture, no venom, or I'd be feeling much worse.'

Hugh arrived. His hair was sticking up around his face, which was creased and tense. He went straight to the coffee machine, then stopped. 'Of course. No water. Look, bugger it, I'm going to use a bit.'

Hugh took one of the bottles then and tipped some into the coffee maker.

'Hey, go easy on that, mate,' said Jack.

'Call it my allowance,' said Hugh, without turning around.

Charlotte glanced at Jack and Alex and shook her head slightly.

The four friends sat around the table, chewing at their toast in silence, the remaining water bottles gathered in the middle. Almost empty.

God, the tension was going to kill them before the thirst did. They needed something to do; something to focus their minds.

Then Charlotte noticed the rubbish bin of papers she had brought down from the study yesterday. She had just started to go through it when they'd realised that Laura had disappeared.

The bin was stuffed to the brim. Charlotte pulled out the top layer. Martha didn't seem to have emptied it for a long time; the papers were jammed together hard, like they were about to form sedimentary rock.

Bills, shop receipts, scrap paper screwed into balls. Medical notes, old envelopes and letters. Strips torn from newspapers, turning yellow. It was all in there together. She settled into sorting them.

Hugh cleared his throat. 'So, guys. We've had our rest. We have to face this. We'll have to walk out. There's no other way.' He lifted his chin. 'And if we're going to do it, might as well be now. It's only going to get warmer.'

This was greeted with silence. Charlotte looked outside. The morning sun was very low. The air wasn't cool, but it was way less hot than during the day. She turned again to the papers. That task was way simpler than this decision.

'Perhaps someone will come.' Alex sounded like he was trying to convince himself. 'If we're not back at work tomorrow, someone will raise the alarm.'

'We've been through this.' Jack's tone was reasonable. 'We don't work together. Will our bosses really put everything together? Or will your boss, or Hugh's boss or anyone's boss just assume we're having a sickie? Let it go a few days and then look into it?'

'And even then they would have to figure out where we actually are. Which is in the middle of nowhere.' Hugh waved out the window.

Charlotte knew that it would take a long time for people to find them. They couldn't stay here and rely on that. But to head outside now, across that landscape, walk all that way up? It was an impossible choice.

She focused in on sorting out the bin and let the discussion drift away to become a background noise, Hugh, Jack and Alex's voices interplaying like a tennis match, back and forth. Back and forth.

From time to time Charlotte would come across a greeting card and glance in it idly.

Then more bills, more papers, more cards. She let her eyes wander across the writing, and a sense arose of the loneliness of Martha's existence, out here in the middle of the bushland on this isolated farm by herself.

But then Charlotte grew still. The cards, letters and records were starting to coalesce into a story.

A somewhat disturbing story.

'Ah, guys.' Charlotte looked up. 'You might want to take a look at these.'

Chapter 53

Documents retrieved from Martha Fletcher's rubbish bin

Extract of letter from Patricia Forrester to Martha Fletcher

. . . I apologise again for dropping in unannounced; I could tell you weren't happy when I first arrived, but I had gotten so worried when all my calls went unanswered and I really wanted to see you. Thank you for the tea and don't worry at all about the cake; the weather has been very humid lately and it doesn't take much for mould to develop.

I know you'll hate me commenting, Martha dear, but I do have to say how concerned I am about you and Robert, living out there on the farm together. It doesn't have to be said that it's hard for the two of you after what happened with poor Ed and I know you said you like being there because it reminds you of him but on the other hand it really is very lonely.

I have to say that I could see the tension between you and Robert. It was obvious straight away and again it's not surprising but it can be a bad idea to let that kind of thing run on and I do wonder again whether you two might consider seeing someone? My niece and her partner found this lovely lady and they only went to a few sessions and she gave them such useful things to consider . . .

Card from James Fletcher to Robert Fletcher with the cover art 'Happy birthday to a dear brother'

Dear Bob

Happy birthday.

From Jim

PS. Thanks for the call. Great to hear from you after all this time. Sorry to hear Martha's not well. Could the doc help?

Letter from Dr Phyllis Simpson to Dr Frank Walker, cc to Martha Fletcher

Dear Dr Walker

Thank you for referring Martha Fletcher to me for consideration of adjustment of medication.

I regret to inform you that Mrs Fletcher did not attend the agreed appointment and all attempts by my office to contact Mrs Fletcher have failed.

Perhaps you could inquire directly with Mrs Fletcher.

Kind regards

Phyllis Simpson

Fellow of the Royal Australian and New Zealand College of Psychiatrists

Letter from Robert Fletcher, handwriting very messy, sealed in an envelope addressed to James Fletcher but not stamped, and screwed up in a ball

I can't bear it I can't bear it, it was awful I had no idea he felt like that and now he's dead he's dead he's dead my boy

We finally read the diary they found in his backpack and he'd said all this stuff about me

And Marthas so angry she keeps saying it was my fault he died although I cant see how it was my fault I was nowhere near him when he died and he was happy when they set out they all were and he wouldn't have chosen to die of thirst its an awful way to go

All those things he said about me that I was cold and angry its awful that's what I used to think about the old man he was such a bastard and I didn't think I was like that

You remember he used to hit us and tell us we were useless and I never did that to Ed not once

I was going to be a different father to the old man I was determined

But Martha said I made Ed unhappy and now he's dead and gone and I cant make it up to him now Id do anything to have him back

I'm so ashamed

Card from James Fletcher to Robert Fletcher

Dear Bob

Very sorry to miss your call. Ellen said you sounded upset. Tried to call you back a few times.

Hoping you're still getting the post.

Call me back when you can mate.

Jim

Torn newspaper extracts from **Nanganook Gazette**

INVESTIGATION UNDER WAY AFTER MAN'S BODY WAS LOCATED AT A LOCAL PROPERTY

Police are investigating the death of a man at a farm in Lost Valley.

About 9 a.m. yesterday police were called to the farm, following a call to 000.

On arrival, officers found the body of a man in his late fifties in one of the farm buildings. He had a gunshot wound to the head.

The man is believed to be one of the owners of the farm.

A crime scene has been established and detectives and specialist forensic officers from Nanganook Area Command are investigating.

Anyone with information about this incident is urged to contact . . .

WIFE OF DEAD MAN RELEASED WITHOUT CHARGE

The wife of a man found dead at his Lost Valley farm has been released after she was questioned by police.

Police discovered the man, in his late fifties, after they attended the farm following a call to 000.

The man had a gunshot wound to the head.

Early this morning, police arrested the man's wife and took her to Nanganook police station for questioning but she was later released without charge.

Police said early inquiries indicate the death is suspicious but it will require detailed post-mortem testing to reveal if he was the victim of homici . . .

DEATH OF LOCAL MAN REMAINS SUSPICIOUS

Police have confirmed they will not proceed with a prosecution in relation to the death of local man Robert Fletcher, due to insufficient evidence.

Fletcher's body was discovered two months ago at a property in Lost Valley in which he lived with his wife Martha Fletcher. He had sustained gunshot wounds to the head.

Martha Fletcher was arrested by police following the discovery of his body but was later released without charge.

Martha and Robert Fletcher were the parents of Ed Fletcher, who died in 2007 while on a hike with his friends in the neighbouring national park.

Three months ago Coroner Jane Warburg of the Glebe Coroner's Court gave an open verdict on Robert Fletcher's death. She found there was insufficient evidence to refer the matter for prosecution, citing significant ambiguity as to who fired the shot that killed Robert Fletcher. 'It is not open to me to determine whether Robert Fletcher's death was accident, homicide or suicide.'

It is understood that Martha Fletcher continues to insist her husband's death was suicide.

Chapter 54

Jack, Hugh, Alex and Charlotte stared at the papers.

'Martha *killed* Robert?' Alex's voice was a whisper.

'I bet she did it.' Hugh shook his head. 'She's clearly cracked.'

'Not necessarily.' Jack's face was tense as he pointed to one of the papers. 'Look at what Robert said to his brother. He was so ashamed of himself. God knows what Ed put in that diary that Robert and Martha eventually got around to reading. So it could have been suicide.'

Charlotte thought Jack sounded like he was trying to convince himself.

Jack went on, 'Or could have been an accident.'

'Looks like they just couldn't find enough evidence.' Charlotte screwed up her face. 'Perhaps the police are still investigating.' A thought occurred to her. 'Perhaps they're keeping an eye on Martha – perhaps they'll come visit.'

'Nice idea,' said Jack. 'But we can't rely on that.'

'Let's not beat around the bush.' Hugh was looking grim. 'This is bad; even worse than we thought. She was arrested. She might have killed Robert. The woman's really dangerous. She's probably not that bothered at the idea of leaving us here with no water to . . . well, to run out of water.'

Jack took a breath. 'It's pretty clear what we have to do, right?'

Three faces turned towards him.

Jack's voice was strangely calm. 'We have to tell Martha. About what really happened. On the walk with Ed. Give her what she wants; what she's wanted all this time. Then maybe she'll let us out.'

There was a very long silence.

Charlotte felt a wave of anxiety. 'But she's so disturbed. She shot at us. Now this business with Robert; that's a real worry. Telling her may make her even more angry.'

Jack turned to her. 'What's the alternative? Wait here until we die of thirst? I think we've tried everything. There's no phone, no radio. We laid the sign outside, but there are no planes.'

His voice was calm and measured. 'I've been thinking. Perhaps we should look at it a bit differently.' He took a breath. 'We all ended up sharing a few little secrets yesterday. And it seemed to me last night that we were all thinking that it was kind of helpful, in the end.

'So, maybe telling Martha will help. Not make her worse.'

Jack paused. 'And then there's Laura. We don't know what she's up to, whether she's in trouble too. But, whether I'm biased or not, I think we owe it to her to give her the benefit of the doubt. We need to press Martha into some kind of discussion. If Laura is in trouble, that's our best way of helping her, too. We can't just up and leave.'

Charlotte opened her mouth and closed it again. Hanging in the air between them was the memory of the last time they had left a friend behind. Charlotte looked between Alex and

Hugh. Hugh was staring thoughtfully at Jack. Alex was shaking his head.

Alex stood up. 'No. We can't tell her.' He began to pace across the kitchen, his bandaged ankle making him limp slightly. 'We don't know how she'll react, what she might do.' He went on, as though talking to himself more than anyone.

Jack kept quiet. Smart Jack, thought Charlotte, letting Alex walk it out.

Eventually Alex slowed. Jack turned to him, then looked back at Hugh and Charlotte.

Charlotte moved her head, nodding gradually. She saw Hugh do the same. Then Alex sighed and finally he also nodded. He looked terribly uncomfortable.

'When?' asked Hugh.

Jack sat forward and put both hands on the table. 'Right now.'

'How will we . . .?'

'We'll try the two-way radio.'

A few minutes later, they were all gathered around the small black box.

Jack pressed the button. 'Martha. Hello, Martha, are you there?'

There was a long silence. Charlotte realised she was holding her breath, then let it out. Jack tried again, then again.

Charlotte felt her hands shaking and sat down. After all the stress of the decision, was this not even going to work?

As the others kept trying to reach Martha, she stood again and went to the window. After ten minutes, the room fell silent once more.

Then the radio suddenly crackled. A voice barked. 'What?'

Charlotte felt a spurt of adrenaline.

Jack cleared his throat. 'Martha? Is that you?' He took a breath. 'It's Jack and Hugh, Charlotte and Alex. We've got something we want to say to you.' He paused.

'Yes?'

'We want to tell you about the walk. What happened, with Ed.'

An even longer silence.

'You all ready to be honest, this time?'

'Yes, Martha.'

'You'd better not be messing with me.'

'No, we're not. We're ready to tell you everything.'

'Right. I'm coming.'

Then there was silence. Jack tried to keep the conversation going, but there was no answering talk.

'Crap. Is she actually coming here?' Hugh asked. 'Wait. Where's she coming from? We'd better watch out for her.'

Charlotte felt her stomach shift. 'She's got that damned gun.'

'We'll keep a lookout.' Jack's voice was still calm. 'I'll lock the front door. Then, Alex, you and I can look out the sitting room window towards the side. Hugh can wait here with Charlotte and watch out the back. She's most likely to come that way, from the pump house.'

Charlotte stood next to the kitchen window. She held Hugh's hand. The cool air of the early morning had already begun to dissipate now the sun had appeared above the cliffs. Outside there was a faint whirring noise as the insects started up.

She scanned the paddocks, but there was no little figure.

Hugh let out a humourless laugh. 'Perhaps we've got it all wrong. Maybe she'll drop in by helicopter.'

But then Charlotte clutched Hugh and pointed. 'There she is!'

There was movement at the top of the hill in the direction of the pump house. A black shape detached from the group of trees. It was moving. Hugh called to Alex and Jack, and in a moment they all stood in the kitchen.

The figure moved towards them across the paddock.

Charlotte's blood was thumping in her ears. She took a slow breath.

'Definitely her.' Jack's voice was tense.

The figure kept moving towards them at a steady pace.

But then Alex said, 'Oh, Christ. She's got the rifle.'

Charlotte could hear the others' intake of breath.

'It's over her shoulder.' Hugh spoke lightly.

He was right, the long black line was at least pointed up and back away from them.

Jack pressed at the radio button. 'Martha. Hello.'

They saw Martha raise her other arm. The radio crackled. Her voice, in the room again, a single syllable. 'What?'

'Martha, we're nervous about that gun you've got. How about you leave it out there?'

But the figure just dropped her hand and kept walking, and the radio remained silent.

Hugh took a long breath. 'Okay, so there's Martha.' He paused. 'But where's Laura?'

Chapter 55

One day previously

Laura stood in the doorway of the pump house, her eyes fixed on the ominous black line of the gun that was leaning against the far wall.

'Laura. I'm disappointed. I really expected so much better of you.' Martha shook her head and rose to her feet.

She took a couple of steps towards Laura.

Martha followed the line of Laura's gaze towards the weapon, then turned back and said, 'Oh, don't worry about that. I just brought it in case of dingoes.'

That didn't sound right to Laura. Why would you need a gun for a dingo? But she was happy that it was staying against the wall.

'Oh, my dear.' Martha's face shifted. 'Sit down. We'll have a good talk.' Martha turned and scrabbled in a bag near the wall. She withdrew a Thermos and a couple of mugs.

'I've got coffee.' Martha gave a gay laugh. 'Have to keep myself going out here.' She waved at the bench that lined one of the walls. 'Sit down, rest. It's hot.'

Laura perched cautiously on the edge of the bench. She would have to approach this very carefully.

Martha poured out some liquid from the Thermos and handed Laura a mug.

'Look, Martha. The walk—'

'Oh, let's leave all that for the moment. You and I haven't had a chance to have a proper catch-up since you got here. Tell me, how have you been? It's a tough time for you.'

Laura stopped. So Martha wanted to chat. That was fine; she could do some small talk for a while, perhaps soften Martha up before returning to the topic of the walk. She took a breath.

'I've been okay. Been seeing the doctor regularly.' She started off on her well-worn spiel about her treatment.

The minutes ticked on as the two women talked.

After a while, Laura blinked. She peered into her coffee cup, but it was empty. The coffee wasn't working. She felt more tired, not less.

Martha looked at Laura with concern. 'You look so tired.'

Laura felt a slight giddiness. 'Yeah, I don't feel great.' She tried a smile. She really did feel very weary. Her eyelids were so heavy.

Martha said, 'How about you lie down for a moment?'

No, that wasn't a good idea. She'd come here for a very important purpose, and she had to get on with it. If she could only remember exactly what it was that she needed to talk to Martha about. 'But what about . . .?' Laura was having trouble forming her words. Her tongue felt thick and heavy.

'Never mind about that now. I really think you'd better lie down.'

She saw Martha reach for her arm, and she started to kneel to the ground, before the ringing in her ears grew louder, the ground rushed up at her, and everything went black.

Chapter 56

Hugh stood with Alex, Jack and Charlotte at the kitchen window, watching Martha's every move as she walked towards them. He was transfixed.

Now she was crossing the home paddock. She was at the gate. And then she was walking across the yard. She had a bag slung over her shoulder. She passed their help sign without a glance.

It seemed like she was moving in slow motion. The early-morning light caught her grey hair as she moved, creating a halo.

The rifle was resting over her shoulder, the barrel pointed up and away. That was something, at least. She stepped up on to the back veranda.

Hugh took a careful breath. She was mere metres away. He was shocked by her appearance, which had changed dramatically since Friday evening. The muscles of her face seemed to have moved in all different directions. Her hair was wild and her eyes were wide open, as if facing an ongoing shock.

She stared at each of them in turn, as though committing their faces to memory. Her jaw was tight. He noticed the fast rise and fall of her chest and his own adrenaline moved up a notch.

She gazed at them through the glass, and they all gazed back.

He took a step closer to his friends. His heart was hammering and his throat was dry.

Hugh heard Jack speak. 'Martha. Put the gun down. Please.' His voice wavered a little.

Martha stared back at them, her face set.

'Come on, Martha. It's just us. We'll all talk about this calmly.'

Eventually she spoke. 'No. I don't think so. Four of you, one of me.'

'Martha, we're really worried. I mean, yesterday you shot at us.'

She moved her hand as if to wave away his words. 'Don't be silly. I wasn't going to hit you. But you were trying to leave the house. I couldn't let you leave, not before you had been honest with me.'

She moved, and Hugh heard his friends' intake of breath with his own, but she was just pacing up and down on the veranda boards.

'Well, you won't escape now. So, I'll come in.'

'Sure. Come in. We'll talk.' Jack had slipped into the role of negotiator. 'But put the gun down first.'

'Open the door.'

She moved the rifle from her shoulder, and Hugh stepped back in unison with the others. He heard Charlotte gasp next to him.

'Martha. Please.' It was Jack again.

Then she popped the bolt on the weapon. She put it back over her shoulder. 'Now I'll come in.'

Jack kept his eyes on Martha but murmured out of the side of his mouth. 'I think that's the best we can do. We could get to her before she has time to fire it.'

'Open the door. Then move backwards. All of you.' Martha sounded determined.

Jack nodded slowly. He moved forward, unlatched the door and pulled it inwards. Then he stepped carefully backwards, along with the others.

Martha stepped in through the doorway.

Chapter 57

One hour earlier

Laura opened her eyes. She was lying on her back. There was a hard surface underneath her body, although her head was resting on something soft.

She stared, confused, at the rough wood beams above her, the brick walls on all sides. Dim light pushed through a small window. Where on earth was she?

Her head hurt. It was hard to think straight. Short, disjointed images started to return to her. Then she remembered.

The pump house. She had walked out here to talk to Martha. She had told Martha the real story of the walk. She had done the thing that had been dragging at her for so long.

And then Martha had become so very angry. Again.

Martha's anger had always been unfair. Her resentment that Ed had not survived the bush walk had always been directed at Hugh, Charlotte, Alex and Jack, but very clearly not at Laura. It was important to remember that this was unfair, because Laura believed everyone should try to be fair, in life.

But still, Martha's position had been hard to resist. It had actually felt pretty good, because if Martha was angry at the others but not her, a little voice kept arguing, surely it meant she, Laura, didn't need to feel guilty; that she was still a good person? Laura desperately wanted to believe that was the case.

Lying now in the pump house, Laura rubbed her head. After she had spoken to Martha, had unburdened herself, and Martha had started shouting, Laura had come in here and sat down, and – and then everything had gone dark.

The coffee. Had Martha *drugged* her?

She went to sit up, but a wave of pain washed across her forehead, and she leaned back. She let a minute or two pass, took another slow breath, then rolled onto her side.

Slowly she rose to a sitting position. The building was empty.

'Martha.' Her voice was croaky. She tried again, more loudly, but no one appeared.

Carefully, she got to her feet, swallowing against her nausea. She sat on the bench for a moment, calling again.

There was a bottle of water on the floor, next to where she had been lying, and she reached for it but then stopped, remembering the coffee.

Laura took a slow breath. Martha was so disturbed. It was important to keep seeing the older woman clearly, to resist her beliefs.

Because, deny it though Laura might, there was another attraction in Martha's anger.

Deep down, beneath the layers of logical reasoning, beneath her determination to do the right thing, Laura felt the same way as Martha.

She too could not shake the belief that it was the fault of Alex, Charlotte, Jack and Hugh that her Ed, her dear Ed, had died.

The fact was, she too was angry – furiously, blood-thumpingly angry – at the four people she wanted to believe were her friends.

She always made sure to quash this poisonous thought with vigour when it appeared. Anger was a destructive and divisive emotion. And this was a terrible belief. Most of the time she was able to push it away and deny it, but in her weakest moments, the anger came roaring back, undeniable, a powerfully addictive stimulant.

Now she stood. These feelings were so uncomfortable, so wrong; she must put them away. One hand on the wall, she carefully made her way to the door.

The valley was in front of her, the grasses waving in a gentle shift of air. The cliffs looked down on all sides. But something didn't seem right.

The light was different, that was it. She was sure it was quite different than when she had arrived. But it really didn't make sense – because it seemed *earlier* than when she had walked out here, not later. What on earth was the time? How long had she been here? Surely she hadn't slept through a whole night?

She called again to Martha, but there was no answer, no figure appearing in the surrounding paddock.

She turned back to the inside of the hut. She frowned. There was something missing.

She stared across the hut to the opposite wall, to the place where, she was sure, that bloody gun had been sitting when she arrived.

It wasn't there now.

And where on earth was Martha?

Laura remembered again the story she had told Martha, and then another memory slotted into place. The red drink bottle that Martha had produced. The reason why Martha had become so angry and claimed that Laura was still not being honest.

And then Laura remembered the particular scene from the walk with Ed that had come back to her so vividly at the sight of the red bottle. The person who had been fiddling with Ed's bag.

Laura turned and, with a stumbling gait that gradually grew faster, set out across the paddock towards the house.

Chapter 58

Martha stepped into the room and looked from face to face. Here they were before her, Ed's friends, finally penitent.

'Martha.' Jack's voice was firmer now. 'We—'

But she cut him off. 'I've been quite sure, all along, you know. That you weren't being honest. I could tell.' Her voice was loud and fast.

She paused. None of them moved a muscle.

'I invited you here, to my home. I thought we could talk properly, even have a nice weekend. I gave you every chance to own up, over dinner. If you had only been big enough to say, to consider just for a moment what I was going through, and to give me the truth. To show some sort of regret.'

Martha glared. Silence.

'But you wouldn't, even now when all these years have passed and you're safe in your new lives.

'And then after dinner, in the kitchen – you were actually laughing! Laughing, on the anniversary of my boy's death.

'I knew then. You weren't going to just tell me. You needed

299

to suffer, like Ed suffered. To be scared. To be thirsty. To have no one to help you.

'So, I did what I had planned.'

She paused again. God, you are all so full of secrets. You couldn't even be honest with each other. Anything from your past that you didn't want to share, you kept to yourselves, no matter how it affected other people.

'And even when I asked you again, even after you were trapped, you still wouldn't talk! When all you had to do was tell me the truth.

'But you've had time to think about that now, haven't you? To practise being honest with each other about all those little secrets, to talk to each other properly.'

Staring at Ed's friends, she lifted her chin. 'And now you're ready to talk to me.'

Four faces nodded, their eyes wide.

Martha dropped her bag to the ground but kept hold of the gun.

They had been lying to her all this time; she knew it. She knew they were to blame for her son's death. And now she was almost there; she was about to get the truth; to experience that sweet relief.

She spoke loudly and clearly. 'On the walk. Ten years ago. With Ed.' She slowed, so there was a pause between each word. 'What really happened?'

Hugh opened his mouth to speak. Alex and Charlotte also started to talk. Their words poured out, tumbling over each other.

Then Jack held his hand up.

'Martha. We'll tell you. But what you have to understand is, by the time it happened, we were already totally beside ourselves.'

300

Chapter 59

Ten years previously

'Can we hold up for a moment?' Charlotte stopped and heaved a sigh.

Ed turned. 'Of course,' he said but, because he was tired, he couldn't keep the impatience from his voice.

The narrow track they had been following had opened out into a rocky clearing, bushes pressing in on all sides, and a high ceiling of tree crowns above. A massive turpentine tree stood to one side, over a metre in diameter, the trunk covered in furry bark.

The rest of the group threaded into the clearing, fanning themselves. Ed could see all their faces were red and their foreheads were creased with tension. They began to swing their packs down. Nobody spoke. The air was warm and still. The sun burned around the shadows. Cicadas strung out their long, ratcheting cries.

Charlotte dumped her pack with an angry thud and dropped down to sit on a rock. She set her teeth together. 'I wish you'd bloody well got that water source right, Ed,' she said under her breath.

'What was that?'

'I said—'

'I heard you.' He glared at her. He could hardly trust himself to speak. 'Yes, thank you, Charlotte. You and me and all of us.'

'And my foot is killing me.' Her voice was tight and irritable.

Ed breathed out sharply and kicked at a bush. Was he supposed to fix her foot as well as find the water? His own heel was beginning to sing with the beginning of a blister. 'Oh, treat it as life experience, Charlotte. A rare opportunity for you to be slightly uncomfortable.' Ed knew he shouldn't talk like that, but the words just rushed out, his voice straining with sarcasm.

'What's that supposed to mean?'

'I mean, we're all uncomfortable. We're all thirsty. We're all tired and sore.' Ed was sick of feeling the resentment radiating off his friends. Having a go at Charlotte was providing long overdue relief. 'And you're sounding just a bit like a poor little rich girl.' He definitely shouldn't have said that either, but again, it just came out.

Charlotte stood, her face furious. 'You're not too proud to brown nose this "rich girl". The famous Ed charm, deployed to get what you want.'

How dare she? Charlotte had been completely enjoying herself when he'd asked her about an internship with her father. He bet it was because they'd got together at the country party and then he hadn't pursued her afterwards. 'Don't give me that! You were playing with me.'

Charlotte's chest was heaving as she glared at him. Alex stepped forward. 'Hey, guys. How about everyone take a breath?'

Ed felt more tension rise. Great, Alex was going to do his peacemaker routine, making Ed look bad. His eyes still fixed on Charlotte, Ed said tightly, 'We don't need your help, Alex.'

'I'm just saying—'

'I said, we don't need your help.' Ed turned to Alex, glaring. He tipped his head sideways. 'Saintly Alex. Lovely Alex, kind Alex. You're so good, aren't you?' His eyes narrowed. 'Don't you want everyone to know exactly how good you are?' His voice was heavy with meaning. If Alex wasn't careful, he'd tell everyone about how he'd stolen that money from Hugh. Let them understand what kind of a saint he actually was.

Alex reared back as though Ed had hit him.

'Hey, steady on there, mate,' said Hugh, looking warily at Ed.

Ed felt a rush of shame, which only made him more angry. He shouldn't have said that, either. But it was too late now. 'I guess no one's perfect.' His voice was still sarcastic. 'Not even me.'

'I think we're all realising that,' said Hugh.

'And what's that supposed to mean?' Ed's energy leapt up again, and he turned to Hugh.

'What do you think it means?' Hugh's face was tense. 'Why are we in this bloody mess? You were in charge. You were so sure of the bloody route. Like Charlotte said, if that creek at our campsite was so important for us, you should have been one hundred per cent sure that it was always reliable.'

Ed had been thinking exactly that, ever since the moment they had laid eyes on the dry creek bed the previous evening.

Now he was seriously anxious about the safety of the group, of his friends. That horrible question kept popping up in his mind:

would they actually make it out of here? And if they didn't, it would be his fault. To protect him from this unbearable thought, his anger came rushing in again.

'All my fault, huh? At least I'm being a real leader. Something you've never been.' His aggression rose up in a hot surge. He'd wipe that look off Hugh's face. He stepped towards him. 'The great sportsman Hugh, always handy with a shoulder tackle. But not so handy with making the hard decisions. Nothing that takes real courage.'

Hugh stepped up towards Ed, sticking his chin out. 'Say that again.' His voice was low.

'Yeah, that's right, square up. That's what you're known for. Being a great big thug. Go on, hit me. That's your greatest skill, after all. You coward.'

The next instant Hugh pulled his fist back and swung it towards Ed. It landed on his jaw.

The pain was astonishing. Ed staggered backwards for a moment. But then his adrenaline kicked in and he ran back at Hugh. Hugh was just pulling his arm back to punch Ed again when Jack and Alex leapt forward.

Jack grabbed Hugh and Alex pinned Ed's arms to his sides.

'Fuck's sake, *stop*!' Jack bellowed.

Ed struggled against Alex's grip. But then he stilled and shook off Alex's arms. He could see Hugh doing the same with Jack. The clearing was silent, but for the sound of panting breath.

Charlotte and Laura stood frozen.

Laura jerked into movement. She hurried to Ed, still limping with her sore ankle, and put her hand to his jaw. She stared into his eyes, her face creased with concern. He looked into her eyes. Those beautiful eyes.

Chapter 60

Ten years previously

Jack was on the other side of the clearing, watching. He couldn't take his eyes off Laura and the expression on her face as she gazed at Ed.

A sinking feeling gripped his stomach, as little incidents from the past couple of days started to click into place. Her coolness as he tried to take her hand. Her choice of tent. Ed rushing forward when she hurt her foot, as though it were his job to look after her.

Ed and Laura were oblivious. Laura was murmuring gently to Ed; he was staring back at her.

Jack tried to speak but his voice wasn't working. Then he managed, 'Laura? What the hell?'

Eventually, Ed turned to him. But Laura was still looking at Ed.

Jack's voice wavered. 'Laura? What's going on?'

Laura finally seemed to notice Jack. She pulled her hands from Ed's face and turned. Her eyes immediately dropped to the ground.

Jack turned to Alex, Hugh and Charlotte, as though the answer lay with them. The only one who met his eye was Charlotte.

Jack's face hardened. 'Laura? His voice was louder. He stepped quickly across the clearing, stood right in front of her. 'Are you kidding me? Are you and Ed . . .?'

She was still looking at the ground. She let out a small sigh.

He reached out and brought her chin up gently so she had to look at him. When he saw her expression, his face darkened even more.

'Is it true?' Each word was a stone.

'Jack, we—' Laura tried to speak, but Jack dropped his hand and turned to Ed.

His voice was slow and deliberate. 'You fucking arsehole.'

The guy was meant to be his best mate. With his girlfriend.

Jack brought his fist forward and landed a punch hard in Ed's face. As the impact sounded across the clearing, the others gasped.

Jack and Ed were clenched together. Jack heard shouting, felt Ed's body under his fists, felt blows landing on his own body.

Laura and Charlotte both shrieked. Hugh and Alex were hovering, trying to get in to break up the fight.

Then Jack landed another heavy blow on the side of Ed's face, and Ed staggered sideways and fell on the ground.

Jack stood over him. 'Get up! You piece of shit!'

Ed's chest was heaving. He hauled himself to his feet. His face was red and contorted, his lower jaw thrust forward, his teeth bared. He let out a long slow groan of fury. He glared at Jack, then Hugh, Alex and Charlotte.

'Fuck you!' Ed bellowed. He struggled to speak. 'Fuck you all!' He staggered backwards. He picked up his pack, swung it

over his shoulder, then stumbled from the clearing and, in a
limping run, disappeared along the path.

Chapter 61

Ten years previously

The sound of Ed stomping away along the path, his pack bashing against bushes, quickly faded.

The fury and adrenaline that had surged within Hugh, overtaking him like a cloud of hot gas, had dropped away. He was aware of the pain on his knuckles. He could hear the rasping breath of his other friends. And with the return of his senses had come the old weight of regret and shame. He'd lost control, yet again.

He kicked his foot against a rock and ripped at a branch that hung in his face. 'Goddamn it!'

Alex's face was twisted in anxiety. Jack still looked furious, his chest heaving, his fists clenched at his sides. No wonder – what a thing to find out about your girlfriend. With your best mate.

Laura was weeping. Charlotte stood with her hands on her mouth.

Jack turned to Laura. 'Are you really serious that this—?'

'Jack.' Laura drew a long shuddering breath. 'I know you're angry. Of course you're angry. But can we please not do this right now? It's not going to help. We're all exhausted, we're all thirsty.' She threw the words out through heaving breaths.

Jack's voice rose. 'When would be a good time to talk, then? When exactly were you planning to talk?'

Laura collapsed onto a rock and put her face in her hands. Her weeping grew louder.

Hugh put a hand on Jack's shoulder. 'Maybe give it a bit?'

'You can talk!' Jack threw Hugh's arm off and stomped to the other side of the clearing.

The bush noises began to creep back into the thick silence.

After some minutes had passed, Alex looked around. 'Ed's taking his time.'

'He'll be back soon.' Hugh pursed his lips.

Laura stood up. 'Ed!' she shouted. 'Come back. We'll sort it out.' After a moment she said, 'I'm going after him.'

'We can't all go running off into the bush.' Hugh made an effort to keep his voice firm. 'Give it a bit longer. He'll be back.'

She looked at him then sank back down again.

Another ten minutes of silence.

Laura stood up again and bellowed. 'Ed!'

Alex looked at Hugh. 'Hey, maybe a few of us should . . .?'

Hugh paused, then nodded. 'Okay. You and me. You wait here.' Hugh gestured at Charlotte and Laura.

'I'm coming too.' Laura stood.

'No, you stay here in case Ed returns. That way you can keep the weight off your ankle.' Hugh turned to the others. It would be best if Jack did not come across Ed without someone else there too. 'Jack and I can go that way. Alex can go towards that ridge. Now, check the time. Back here in no more than thirty

309

minutes. That's the sun. Keep it on the same side of you. Don't bloody get lost yourself. Stick to the track.'

Hugh, Jack and Alex set off, leaving their big packs with Laura and Charlotte.

Hugh made his way along the path with urgent steps, scanning the grey-green bush. Jack was right behind him. But, shout though they might, there was no answering call from Ed. No coloured pack visible through the leaves.

Hugh checked his watch. They'd have to return. He turned to Jack, who hadn't said a word during the whole search. He just nodded and followed Hugh.

When Hugh and Jack returned to the clearing without Ed, Hugh saw Charlotte and Laura's faces fall.

Laura slumped. She wrapped her arms around her torso. 'Oh god. I can't bear it. What if he's hurt?'

'He's probably just still pissed off.' Hugh tried to relax his own tense features.

'And where's Alex?' Laura turned to look along the path.

Yes, where the bloody hell was Alex? Trust him to get himself lost too.

Hugh was more relieved than he wanted to admit when they heard footsteps and Alex appeared in the clearing.

Alex dropped his day pack to the ground and collapsed, his face against his knees.

Charlotte patted his back. 'You did your best.'

Alex just shook his head, his face still buried.

The sun moved slowly overhead as they waited. The shadows crept across the dirt. Hugh found himself gazing at a group of ants busying themselves, oblivious to the rising tension in the clearing.

'Guys.' Hugh's voice was slow. 'I hate to say it. But you know we can't stay here.'

'What do you mean?' Laura cried. 'We can't leave him.'

'We can't stay here for ever,' said Hugh.

'Argue all you like, I'm not going.' Laura stuck her chin up.

'What, you're going to stay here by yourself?'

'Someone will stay with me.' She looked at the others in turn, but none would meet her eye. 'Alex?'

Alex's face tensed.

'Jack? Charlotte?' Laura looked at them in turn, but they stared at the ground. 'Are you all kidding me? You're going to leave without Ed?'

'We're all thirsty, Laura.' Hugh could see Jack was trying to keep his voice even. 'We can't stay. We have to get to the river, and then we can go get help. That's the best thing we can do for Ed now.'

'Well, if you hadn't punched him, we wouldn't be having this conversation,' Laura said, her voice rising.

'This is my fault?' Jack's face lit up with fury. 'If you hadn't been fucking him, we wouldn't have had the fight!'

Laura drew back in shock.

'Hey, we were all in that argument,' Hugh began. It felt weird, being the voice of reason. 'We all said things we shouldn't have.' He himself really should not have lashed out at Ed and said the things he did. But then the others had shouted some pretty unpleasant stuff too.

Indeed, Hugh could see the others' shame in the discomfort written all over their faces. Jack and Alex, Laura and Charlotte; all of them, full of regret.

'But now is not the time to hash it all over.' Hugh made his voice calm.

'Why is he not back by now?' Laura cut in. 'It's been ages. He must be lost. We have to stay.'

'He'll be so thirsty, after running off.' Charlotte's voice was stiff with anxiety.

'He has more water than us,' Hugh snapped. 'Remember, he had that second red platypus bottle that he was so smug about.' Thoughts of that water sloshing in Ed's bottle had been an extra irritant to Hugh during the morning's thirsty walking. 'Did you notice he wasn't offering to share that with us?'

Laura frowned, and Jack shook his head.

Alex jerked sideways, kicking at the ground. 'Christ!' His face twisted. He began to pace from side to side. He opened his mouth to speak but then closed it again, then turned away.

'Perhaps he found a tributary to the river.' Hugh forced himself to continue calmly. 'And can't find his way back. So he's making his way down to the main river.'

'And what if he's not?' Laura's voice rose. 'What if he's lost? We can't leave him here.'

'If he's lost, then the best thing we can do is get out of here, get help and get a search team organised.' Hugh looked intently at Laura.

Laura stared back. Then her face fell, and she gave a short nod. 'Five more minutes.'

They waited. Now and then, one would swat a mosquito or fly from their face, but no one spoke. No one met the others' eyes.

Hugh stood. 'Okay, guys.' He made sure his voice was gentle. 'There's no putting it off any more. We have to go. Now.'

He saw Laura's face crumble.

'I don't want to be too grim, but it seems to me that if we don't move, there is a chance that we could all actually die here.'

Hugh's voice rose in urgency. 'It's getting very hot, we don't have water. We have to get to that river. We haven't got any more time to wait.'

Hugh saw Jack let out a breath. He looked at the others. He saw his own misery reflected in their faces.

Alex was pacing to and fro across the clearing, his face a study of anxiety. The guy looked like he was about to explode.

Hugh went on calmly. 'We can get water, then we can get back to the house.'

Charlotte gave a slow nod. 'Okay. We can't do anything more here. Back at the house, we can organise a proper search.'

Laura started to cry.

Charlotte put her arm around Laura and helped her to her feet.

They swung their packs on their backs. Laura looked at the others. She shook her head again, but then gave one nod.

With slow, heavy steps and many backward glances, they threaded their way out of the clearing and set off along the track towards the river.

Chapter 62

Martha felt the rifle beneath her fingers. She knew how to use it, she was comfortable with it. Robert had taught her how to handle it, many years ago, out in the paddocks, and she had practised from time to time. If you lived on a farm you needed to know how to handle a gun.

The kids looked so scared. She didn't care. It was good that they were suffering. They deserved it. She had wanted them to be thirsty, to be afraid, to feel alone and terrified. To suffer like Ed had suffered.

Now Jack was looking at her intently. 'Martha, we were still hoping that when we got to the river Ed would be waiting for us.'

Jack's voice sounded so reasonable, as though what they had done was somehow understandable.

'Maybe looking a bit sheepish because he'd lost it and stormed off,' Jack went on. 'But he wasn't there. And it was awful. Just awful. But then at that point we knew we'd have to get out, as fast as possible, get help. You remember; we ran towards you across the paddock. You and Robert came to meet us.'

Jack's face was crumbling. 'And then, when the ranger asked us what happened, how Ed had become separated from us –' he stopped and looked at the others '– we were just too ashamed to admit it. That we'd had that big fight with our friend, and it had gotten violent. And now he was missing. We were feeling so very guilty.'

Charlotte said, 'We've all felt it, ever since. Guilty. That we survived.'

'And we didn't want to tell you about the fight because . . .' Jack looked at the others. 'I mean, at first, we told ourselves it was because it would stir things up for you; that it wouldn't help; that you'd be too upset.

'But really, it's this: we thought that telling you would make us feel even more ashamed.' His voice slowed. 'We are so very sorry.'

Martha glared at them – Charlotte, Alex, Jack and Hugh. Her breath hissed through her clenched teeth. They gazed back, their eyes wide, their faces tense.

These shivering children. These fragile teenagers hidden in adult bodies. They had kept their story within their hearts for ten long years. Now their protective layer was ripped off.

She felt a shift in the room, as if the air had thickened and become hard to breathe. As though their shame had left their bodies and was floating in the room like a dark wraith.

'So.' Martha spat the word out. 'You drove him away. You drove my boy away. And then you left him behind.'

Jack's voice creaked. 'Martha, we waited and waited.'

She snapped, 'Enough! Finish the story. You need to tell me everything.'

Jack glanced at the others. 'We have. We've told you everything, now.'

She stamped her foot and the friends jumped. 'You're still lying to me! I can't believe that you still won't be honest.'

'Really, Martha, we've told you all of it.' Charlotte voice was low and tense.

'No, you haven't!' she shrieked. She fumbled in her bag then thrust it towards them, the battered red drink bottle.

They all gazed at the bottle. She watched their faces shift.

'That's Ed's drink bottle.' Hugh looked fascinated. He turned to the others. 'Remember? The one he had on the walk. The second one, that they never found.' He turned back to Martha. 'Where did you get that?'

'I found it in the laundry. When it started falling down last year. Maybe the year before. Someone brought it back from the walk and hid it there.' Martha spat the words out. 'Someone stole my boy's water; the water that he needed to survive.'

She glared, but none of them spoke. She saw them glance between each other. Were they still going to keep up this charade, after everything?

'Martha – I – we.' Charlotte looked between the others. 'We don't have any idea.'

'Stop *lying* to me!'

There was a long silence.

Then, out of the corner of her vision Martha noticed a movement and another voice spoke.

'It was Jack.'

They all turned.

There was Laura, silhouetted in the doorway, breathing heavily and steadying herself against the door frame.

The other four friends gasped. Then they all started to talk at once.

Laura held her hand up and the others fell silent. She turned to Jack. 'It was you, wasn't it?'

Jack stared at her. 'What? What the hell are you talking about?'

'Jack, you took the water bottle. Didn't you?'

Chapter 63

'It was on the walk. Do you remember when I twisted my ankle, and I fell over? You and Ed both rushed towards me. And then you had to get the first aid kit out of Ed's bag.

'I saw you, Jack, I saw you looking through his bag and then turn back to your own bag and do something, I couldn't see what you were doing but it took a little while and I remember wondering what it was.' Laura gazed intently at Jack.

'And when Martha told me about finding the bottle, I remembered that whole scene. It must have been you who took his bottle at that moment.' Laura was still standing in the doorway as she spoke.

Hugh was judging the space between Martha and his friends. It was hard to guess how far it really was. It felt a bit like it kept expanding and contracting, even as Laura was talking.

'And I was confused, because at that point you hadn't yet found out about me and Ed, but then I also remembered that Ed had rushed towards me first, and you had noticed, and I saw the look on your face, and what I think is that you'd figured it out. Even if you didn't want to admit it.'

Jack burst out. 'No. That's not what happened.'

Hugh's eyes were fixed on the gun, Martha's hands holding the gun.

Laura stepped forward into the room. 'It's okay, Jack. I'm sure you were thirsty. And you were feeling suspicious and angry, and the bottle would have been just there, and so why not take it, right?'

'Laura, no.'

'Enough!' Martha shrieked, and they all fell silent. 'Enough with your lying and your arguing. You're still at it, after all these years, unable to take the blame. Look at you all! You're all so happy, so smug. So *alive*. I just cannot bear it.' Martha spoke through gritted teeth. 'That you all go on, living your lives, while he lies dead in the ground.'

In a flash, Martha suddenly shot the bolt into place on the rifle. Hugh's heart leapt but, before they could do anything, the rifle was primed and Martha raised it to her shoulder.

Now Hugh really couldn't breathe. Martha waved her weapon wildly.

She turned to Charlotte. 'You! You're even going to have a child. My Ed will never have a child.' Her voice rose to a shout. 'I will never be a grandmother.'

She took gasping breaths. Her voice gathered into a sob. 'When I heard that you were pregnant . . . that's when I decided that it was really time to confront you all.'

Charlotte started backwards.

Adrenaline burst across Hugh's chest and without a thought he stepped in front of Charlotte, but Martha ignored him.

'You shouldn't be allowed to have a child.' Martha spoke

through gritted teeth. 'To have that joy. That Ed will never have. That I will never have. You can go first.'

Hugh opened his mouth, but before he could speak Alex stepped forward. He spread his arms out in front of his friends.

'Stop. Martha.' Alex's face was wobbling, but his voice was steady. 'If you're going to take someone, take me. They don't know this.' He waved at the others, his eyes fixed on Martha's. 'But it was me.'

Chapter 64

Ten years previously

Alex lay in his sleeping bag, staring at the tent above him. Ed lay near him snoring softly. He could hear bird calls. He was thirsty. But stronger than the thirst was the anxiety.

He wasn't going to make it, he knew. He would die of thirst before they reached the river. He already felt sick in his stomach. The anticipation of what it was going to be like was overwhelming; he would have to walk, and it would be hot, and he would be carrying his heavy bag, and there would not be enough water.

Soon he could hear stirring from the other tents and he wriggled out of his bag. It was a relief to talk to the others, to push his worry away with conversation. He made a point of noticing the bush around them, which, after all, was beautiful and the reason why they were here, and it would help him be in the moment and away from his anxiety.

But the thoughts snuck up behind him and ran on in the background, making his heart thud and his throat close up. He felt the urge to yell, to run away.

He kept thinking of his water bottle, with its meagre freight of liquid. He probably only had about a fifth of a bottle left. Perhaps less.

He concentrated on the tasks. Cleaning the breakfast things away. Packing his bag. Folding up the tents. Making conversation; words that sat in the air, brittle against his feelings, as they all worked steadily to pack up the site.

He was standing by himself, putting his cutlery into his bag, when he saw it.

Ed's bag. It was open. It was just sitting there.

And in the bag: Ed's red platypus water bottle.

Alex could see inches of precious water through the clear red plastic. It was still almost full.

He looked away, but the bottle sat there, in the bag and in his mind, as he went on with the tasks.

The bag was still there. Alex stared at it. He chewed his lip. He knew he shouldn't do it. Alex looked around. Ed was across the campsite with the others. He was helping them with the tents.

Alex reached out his hand. He snatched the bottle from the bag.

He stepped backwards, behind a bush.

Then he brought Ed's bottle to his lips and tipped in the liquid. It flooded into his mouth, and he gulped and gulped again. The pleasure was exquisite.

Then he pulled the bottle away. It was not full any more. Perhaps a half, perhaps a third. A wave of guilt and regret flooded over him.

He turned back to the bag, desperate now to return the bottle. But Ed had walked back across the clearing, and Alex was right in his sightline. Alex quickly slid the red bottle into his own pack.

'Make sure you collect all the tent poles,' Ed called. 'Has anyone seen my small pack?' Alex could see him frowning.

Alex picked up Ed's bag. Could he get the bottle back in before Ed saw?

But now Ed was looking straight towards Alex.

'Here you go.' The words came out of Alex's mouth, despite himself, and Alex handed over the bag, unable to take his eyes off it.

Ed took the bag.

He was going to notice that it was lighter. He was going to check for his second bottle. Alex's heart began to hammer again.

He would be found out. Ed would be furious. He would tell everyone. And he would tell them, too, about Alex taking Hugh's money at the country party. This second transgression would mean Ed obviously could keep silent no more. They had a thief in their midst. Alex would be hounded away.

His breathing grew ragged.

But Ed did none of those things. 'Thanks. Hey, Jack, make sure you grab the rubbish near that rock.'

It seemed like only a minute later to Alex that the clearing had been emptied and they were all swinging their packs up onto their backs, then making their way out of the campsite.

As they fell into a rhythmic pace, Alex could hardly tear his eyes from Ed's small pack with its now-depleted freight.

Every time they stopped for a rest, Alex looked, and looked again for his chance. If he could only slip the red bottle in, Ed might still be none the wiser. Even if he noticed there was less water, he wouldn't know who'd taken it, and the others would just tell him that he was imagining it, that he had drunk it and not remembered.

If only he could get that bottle back in. He almost managed it when Laura hurt her foot, but then Jack had turned to the bag to get the first aid kit.

Then they stopped and the fight broke out, and suddenly Ed stormed off, and he was gone.

And the minutes ticked on, and Ed still didn't appear, and he was out there, in the merciless bush. Without his water.

Chapter 65

Alex's breath came in sobs. Tears stung his eyes as he looked between his friends and Martha.

Alex could see the scene before him still. 'I was thirsty. I needed water.' He felt his throat go dry, as it had back then. 'It was there. It was just a moment.' He turned to his friends. 'I snatched up the bottle, and then it had happened. It was done and it was over. And I've been trying to make up for it, ever since. I've been trying to make up for everything.'

For Ed's water. For Hugh's money. For everything he'd done on that hideous trip. For the shamefulness at his very heart.

Alex had no shortage of memories that could flood him in shame. He had done bad things. He had taken Hugh's money. And then he had taken Ed's water. Even taking those damn patty cakes at his grandfather's funeral. But pushed way to the back of his memories, where it couldn't fall out unexpectedly, was the one that stung him more than anything.

Sitting by himself on the carpet at the house of one of his mother's friends, playing with the toy car he'd brought with him. Then becoming aware of the pressure in his bladder. Pulling at his mother's arm and whispering that he needed the toilet. Her angry snap at him, *just wait!* Hovering, then eventually sitting down. The feel of the synthetic wool of the carpet against his legs. Then, the terrible warmth spreading down his thighs. Seeing the expanding pool of dampness on the carpet. His mother's barking shout, when the odour of the urine alerted her to what had happened. Her furious face. The friend, turning away, but not before he'd caught her look of disgust.

And then the crushing shame, and the realisation, just then, at that very moment, that he was loathsome. A sudden sense of understanding, of vague instincts gaining clarity and logic. Of incidents and memories clicking into place. They all suddenly made sense.

Now he was an adult, he knew, logically, that a kid wetting himself was normal. He could tell himself it didn't mean he was disgusting or hateful.

But deep down, way down, he couldn't shake his belief. It hadn't just been a kid's vulnerability. It was an insight into his true nature.

He started to weep.

Laura took a step towards him, but he held up his hand. He didn't deserve her sympathy, not one little bit. He choked back the sobs. He must explain.

'And when we got back to the house, I still had the bottle and I realised I had to get rid of it. I couldn't think what to do. I thought I might slip it back into Ed's bag, when he got back. We were all still thinking, still hoping, that Ed would be found in time and brought home.

'But time went on and he wasn't found. And then we got the horrible news. And I still had the bottle.

'I couldn't leave it with my things, in case they were searched. I couldn't just leave it lying around the house; someone would find it after we left and realise it had been taken.

'So I shoved it into one of the walls that were being built in that laundry wing. I pulled at one of the wall sheets that was a bit loose, and shoved the bottle in, and pushed the sheet back and I thought the wall would get sealed up, and it would be gone for ever and then no one would ever know.

'And even this weekend, when we thought about being more honest with Martha, I was just desperate for us all to stay silent, in case something came out, someone remembered something about me and that goddamned bottle.'

Martha's face hardened. She moved her gun down from her shoulder. Before anyone had a chance to react, she clicked it together.

She moved it towards them.

Their sudden intake of breath was audible.

She turned suddenly. 'I'm always here, with Ed out there, and I can't help him.' Her voice rose. 'He needs me. He's my boy. He's lying out there, thirsty, and I can't help him.'

Chapter 66

Ten years previously

Ed staggered along the path, away from his friends in the clearing. His pack was slung over one shoulder, tipping him sideways, and he limped against a pain in one ankle. But on he went. He couldn't bear the sight of them any more; he just could not be near them for one second longer.

His breath tore at his throat in dry gasps. His anger fuelled his limbs as he hobbled in a run, faster and faster, as fast as he could. He pushed himself onwards, blind to the bush around him, feeling the air blasting his throat and the pain in his muscles as a relief from his anger.

His mind pulsed with rage. His friends had turned on him. They had betrayed him. They had attacked him.

Fuck them. Let them wait for him. Let them worry. They'd wish they hadn't treated him like that.

Eventually his legs and arms grew heavy, and the rasp of air in his throat was too painful, and he slowed. He was aware of a great thirst.

He swung his bag from his back and pulled out his clear water bottle and took a swig. The liquid down his throat was so soothing. He knew he shouldn't take another swig but he did anyway. The pleasure was so great.

He eased himself onto a rock and looked around. On all sides the bush looked the same: scrub, tree trunks and a canopy of gum leaves above. The fact that there were no distinguishing marks in any direction was a bit eerie. Little noises pushed through the quiet of the bush. Insect chirps. Bird calls.

Then he got up and walked on again, breathing in the sharp gum smell, watching the sunlight on the leaves. After a while he felt calmer. He supposed he'd better get back to them. No matter how irritating they were, no matter how angry everyone was, they really had to get to that river and get out of the bush.

He swung his pack up and turned. That was the way he had come. He was sure.

But, as he walked, it was as though his way ahead danced about. Was the path this way to the left? Or that way, between those two trees? He was almost certain he had clambered over that rock.

Now he looked more closely, it wasn't even clear there was a path. Just dirt scattered with leaves, just like the rest of the ground.

A sharp trickle of fear ran over his skin.

He was so thirsty. His throat was much drier. He supposed all that running earlier hadn't helped. And it was so very hot. He knew he should ration the water, but one more sip wouldn't help.

He got out his clear bottle and took a sip. Then another. His thirst was so strong, so irresistible. He lifted the bottle for another sip, tipped it higher and higher before the liquid hit his tongue, and felt again that extraordinary pleasure.

The bush really did look identical on all sides. He scanned the ground. He had to admit it now: there was nothing that looked like a path.

His breath came faster, and he felt his pulse thrum.

Lost. The word sat in his mind, like a black hole drawing everything in.

Ed forced himself to stand. He took a breath. He needed to stay calm. His friends might actually be very close. He began to call out their names. He heard his own voice thrown back at him from the rock ledges nearby and paused. But the buzzing and whispering of the bush that came back to him held no human sound.

He walked on for a while. Then he began to think that he had set out in the wrong direction, so he retraced his steps. Bushes pulled at him, but he forced his way through. He stumbled over rough rocks. He felt the sun burn against his skin.

The thirst was overwhelming now.

He had another bottle, he remembered now; the red one. He scrabbled through his pack. He couldn't find the bottle.

He tipped everything out on the ground. No red bottle.

His head felt so fuzzy. Perhaps he was confused. Had he dropped it? Left it somewhere?

He stared at his pack, his scattered things.

No more water. This was bad.

Ed's eyes fluttered open. Then closed.

Then open again.

He could see bush all around. It seemed to be pulsating, the leaves and bushes coming closer and retreating in rhythmic waves. He stared. It was like some amazing drug experience.

He swayed as he scrambled to his feet. A wave of anger broke over him as he remembered what had happened just moments before.

But now the anger was draining away, and he struggled to keep hold of it as it was replaced by a stronger and stronger stab of fear.

He was standing at the bottom of a wall of rock. Its sheer grey face stretched above. On the other side the scrub was thick with leaves.

He had tried and failed to climb that rock face; he just could not get himself up there. He was too exhausted. There was no way.

He would have to find another way out. Another spurt of fear lent him some energy, and he pressed forward through the bushes.

As he stumbled on, scenes from the walk with his friends came back to him. The walk seemed like an awfully long time ago.

Other memories rose up at him, all mixed up. When they had all started high school together. His time at the little local school, a long drive away. Out in one of the paddocks in the middle of the long grass, looking up at his dad. He must have been very small because the grass was really tall.

A little later he woke again. He was lying in a small clearing that was almost perfectly round. There were four large grass trees, with their rough black trunks and spikes. It was like the space had been out here waiting for him.

Everything was quiet. He was alone.

He clambered to his feet. He was so heavy. It was such an effort.

His throat was so dry. That crushing thirst. His breath was coming in little gasps now.

His knees felt so weak. He tried to keep them straight, but they wobbled and gave way, and he sank to the ground.

He looked around at the pitiless bush.

He tried to speak, but there was not enough air.

His torso tipped forward, as if in supplication. But there was no answering benediction. No relief. No help.

His face neared the ground. The dirt was millimetres from his mouth.

Another breath.

A pause.

The heat gathered around him.

A crow alighted on a nearby branch. It sat there, watchful.

Ants, busy on the ground, ran over his legs. An insect flew onto his arm and took a minuscule bite. Flies circled his face.

His dark curls lay still.

Finally, there was silence. Not even breath. No pulse of blood.

Ed's eyes were open, but they saw nothing.

Chapter 67

'I can't get out of here.' Martha's voice came in short gasps as she glared across the kitchen. 'I can never leave. I'm always here, waiting for my boy to come home. And he'll never come home. So. You have to pay.'

'We have paid.' Jack's voice was urgent. 'We have all *paid*. Can't you see that?'

Charlotte sobbed and wavered, then took a step forward, and at her movement Martha turned.

In that instant, Hugh leapt forward.

Martha turned back at him with the rifle, but he had already grabbed the kitchen table and upended it towards her like a wall and she fell backwards.

'Run!' he screamed.

It felt like for ever, but it was only a millisecond, then Charlotte, Laura, Alex and Jack dashed from the room.

Hugh could see Martha scrambling to her feet.

She was holding the rifle.

For a moment he thought of charging at her, but it was too

late, and he turned and followed the others, slamming the door behind him.

In the hallway he could see Jack fiddling with the front door.

Terror was written across the four faces.

'I can't get it unlocked.' Jack's expression was desperate.

They could hear the creak of the kitchen door opening behind them.

'There's no time! Up the stairs.'

As one, they turned and flew up the stairs, Hugh half-carrying Charlotte, Jack and Alex heedless of their injuries.

A sharp crack sounded. Five yells.

There wasn't time to plan. There was only splintered thought. Get away from Martha. Get away from that gun.

Hugh was along the hallway, pulling at the ladder to the roof. His breath was in his throat. He could hear the others panting.

'Up here. We'll pull it up behind us.'

Up they went, one by one, so fast they couldn't feel the ladder beneath their feet.

Hugh was last, his glance darting between the legs disappearing upstairs and the corridor behind him.

Now he could see Martha rounding the corner from the stairs.

He leapt forward and yanked at the old dresser, pulling it across the hall. It might slow her down.

Another deafening crack, and he jumped.

He dashed back and flew up the ladder, his feet clattering.

The others stood at the top, staring at him anxiously.

'We'll pull it up. She can't get up here.'

Hugh knelt down and yanked at the metal, but with a sickening feeling he realised that the ladder was only operable from the floor below.

His eyes flew around the attic. 'Pull those boxes across.'

Jack grabbed one end of a box, Alex the other. They had most of the opening covered.

At the back of his mind, behind his panic, Hugh registered a dim pulsing noise, strangely familiar. It seemed to be coming from outside.

But then they heard the sound of Martha's laboured breathing.

Her feet sounding on the ladder. Slowly. Inexorably. One foot after the other.

Charlotte was already opening the window out onto the ledge. She was panting, but her face was set. Then she was clambering through.

Alex looked between the window and the opening to the ladder then darted after Charlotte.

Jack followed Alex.

Hugh hesitated, but only for a moment.

Behind him he heard the scraping sound of the boxes against the attic floor.

He went through the window.

He had half an instant to see the vast, sunlit valley open up before him then he immediately turned to where Charlotte was huddled against the edge of the terrace. She glanced down towards the ground far below but then turned back to him, her face frozen with terror. She clutched at Laura. Alex and Jack were standing in front of them.

Hugh glanced around wildly. There was nothing on the terrace that could be used as a weapon or a barrier.

Nothing.

The door opened behind him.

That pulsing noise was growing louder and louder.

He stood in front of Charlotte, making himself as large as he could.

His blood, thundering in his ears, almost drowned out the panting breaths of his friends.

They all watched, transfixed, as the door to the terrace opened.

The noise that Hugh had noticed was now a ratcheting moan, and with a shock, he realised what it was.

But then Martha's head emerged from the terrace door. Then the ominous dark line of the rifle. Then the rest of her body.

She straightened.

She stared at them.

She pulled the gun out.

'So. This is how it will be.'

Hugh heard Jack's intake of breath. He heard Charlotte whimper.

Hugh could now see the helicopter, approaching across the valley from behind Martha. It was blue. A police helicopter. He thought he could make out a figure in the open side door.

His glance flicked over the low wall of the terrace, down towards the ground. Such a long way down.

'Martha.' Hugh could hardly get the word out.

The helicopter was still some way off, but the ratcheting was getting louder. Would it get here in time?

'Enough talking. Now you're going to pay.' Martha's expression was rigid. She did not glance away. It was as though she couldn't even hear the growing noise coming from behind her.

Hugh felt rather than saw Alex step past him. He was taking slow steps towards Martha.

Hugh's eyes darted between the helicopter and Martha. The figure in the aircraft seemed to be holding a gun. Could they see what was happening on the rooftop? Were they close enough to use it?

'Stop.' Martha's voice was hard. 'Or I'll shoot you. I'll do it. I will.'

Alex turned and looked at his friends. He looked into their eyes, one by one.

Hugh felt like Alex's glance was searing right through him.

'I know,' Alex breathed. 'I deserve it.' He turned back to Martha and continued towards her.

Chapter 68

It happened in an instant.

A sharp crack sounded.

Alex stood suspended in the air for a moment, then he fell. Sideways, against the low terrace wall.

His legs collapsed against the wall, but his body kept going, over the wall, out towards that huge drop.

He was still moving; he was going over.

Alex disappeared over the edge of the roof.

Martha started back. The gun fell from her hands, clattering against the terrace.

Jack leapt forward and picked up the weapon.

Then slowly, irresistibly, Hugh, Laura, Jack and Charlotte inched towards the edge of the terrace and peered over.

Far below, Alex lay sprawled on the roof of the laundry building.

It felt like they all stood frozen for an age, but it was really only a second, then everyone sprang into motion.

Hugh stepped forward and grasped Martha's arm. It was tiny beneath his large fist.

Jack unbolted the rifle. Then Jack, Laura and Charlotte pushed past Hugh, through the window, back into the attic.

Across the attic and down the ladder. Along the hall they flew, then down the stairs, up the hall, across the kitchen and outside.

'Alex!' It seemed like everyone was screaming at once.

Laura was trying to climb up the cracked and broken walls towards the laundry roof.

'Oh my god, he's bleeding.' Laura had managed to get high enough to peer onto the roof.

The moan of the helicopter shifted down a note as it floated down towards the paddock next to the house. As the blades of the aircraft slowed, two figures emerged and ran, crouched, towards the house.

The kitchen door opened. Hugh was pushing Martha through. Martha's expression was completely vacant. She was staring fixedly, as though she could see through to the other side of the earth.

Laura talked urgently to Alex, as though he could hear her. As though there was hope. 'We've got you. Stay with us.'

Now she was kneeling on the buckled metal of the roof.

'He's not responding.'

She shouted his name. She grabbed at Alex's shirt, pressing it against his shoulder, but it was immediately soaked in red.

'Alex, Alex, listen. Stay with me.' Her breath caught in her throat.

'We'll take over from here.'

Then Laura realised two uniformed figures had appeared at the laundry, carrying bulky packs. Two more were running behind them. The helicopter was now sitting in the next paddock.

Then the officers were on the roof of the laundry, kneeling over Alex. Laura slithered backwards, staring in shock.

The officers were calmly but steadily unpacking their bags, turning between Alex's prone body and their equipment.

They conferred in quiet voices; they kept turning back towards Alex.

On and on they worked.

Jack, Hugh, Laura and Charlotte stared, their eyes fixed on the uniformed figures.

But Alex lay, unresponsive.

Chapter 69

A magpie alighted on a fence post outside the Fletcher homestead and twitched its head, watching.

The house, so quiet for a day and a night, had come alive in the morning light.

First to arrive, in a roar of rotor blades, a helicopter had landed in a nearby paddock, flattening the grasses and sending birds and animals fleeing. Heads down, figures had run across the paddock and towards the house. Then the helicopter sat motionless in the paddock, like a giant insect.

Not long afterwards an ambulance appeared, racing along the thin line of road like a little white toy against the immensity of the valley. It now stood in the front yard of the house, its bright colours out of place against the muted grey-yellow of the landscape and the weathered old house.

Soon after that, two police vans had raced across the valley, up the track and into the yard and pulled up near the ambulance.

Now, a little later, people in uniforms were making their way in and out of the house, fetching bottles and equipment from the vans.

They hurried. Their voices were urgent.

Whatever was happening was more activity than this house had seen for a very long time.

Then two figures emerged, another lying on a stretcher between them. The stretcher was loaded into the back of the ambulance.

The lights started flashing, and the van bumped quickly down the track towards the road.

The magpie noticed a twitching gecko, paused and suddenly darted from the fence.

Martha sat frozen, two police officers standing near. They questioned her, they tried again and again, but she said nothing, her face not moving as she stared and stared. Eventually, they let her just sit, with an officer standing near.

Hugh, Jack, Charlotte and Laura sat huddled together in the sitting room. At long last they had sated their thirst. The paramedics had provided bottled water, and later a couple of police officers had made their way to the pump house and turned the crank that connected the house back to the main water supply. The paramedics had wrapped each of them in silver space blankets. One of them had treated Jack's snakebite, shaking her head and murmuring that he had been lucky.

At one point an officer appeared with a tray of hot drinks. 'Your mate's still alive. They're hopeful. That crumpled roof broke his fall.'

The friends asked disjoined questions. The officers replied calmly. It seemed that a plane crossing the valley earlier that morning had noticed the help sign and called it in. When the call was patched through to Nanganook police station, the officers had recognised the description of the location as the old Fletcher house and they were immediately concerned. The suspicions around Robert Fletcher's death were still fresh in their minds. So when they had tried to phone but the call wouldn't connect, they'd grown alarmed and sent the helicopter.

Now, outside, the police were taking photographs. More officers were working upstairs.

The police had no trouble interviewing the four friends. They talked and talked, interrupting each other as they remembered more details, the silver blankets crackling.

The officers nodded and took notes, looking at them with careful, assessing gazes. Their questions went on and on, circling back and forth.

And when did you notice the water was cut off? . . . Do you think she was actually firing at you? . . . And you're sure the modem was gone? . . . Can you show me this email invitation?

Jack clutched at his water bottle, not wanting to let it go even though it was his third and it was almost empty. The officer handed him another one without saying anything and he clutched that too.

Hugh kept his arm around Charlotte. He blinked his eyes as he spoke, surprised by the emotion that kept threatening to overwhelm him.

Under the silver blanket, Charlotte still felt cold throughout all her limbs.

Laura had deliberately sat so she could see the doorway. She didn't want Martha reappearing behind her.

Finally, the questions stopped. The officers stood and conferred in a corner, murmured to each other quietly.

Then there was a movement in the doorway. Martha was being walked outside by two officers. She was still staring, her expression vacant. When she saw the four friends she stopped and turned and her face crumpled.

Her mouth kept working but no words emerged, and then the officers led her away.

Jack, Laura, Charlotte and Hugh sat, all talk over, their whirling minds beginning to slow.

The police were in the hallway conferring. Then the officer who had accompanied Martha out to the van returned to the living room. His expression seemed a little more sympathetic than it had before. 'How are you guys going now?'

Laura stirred. 'How do you think we're going?'

The officer said, 'Getting into the van seemed to set something off in her.' He indicated back towards the police van. 'She started spilling it all out. Telling us what she did. All fits with what you've said.'

'So, you believe us now?' asked Hugh.

The officer put up his hands placatingly. 'No one is accusing you of lying. You mentioned some notes she'd left for you. Accusing you of things, and you didn't know how she would have known?'

The officer turned to Laura. 'Because she didn't get it from you, right?'

Laura shook her head. 'Like I said. Ed hadn't talked about any of that stuff.'

The officer went on. 'She told me that she read it all in some diary kept by your mate Ed. Said it was in the pack they found in the bush after they'd found his body. Said she and her husband couldn't face it, for years. But then they had finally made themselves read it. And apparently, Ed had written about those things, about you guys.'

The officer looked about the room, then out through the window. 'Sounds like she's been out here, all by herself all these years, nothing to do but dwell on it all. Dreaming up this whole show for you.'

Hugh let out a long breath. He turned to Laura. 'I'm sorry I suspected you. I just thought there was no other way for Martha to have known that stuff other than from Ed telling you, and then you telling her. And, I mean, you'd disappeared on us. Like you might have gone to help her, been in on it all.'

Laura shook her head. 'It's okay. I know it looked really dodgy.'

She turned to the officer. 'I reckon when I was with her out there at the pump house, she drugged me. Did she say anything about that?'

The officer nodded. 'That's right. Said she couldn't send you back to the house once you knew where she was. But didn't want you interfering, so she gave you her own sleeping pills.'

Laura said, 'Must be bloody strong pills. I was out for the whole night.'

'If Martha was seriously anxious, she'd need a really strong dose to knock herself out at night,' said Jack. 'But you wouldn't have been used to them.'

One of the other officers stuck her head in the room and called her colleague away.

Laura looked from face to face. 'I thought I could help. I thought, she trusts me, I'll go see her and I can tell her the full story, maybe she'll settle down, let us go. But she got mad when I couldn't explain about the bottle.'

Hugh leaned back. 'Laura, she was already mad.'

'In both senses,' said Jack.

Laura's face crumpled. She curled her legs up and put her face against her knees. Charlotte patted her back, her own face twisted.

They all sat in silence, in the dusty room in the old house in the lonely valley, thinking of their friend who had died in the merciless bush and the other friend, now just clinging to life.

Hours later, they gathered on the front veranda of the homestead, their belongings heaped together, their cars filled with petrol the police had brought.

They were all still stiff with shock. They had stared, hardly believing their eyes, as Alex was carried out on a stretcher. Every time they remembered his crumpled body lying on the laundry roof, they felt a fresh stab of anxiety.

As they stood looking out on the front yard, each pictured their arrival in that very place just a couple of days before: already apprehensive, but with no idea of what lay ahead.

Now they clung to each other in farewell. Then they loaded their bags in their cars and settled in, pulled the doors closed.

Jack took Alex's car, Laura followed, and Hugh and Charlotte drove out last. One of the police cars was going to accompany them. The cars bumped down the track towards the road. They rolled onto the bitumen and wound their way through the paddocks that stretched across the gentle hills.

They entered the forest at the base of the cliffs. They drove, this way and that, up the hairpin bends until they reached the top.

They passed the cafe. They twisted and turned through the

thick forest. Along the winding highway, through hamlets and villages and towns.

Joining the string of cars along the motorway, they gathered speed, burrowing back into the city, back into their lives.

Chapter 70

Three weeks later

Jack, Hugh, Charlotte and Laura stood around Alex, who was lying on the hospital bed. Jack was suddenly reminded of that previous hospital visit all those years ago after Ed's death, when Alex lay in a very similar cubicle, his bandaged wrists lying on the covers like a reproach to them all.

But this was a much happier occasion. For a start, now they were all looking at Alex with admiration rather than pity.

'Mate, you just had to be the hero, right?' Hugh's words sounded sarcastic but his smile was affectionate.

'Oh I dunno.' Alex couldn't even manage a smile. 'It was more instinct than anything.'

'I think it was very brave.' Laura patted Alex's hand. 'Even if very foolhardy. Martha was holding a real gun.'

'Believe me, I know it.' Alex glanced towards his shoulder.

Jack winced. The bullet had pierced Alex's shoulder and exited again, but had passed dangerously close to his spine. He had lost a lot of blood at the farmhouse.

'Anyway, we've been over all this.' Alex looked around at the group. 'How are you guys going?'

Jack studied Alex's face. There was something sitting behind his stoic expression and Jack couldn't quite put his finger on it. He should be pretty happy; the surgeons had predicted he would eventually get back most of the use of his right arm. He'd been lucky with where the bullet had entered, and lucky that the paramedics had got to him so quickly.

But perhaps Alex was thinking about the long months of rehabilitation ahead. When he left hospital he would still have many hard physio sessions ahead of him.

Jack glanced at Hugh and Charlotte. Hugh had his arm around his wife and Charlotte looked more relaxed than she had for a long time.

Charlotte rubbed her stomach. 'I'm good – as good as I can be with this uncomfortable being getting larger by the second.' She smiled up at Hugh. 'And I think we're just about ready for him.'

'Him?' Laura raised her eyebrows.

'Yes, we found out at the scan the other day.' Charlotte gave Hugh a questioning look and he nodded. 'And, we might as well tell you – we've decided to call him Alex.' She smiled at Alex. 'Hopefully he can be brave like you.'

Alex looked horrified. 'Guys, no! You can't do that.'

Alex was really not comfortable with all this adulation, Jack thought. Not surprising. He'd never exactly been the centre of attention in their group. That honour had always belonged to Ed.

Hugh shook his head. 'Too late, mate. It's all decided.'

'But . . .'

'Oh shut up, Alex.' Hugh turned to Laura. 'How are you? Your treatment going okay?'

'Not too bad thanks. And . . .' Laura paused. 'Possibly too much information, but I've decided to have the mastectomy. It will be grim, I know. But life is precious and I need to do everything to keep it.'

'Good for you, Laur.' Jack smiled at her.

It was easy to be friendly now. Their hideous weekend at the Fletcher farm had taught him that he didn't need Laura any more. It was his old self who had loved her, the boy who had walked into the bush with five young friends. Everything they'd been through on that endless weekend; everything he had been through – confessing his drug dealing; screwing up his courage to go to rescue Alex when he'd twisted his foot – had clarified his thinking. He'd been clinging to the idea of Laura as she'd been then, hoping to return to that more innocent time.

'I'm also going to give up that godawful admin role and find a job at a charity,' Laura went on. 'I have to live by my values.'

Jack smiled. That note of piety had always been there when she spoke like that, but now it was easier for him to admit to himself that actually it could be quite irritating.

'There was something else I wanted to say.' Laura's expression grew more serious. 'Basically . . . sorry. I was angry at you all about what happened on our walk. I was fixated on the fact that you'd all had the argument with Ed, and I thought you'd driven him away, to his death.' She took a breath.

'But really I was angry at you to mask my own guilt. Because – I have to admit this – if Ed and I had been more brave, if we'd told you about us when we should have, before the walk, then we probably wouldn't even have gone on that trip. And if we had gone, there wouldn't have been that awful secret at the heart of it, waiting to explode.

'I know, I know – that's not the only reason why he ran off and got lost. But it's possible we might have avoided the whole disaster. So, I'm sorry. I'm really sorry that I wasn't more brave.'

Jack could hear the muffled noise of traffic outside as the room fell silent.

'Anyway, Jack.' Laura put on a brighter voice. 'You've got some news?'

'Yep, big news. I've decided to put my PhD out of its misery. Been doing it for all the wrong reasons. I need to get a real job. Figure out what to do with my life.'

'Not medicine?' Hugh asked.

'Nope. I don't need to be Dr Zhang to be worthwhile. Just a regular job. Something ordinary.'

'Yes.' Laura tipped her head on the side. 'But that wasn't the news I meant.'

'Oh, right. Yeah. Well, in the spirit of telling people things, which we all did an awful lot of at Martha's, I told Julie about Ed. What happened on the hike with him. All of it.'

'And . . .?' Charlotte looked curious.

'And, she said it explained a lot, and asked why the hell didn't I tell her earlier.'

It had been a very good question, one that Jack struggled to answer now. Keeping it secret, keeping everything secret, had felt so important at the time. Now, with things out in the open – not just all his own dark, hidden memories, but those of his friends too – everything felt so much freer, more at ease, between them. Almost like it had been back at school, before the walk and Ed's death, and everything that came in the wake of that.

'So is she going to take you back?'

'I think that's still to be decided.' Jack glanced out the window.

'But it's probably a good sign that she dropped me off here and she's waiting outside so we can go get a coffee.'

The others whooped and he grinned.

'Well don't let us keep you from your spade work.' Hugh nudged Jack.

'Hugh's right.' Alex nodded. 'Thanks for coming, guys, but I bet you've all got other things to be doing.'

Alex really seemed to want them to leave, thought Jack. They hadn't yet talked about Martha, sitting in a cell with the attempted murder charge hanging over her, psychologists circling while her lawyer worked out whether a diagnosis was a good idea. But then there really wasn't much to say about that.

Hugh rolled his eyes. 'Hey, happy to be here. I'd only be spending yet another hour choosing one of the identical shades of greige Charl wants for the nursery.'

He grinned as Charlotte gave him a little shove.

Laura looked around. 'Still, Alex might be getting tired. Could be time to go.'

It took another few minutes of hugs and goodbyes before they began to file from the room.

Jack looked back at Alex one last time, but Alex was already gazing out the window, as if he'd forgotten the friends were ever there. It was all clearly still very much on his mind.

Jack thought of their younger selves, with all their longings and fears, standing in a clearing far out in the wilderness, the words of a vicious argument still echoing in their heads.

And poor Alex – still so riddled with shame about that one brief act of taking Ed's water bottle. He'd been so guilt-ridden, now he'd literally taken a bullet for it.

Such a harsh atonement for a moment's self-interest.

352

Chapter 71

Ten years previously

Alex scanned the bush. It would be so wonderful to find Ed. He could imagine the others' faces if he were able to return, having found him.

He tramped on, scanning the bush. He must remember the time, though, and be back at the clearing when Hugh had specified.

But the minutes ticked past, and there was no Ed.

Then suddenly he stopped. He could hardly believe his eyes. He stared. Was he hallucinating?

The steep ground, thick with bushes and trees, rock ledges and sudden drops – and then a human figure. Finally, finally. Thank god.

'Ed,' he breathed. Then, more loudly, as though to convince himself, 'Ed!'

A smile broke across his face. Relief washed over him, so sweet it was like a wave of cool water on his skin.

But Ed looked awful. It was as though days, not hours had passed. His face was haggard, his expression desperate. There was a vivid red mark on the side of his face, already tinged with purple.

He opened his mouth. He took a step towards Alex.

Alex stepped forward and grasped his arms. 'Mate. It's okay. I've got you.'

'Water?'

Alex nodded. Of course. He swung down his day pack and opened it.

He almost pulled out Ed's red platypus drink bottle but stopped himself just in time.

There was just a little liquid left in his own bottle. He held it out, and Ed grabbed it, and downed the lot with one swallow.

Alex tried not to flinch. 'It's okay, mate. The others aren't too far away. Just a few minutes back along this path. Around this ridge. We'll be all right. I'll take you back, no worries.' Alex was so relieved to see Ed that he was babbling.

It took a moment, but the water seemed to revive Ed a little. His face creased. 'Bloody stupid,' he said.

Alex assumed he was talking about himself, storming off like that.

'Where's your pack, mate?'

Ed just shook his head and waved backwards. 'Too heavy. Had to put it down.'

That wasn't great. But the main thing was that Ed was found, Alex could take him back to the others, then it wouldn't be long before they were all at the river.

'Back this way, mate. Do you need to lean on me?'

Alex grasped Ed's shoulder, but Ed threw it off and stood on his own, so Alex set off down the path. He kept glancing backwards but could hear Ed's slow steps just behind him.

They walked for a couple of minutes before it happened.

Perhaps Alex was going too fast, or perhaps it was just that Ed was feeling weak and was walking over rocky ground.

Ed stumbled, then pitched forward against Alex. Alex staggered and just managed to miss the sudden drop in the rocks to their right. Ed grabbed at Alex but missed and pulled at Alex's day pack. Alex heard the zipping sound of his bag coming open.

Alex stumbled sideways with the force of Ed yanking his bag, and then suddenly they were both lying on the ground.

'Sorry. I'm sorry,' Ed managed.

'No worries. No harm done.' Alex stared at Ed's drawn face.

But Ed didn't stare back. Ed's gaze was fixed on the ground.

Alex followed the line of his sight. Then his blood seemed to freeze in his veins.

When Alex's pack came open, some of the contents had fallen out.

And lying among them was the red drink bottle with the platypus sticker.

Hours seemed to tick past as they both stared at it.

Then Ed turned to him. His voice croaked, but the words were clear enough. 'You stole it. You bastard.'

Alex opened his mouth but couldn't think of anything to say.

'You dirty thief.'

'Wait – I just—'

'What? Any excuse? Anything?'

Ed's lip curled contemptuously. His voice grew stronger. 'You always were a sick little thief. You got another chance after you took Hugh's money at the party. Thought you might change.'

Alex held up his hands, as though to ward off the hideous words, but they kept coming.

'But once a thief, always a thief.'

Tears were pricking at Alex's eyes.

Ed was shaking his head in disgust. 'That's it. I'm telling the others. They need to know what you're really like.'

Ed scrambled to his feet, reaching for the red bottle, but swayed as he rose and instead of picking it up, he knocked it so it rolled along the rock face. He lurched after it, but too late.

The bottle disappeared over the edge of the rock. They heard a clank as it bounced down.

'Shit!' Ed's face creased in horror.

They both edged forward and peered over the rock ledge. The bottle lay metres below them.

Ed's face shifted. 'We have to get it.'

Alex saw the long drop. 'I dunno. That's a long way down.'

'It's the only water we have. Of course, *you* can't be bothered getting it, but I'm bloody thirsty.'

Alex stood silently as Ed began to scramble down the side of the rock. Ed really should not be doing that. At one point Ed slipped and Alex caught his breath.

Ed slid down the rest of the sheer face and hit the bottom with a soft cry. Then he straightened. He grabbed the bottle and took a sip, then gave it a slight shake.

'Can't believe you were going to leave this here.'

Alex saw Ed way below him, as though through a tunnel. He seemed to be a long way down. Those rock faces were so steep and sheer.

Ed tried to climb while holding the bottle, but he couldn't get far with one hand. He tried to shove it in his shorts pocket, but it wouldn't fit. He shoved it in the back of his shorts against the waist band, but he hadn't climbed very far before it slipped out and tumbled down the rocks. He climbed down, tried to put the bottle in the front of the shorts, but it slipped out yet again.

He slithered back to the ground and picked up the bottle.

'You'll have to take it.' Ed stared up at Alex and made to throw it.

Alex nodded.

The red bottle came sailing up through the air. Alex grabbed it.

'Don't bloody drink any.'

Alex nodded. He put it carefully in his pack straight away, his hands shaking.

'That's mine, mate. Better be there when I get up.'

Ed scrambled up the rocks from the clearing below. But he didn't get very far before he had to stop and scan the rocks again.

'Shit. There's no fucking holds.'

Ed slipped down then tried another route to the top, but had to stop again.

The minutes ticked past, with Ed's heavy breathing and Alex staring down, transfixed.

Ed slithered to the ground again, and bent down against his knees, breathing heavily.

'That's hard work. I don't feel great.'

He turned and managed to get about a metre further up.

'You're going to have to help me. Alex, do you hear? If you lie down then reach your arms down, you should be able to grab me.'

Alex looked at the distance between them. 'It's too far,' he croaked.

Ed paused for a second, thinking. 'Okay, so hang your pack down. I'll hold onto that while I scramble up.'

Alex stared at Ed.

Ed stared back. 'What are you waiting for?'

Ed seemed so very far away. The rock face between them seemed to grow longer and longer.

Ed seemed to be receding, while a buzzing noise sounded in Alex's head.

All he could hear were Ed's earlier words, echoing, over and over.

Once a thief, always a thief.

The buzzing grew louder.

I'm telling the others . . .

Alex could not let Ed tell anyone about the bottle. The theft of Hugh's money at the country party was bad enough. But taking someone's desperately needed water? There were no words for such a deed. He would be exposed, his shameful, loathsome true nature there for all to see.

He could not let everyone find out what he was really like.

He stared at Ed, transfixed, his thoughts splintering.

The buzzing noise in his head turned into a roar. He could hardly believe the idea that was crowding out all other thought.

He took a step backwards. His feet felt terribly heavy. He took another step.

Ed's face flashed with confusion. 'Alex? What are you doing?'

Alex took another step back.

Ed's face shifted as he began to realise what was happening. 'Alex?' His voice rose to a yell. 'What the hell?'

Alex felt the energy flow back to his legs, and then it was like they were taking him away of their own accord.

'Alex!' Ed's voice was now a shout. 'Get the fuck back here! I'm stuck! I can't get up.'

Alex turned and began to walk.

He could hear Ed's cries behind him, rising to a scream.

Alex began to run. His pace picked up. Faster and faster.

The sound of his breath in his throat and his feet thudding along the dirt began to drown out the fading cries of his friend.

On and on he ran, his breath ragged and his legs screaming, as though if he hurt enough it might burn away his shame.

On and on, through the heartless bush, as though if he ran for long enough he could run away from himself.

Acknowledgements

I am fortunate to have made numerous visits to Varuna, the National Writers' House, whose precious quiet has a magical effect on writer productivity and is broken only by convivial talk with other residents. In particular, Marele Day and my fellow writers in the crime week residency gave me early encouragement, which helped to keep me going through the thickets of the publishing country that lay ahead.

I thank Lisa O'Donnell and Simon Ings, tutors on the Curtis Brown Creative Writing Your Novel course, and my talented fellow students, especially Christina Naughton, Sarah Clutton and Guy for reading full drafts and providing insightful notes.

I am grateful to my agent, Samantha Brace of Peters Fraser and Dunlop, for championing this work, and to my editor, Hannah Wann, and the team at Little, Brown for their excellent suggestions for the manuscript.

At home, Sam and Thomas were patient with my regular disappearances to tap away at my keyboard during the years that led up to this book. Above all, my love and gratitude to Matthew, who has unfailingly supported this long-held dream.